Cast of Characters

Theocritus Lucius Westborough. A little man with a long name and even longer big reputation, he's a classical scholar, an amateur detective, and a good friend of

Johnny Mack. A bluff, old-school Chicago police detective, who always welcomes Westborough's assistance on a complicated case.

Captain Terence ("Terry') O'Ryan. A giant of a cop.

Hezekiah Morse. The victim, he was a retired financier who was a noted book collector.

Sylvia Elaine Morse. His granddaughter and the chief suspect. She was to be left only a terra-cotta statuette of a New Zealand parrot should she choose not to marry

Thomas Raymond Vail. Morse's neighbor who stands to inherit one third of Morse's estate.

Barry Foster. Our narrator, Morse's lawyer, and the man Sylvia really wants to marry.

J. Worthington Wells. A fellow book collector and sometimes bookseller who was among the last to see Morse alive.

Pete Whealon. A paving contractor and book collector who was almost sued for slander by Morse.

Baines. Morse's butler of 20 years, he's been known to play the horses without much luck.

Matilda Sampson. The cook, she enjoys a game of cribbage with Baines.

Ernest Hands. An ex-clerk in a broker's office, he was unsuccessful in an attempt to blackmail Morse.

Giovanni. A bootlegger who knows the price of a rare bottle of wine.

Brenda Carstairs. She provides one of the suspects with a seemingly air-tight alibi.

Lawrence Steelcraft. A partner in Barry's law firm.

George Smith. Dead two years now, he gave the parrot to Morse.

Plus various policeman lawyers secretaries and bankers.

D1260206

In the Theocritus Lucius Westborough canon:

The Fifth Tumbler, 1936
The Death Angel, 1936
Blind Drifts, 1937
The Purple Parrot, 1937
The Man from Tibet, 1938
The Whispering Ear, 1938
Murder Gone Minoan, 1939
(English title: *Clue to the Labyrinth*)
Dragon's Cave, 1940
Poison Jasmine, 1940
Green Shiver, 1941

The Purple Parrot

A Theocritus Lucius Westborough
mystery

Clyde B. Clason

Rue Morgue Press
Lyons, Colorado

The Purple Parrot

978-1-60187-064-3
was first published in 1937

New material in this edition
Copyright © 2012 by
The Rue Morgue Press

Printed by
Pioneer Printing

PRINTED IN THE UNITED STATES OF AMERICA

About the author

CLYDE B. CLASON'S career as a mystery writer took up only five of his 84 years, but in the short span between 1936 and 1941 he produced ten long and very complicated detective novels, all published by the prestigious Doubleday, Doran Crime Club, featuring the elderly historian Professor Theocritus Lucius Westborough.

Born in Denver in 1903, Clason spent many years in Chicago, the setting for several of his novels, including his most famous work, *The Man from Tibet*, before moving to York, Pennsylvania, where he died in 1987. During his early years in Chicago Clason worked as an advertising copywriter and a trade magazine editor, producing books on architecture, period furniture and one book on writing, *How To Write Stories that Sell*. Clason stopped writing mysteries on the eve of World War II, although he published several other books, including *Ark of Venus* (1955), a science fiction novel, and *I am Lucifer* (1960), the confessions of the devil as told to Clason. He also produced several nonfiction works dealing with astronomy as well as *The Delights of the Slide Rule* (1964), his last published book-length work.

Clason left the crime fiction genre never to return, primarily because the postwar mystery fiction world was dominated by what he called the sex and violence school popularized by writers such as Mickey Spillane. He believed that readers—or at least publishers—were no longer interested in his thoughtful and leisurely tales of detection

For more information on Clason see Tom and Enid Schantz' introduction to *Green Shiver*.

PART ONE

Wednesday, November 18

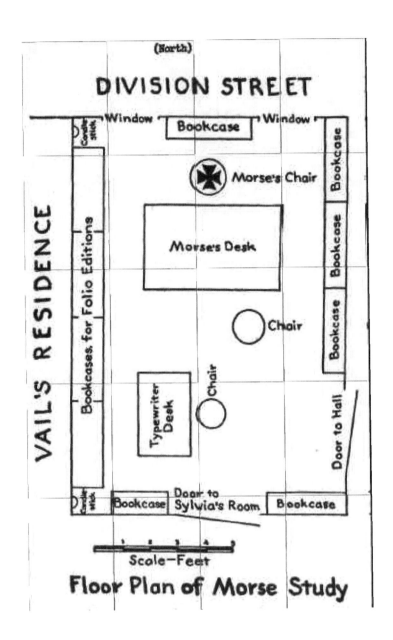

Floor Plan of Morse Study

I

"And to my granddaughter, Sylvia Elaine Morse, in the event she marries other than the aforesaid Thomas Raymond Vail, I give and bequeath only my purple parrot . . ."

The words (I had drafted them myself only a few days before) were singing in my ears as our cab spun northward on Lake Shore Drive. I said aloud:

"I shouldn't let you. If I had the courage I wouldn't let you."

Sylvia only laughed. "Money, Barry? When we have—*this!*"

I gulped down the lump in my throat. I couldn't say anything, couldn't acknowledge my indebtedness. Even though I knew it was the act of a heel to allow her to go on with it I wasn't able to help myself. As far as I was concerned Fate had knocked on the door the first time I'd seen her.

She is a tall girl, dark-haired, and her eyes are of that deep velvety blue found only in fine sapphires. Her face is a delicate oval, and—well, sweet isn't much of a word, but it's the only word I know that comes anywhere near describing Sylvia.

But, when I decided to put down on paper my recollections of what turned out to be one of Chicago's most dramatic murder sensations, I didn't expect to be rhapsodizing this way. Still—Sylvia was the center of all that happened during those few hectic days, and, if I keep my own feelings about her entirely out of this account, it will be as lifeless as a dried out sponge.

Our cab turned left, off Lake Shore Drive, and then made a U turn in the middle of the block to pull up before a three-story house, faced with gray stone and set close to the sidewalk. After I had paid the driver we stood there for a moment uncertainly and watched the cab, a blob of bright canary yellow, melt away in the darkness.

"He must be told tonight," she declared firmly, and that was Sylvia. Courage when it was needed—always.

"I'll take that job myself," I promised. I was unable to keep the grimness from my voice.

"No, Barry, you mustn't. He—oh, I'm not just sure how to explain."

"Well, we'll settle the argument inside."

We climbed the five or six stone steps which led up to the covered vestibule, steps flanked by wrought-iron railings which must have been the last word in elegance during the nineties. The front door was massive and inset with panes of mullioned glass. Perched sadly on it a weather-beaten gargoyle stared at me in stony reproach. As I fumbled for the door key I was reminded of Hezekiah Morse.

The door swung open. " 'Better thou hadst not been born than not to have pleased me better,' " Sylvia quoted softly. She confessed: "Barry, I do feel something like poor Cordelia."

And there was something Lear-like about Hezekiah Morse. Nothing as superficial as a white beard because Morse, with the exception of his bristling mustache, was clean-shaven. No, the resemblance, provided that it didn't exist solely in my own imagination, lay in Morse's dominating imperiousness.

He was built along the general proportions of a grizzly bear, with tremendous hands and a grip that, despite his seventy-two years, was still bone-crushing. Add a large bulbous nose, small, deeply set, slate-colored eyes, and a florid complexion which probably meant a tendency toward apoplexy, and you have the picture of Sylvia's grandfather. I own that I wasn't looking forward with any pleasure to our interview that night.

The front hall was an inky black. "The switch is behind the door, Bar—"

She wasn't allowed to say more. Space and time dissolved momentarily as I pulled her into my arms.

"You're lovely, so lovely! Like all the princesses in all the fairy tales!"

But, if this were a fairy tale, I recognized presently, upstairs was a very fierce old ogre to be placated.

I helped her off with her wrap. It was ermine and had probably cost more than my year's salary. Once again I realized all that I was forcing her to sacrifice. And yet— even then—I was powerless to halt her.

She turned her head, and I saw that her face wore the expression she has when her mind's once and for all fully made up. She's rather like her grandfather then.

"I shall talk to him alone, Barry."

I exclaimed indignantly: "What kind of spineless worm do you think I am?"

"Please." Her hand rested an instant on my sleeve. "He's an old man, you must remember. I owe him a lot. The very least I can do is to tell him myself."

I kissed her.

"We'll have to compromise, I see. Suppose I wait down here for ten minutes and then come up after you. We'll face him together—like John and Lorna before old Sir Ensor. Do you remember?"

Her smile was a little wistful. "I remember that Sir Ensor called them two fools."

"And John answered that they were well content to be two fools together," I replied.

"Well, aren't we?" Her eyes gazed beyond me, into the dim shadows of the upper stairs. "Only I consider it the wisest thing we've ever done, my dear."

The tall clock in the front hall boomed. I counted the strokes; there were exactly a dozen. Their echoes were swallowed by the silence everywhere around us and vanished like ghosts.

"Only ten minutes," I reminded as she started up the stairs. She turned an instant to wave at me.

Silhouetted against the darkness her white taffeta gleamed like a moon ray. Sargent—and Sargent alone—could have done full justice to that portrait. Then she was gone—blotted out by the blackness of the upper hall.

The house became suddenly empty, and I realized then how intently I disliked it. A house of creaking floors, of gloomy hallways. A house, dank and musty, seldom, even in midsummer, visited by the sun. A house which suffocated Sylvia's gaiety beneath Victorian oppression.

Or was I blaming the house when the blame should be placed squarely upon the shoulders of Hezekiah Morse?

Taking off my overcoat I went into the living room to wait my ten minutes. With all the lights on this room wasn't so bad. It would even have been cheerful if flames had been flickering—as they should have been—in the open fireplace under the marble mantel.

I sat down in a lounge chair, which faced the open door to the hall and from which I could keep my eyes fixed on the stairs where I had last seen Sylvia. Lighting a cigarette I reflected that the situation was rather like something out of the *Mikado*. Something fantastic and ludicrous and utterly muddled!

It was I who had drawn up for Hezekiah Morse the document which would so effectually disinherit his granddaughter if she married other than one specified man (who was decidedly not Barry Foster). Sylvia was forbidden, unattainable. Yet I, who should have realized that fact better than any man, had ventured to reach for her nevertheless, helpless in the grip of a force I could not control. And what would be the outcome of it only the gods could conjecture.

Morse loved his granddaughter, yes. Probably as much as it was in his makeup to love anyone. But he couldn't bear to have his will thwarted. And he didn't back down. Those beetling eyebrows, that rugged jaw, showed unmistakably how impossible it was for him to capitulate.

Well, what of it? I asked myself fiercely. Sylvia could come to me without one nickel from her irascible old grandfather, and I asked nothing better. The money didn't matter to her either, she had assured me.

Besides, I wasn't doing so badly myself. I was well on the way to a junior partnership with Steelcraft, Cunningham and Swift. But the catch came right there.

Morse wouldn't forgive easily. It might be more accurate to say that he wouldn't forgive at all. Although I didn't have a better friend in the world than Lawrence Steelcraft would his friendship be enough when Hezekiah Morse began to pull wires? There were plenty he could pull—Morse was well able to make his influence felt in Chicago.

And if Steelcraft were forced to bow his head to the storm? It's never easy at best to locate with a new firm; it might be an impossible task if Hezekiah Morse wanted to hound me, as he probably would. And then what? Wearing out shoe leather walking

hostile streets? Waiting vainly in anterooms where many are called but few are cho-
sen?

And Sylvia? No, I didn't have any right to ask her to share *that* sort of life. I had to
tell Hezekiah Morse that it wasn't true, I wasn't going to marry his granddaughter.
Rising from my chair I took a hasty step toward the door. But to give up Sylvia? I
couldn't!

I sank back, undecided. No, I couldn't see any way between the horns of this
dilemma. Besides, things had gone too far for action now. I could only wait.

Time had dragged interminably, but the hands of my watch stubbornly insisted
that only five minutes had passed. I crushed my cigarette into a convenient ash tray
and thought of Hezekiah Morse.

He would be in his study, of course. That was his favorite room, and he was generally to be found there—among the books which lined its walls from the floor nearly
to the ceiling. Idly, I wondered how many of them there were. Two thousand at the
very least, I estimated. Some dated back to the sixteenth century, rare first editions.
The total value of the collection couldn't be much less than a hundred thousand
dollars. Morse had shown me one book for which alone he'd paid enough to keep an
entire family in decent comfort for a year. Yet he'd considered it to be a great bargain—because it had been printed in 1579 and because, as far as anybody knew,
there was only one other copy in the world.

My thoughts strayed from the study, and I became aware that Morse's house was
surprisingly quiet. Was Sylvia talking to her grandfather upstairs? One would think
their voices could be heard, or at least Morse's rumble. He should, if past experience
were any criterion, be bellowing with a bull's anger by now.

I listened intently, but could discern nothing. The silence continued to envelope
the house in the manner of a thick, heavy gas. Haunting walls of silence! Where were
the servants? Where was Morse? This eerie quiet was like some sinister emanation
from a disturbed Egyptian tomb.

Glancing again at my watch I saw that it was now nine minutes past twelve. And at
that very instant every nook and cranny of the room was alive with sound, its waves
beating their message into my eardrums. A scream! The shrill paroxysm of a soul in
terror. A woman's voice. *Sylvia's!*

I ran to the stairs, dashed up three steps at a time. Memory is vague with regard to
what I had expected to find up there. Perhaps I had envisioned Morse twisting her
arm or some such sadistic nonsense . . . Faintly as in a dream I was conscious of other
footsteps than my own, footsteps that were clattering up the other stairs, the stairs
which descended to the kitchen.

I reached the upper hall, and Sylvia, like a hunted thing seeking refuge, ran into
my arms.

"Barry!" Just that single word repeated over and over. "Barry! Barry!"

She raised her head from my shoulder. Though I live to reach the century mark I
shall still be haunted by the sheer horror which I saw imprisoned on her face.

"Grandfather! In there!"

Her gesture indicated the study, and I tugged at the doorknob. The door met my pull with unexpected resistance. Baines hurried toward us from the far end of the hall, and I was vaguely conscious that it had been his footsteps I had heard on the back stairs.

"It's locked!" I said stupidly. As though doubting my word Baines tried the knob also.

"So it is, sir."

"The other door!" Sylvia cried. "In here!"

I stepped across the threshold of the room she pointed out—her own room I recognized at once. From it a door opened onto the study, a connecting door which now stood open.

A wide circle of light from the tall lamp on Morse's desk illuminated the room, permitting me to see, only too clearly, every hideous, horrible detail.

He was slumped far forward in the chair, his chest resting against the edge of the desk. His fingers were gripped about the handle of a small knife, the blade of which penetrated through the coat of his gray suit, disappearing from view within his very flesh.

"Why it's—it's Mr Morse!" Baines gasped weakly. His voice seemed to be coming from a great distance, an irrelevant element in a kaleidoscopic nightmare.

I lowered my eyes. A red pool had formed on the desk top. A horrible pool of glistening crimson which was trickling drop by drop down to the blue Chinese rug. I glanced hurriedly about the room. It was in no disorder with the single exception of one desk drawer, which had been pulled open as though the desk had been hastily rifled.

I turned my head and found Sylvia shuddering behind me. Her eyes were fascinated, seemingly unable to break away.

And it was then that I saw for the first time, staining the hem of her white gown, that damning red smear!

II

I sent Baines back to the kitchen, acting upon some vague sort of idea that he ought to be at his post when the police arrived. I urged Sylvia to lie down in her own room; it was the only thing I could think of that might make it even a trifle easier for her. She obeyed me, moving mechanically as an automaton; she was too stunned even to cry. I would have liked to shut the study door, to cut off that sight from her eyes, but I knew I had no business disturbing the status quo.

The desk telephone was fortunately well out of the range of that bloody puddle.

Lifting the receiver I dialed "Police 1313." After I had made as brief and noncommittal a statement as possible to the police operator I called Steelcraft. His voice, answering sleepily over the wire, heightened in tense surprise as I told my story. Yet his tones, cool and calm as always, carried assurance, and I felt a trifle easier when I left the telephone. Since my legal experience had been largely limited to probate and corporation work I was unable to predict what course the police would take in such a case as this. But Steelcraft, now forewarned, could be counted on for immediate action in the event that both Sylvia and I should be arrested and held incommunicado. That possibility, however, seemed very remote then.

Before leaving the room I made a hasty reconnaissance. As I have shown in my diagram (frontispiece) mahogany sectional bookcases lined the walls on the four sides of the study. All the bookcase doors were closed, and there was no evidence that anything else in the room had been disturbed. However, I noticed a piece of paper lying upon the floor near the hall door.

I bent to pick it up. Disgustedly, I saw that it was merely an obvious form letter from an advertising agency, which must have blown from the top of the desk. Just in time I stopped myself from tossing it back there. The police, I recalled, would certainly not wish any disturbance of that crimson pool on the glass top, a pool which seemed, as I watched it, to be ominously enlarging. Under the light from the desk lamp it glinted like a molten lake. Slightly nauseated I turned away.

Sylvia sprang anxiously to her feet as I entered her room.

"Barry, why did he do it? Why?"

I shook my head blankly. I was wondering if Hezekiah Morse *had* killed himself. It did not seem at all like him. But if he had not, then who had? Besides ourselves and the servants there was no one else at present in the house.

Or was there?

The place should be searched, of course. But not now, not by me. My first duty was to stay with Sylvia. Besides, if there were such an intruder, he could scarcely escape unobserved now. Unless—

I said quickly, "Did you hear a noise while I was telephoning? A sound like someone moving around?"

"No, nothing."

"Nor I. And the front stairs squeak. You'd think— Oh well, shall we go downstairs?"

A blinding spotlight pierced through the glass of the front door as we reached the bottom of the stairs. The squad car! Flinging the door open I admitted two patrolmen, one of whom trudged at once to the kitchen.

"Picked up the call less than five minutes ago," declared the other, who had taken his station by the front door. "It's only twelve-fifteen now."

"I'm Barry Foster," I told him.

"And I'm Jim Sullivan," he said pleasantly. He was a fair-haired lanky kid, who couldn't have been over twenty-two or twenty-three.

I took Sylvia into the living room. "Dear, can you sit down here in this big chair and not think of it?"

"I can try," she said with a wisp of a smile. She did sit down, but that was as far as she could comply with my instructions. "Barry, why did he do it? Why?"

To that tortured cry I had no answer. Reluctantly I left her, to return to Officer Sullivan.

"He's upstairs." I pitched my voice low so that it would be inaudible to Sylvia. "I'll show you—"

"My job's to keep the door covered," he interrupted. "There 'll be plenty of fellows from headquarters to take care of the rest. Maybe O'Ryan 'll come too."

"O'Ryan?" I repeated for the sake of saying something.

"Captain O'Ryan," he amended. "Water Tower Station. Don't you know this is in his district?"

I hadn't known, but the doorbell pealed again before I was able to confess my ignorance. Sullivan opened it and let in three blue-coated officers. One of them was about as fine a physical specimen as I ever hope to see anywhere. He was at least six feet four, and his shoulders would have shamed an all-American fullback. This giant, I soon found out, was Captain Terence O'Ryan, and he took instant command of the situation.

"Stay by this door," he roared at Sullivan. "Anyone watching at the back?"

"Patrolman Murphy," Sullivan told him.

"All right, let him stay there." For the first time he appeared to be conscious of my presence. "And who might you be?" His manner was bluff, yet not offensive.

"Barry Foster." I added, "I was Morse's attorney."

He asked bluntly, "Where 'd it happen?"

"Upstairs. I'll show you."

He turned to the two patrolmen who had come with him to the house. "Phelan, McCarter, both of you had better come up, too." Our cavalcade filed up the polished steps. When we had reached the upper hall I stopped before the door leading to Morse's room.

"He's in there."

O'Ryan tugged at the doorknob just as I had done. "It's locked."

"There's another door," I explained. "This way."

We entered Sylvia's bedroom, and I noticed O'Ryan's searching glance toward the flounced dressing table with its array of crystal bottles.

"Woman's room," he pronounced. "His daughter's?"

"Granddaughter's," I corrected. "Miss Morse is the only sur—"

But O'Ryan was staring through the open doorway.

"So that's Morse! He looks like he'd been carved up plenty! Well, we'll take this thing in order. Who found him—you or Miss Morse?"

I hesitated before answering. The truth was the best policy in dealing with the police, but—I remembered that smear upon Sylvia's dress. If a lie would help her I didn't mind telling several of them. Then I realized that I couldn't say that we had been together. Baines had already seen me running alone up the steps.

"Well?" O'Ryan demanded irritably. "Was it you?"

"It was Miss Morse," I was forced to answer. "But I was here almost as soon as she was."

"Anyone else in the house? Any servants?"

"Two. Baines—Morse's butler—and Matilda Sampson, the cook."

"Are they downstairs?"

"In the kitchen. At least I told Baines to wait down there."

"Phelan," O'Ryan directed to one of his henchmen, "go down to the end of the hall and down the back staircase and bring up this fellow Baines. There is a back staircase, isn't there?" he asked me.

I admitted that there was, and O'Ryan smiled broadly.

"Usually is in houses like these. What's that little toy sticking into his chest? A paper knife?"

It was—but it had about as keen a double-edged steel blade as you'd find anywhere, I remembered. Morse had picked the thing up in China during his last round-the-world cruise, attracted, I suppose, by the cloisonné handle, which was really a work of art.

"It's his own knife," I said. "I've seen it lying on the desk several times."

"Humph," O'Ryan grunted. "I hope Johnny Mack gets here before long."

"Mack?" I asked. "Who's—"

"Homicide squad," O'Ryan explained tersely. "I'm not so sure this case isn't up his alley."

"You think Morse was murdered?" I ejaculated. Before he could answer, Phelan brought in Baines.

Rather slender in build Baines carried himself with an air of quiet dignity. There was a large bald area upon the top of his head, and he had a solemn face. I had never actually seen Baines smile, although once or twice I had noticed a glint in his pale blue eyes that showed he'd like to. He waited attentively at the door, his head slightly bowed as though to receive his master's final orders.

"What do you know about this?" O'Ryan interrogated gruffly.

"Very little, sir. Miss Sampson and I were together in the kitchen when we heard the scream."

"Scream?" O'Ryan echoed. "Who was doing all the screaming?"

"It sounded like Miss Morse, sir."

"Oh, it did! And did you find her when you ran upstairs?" He studied the butler's face intently. "You did run upstairs, didn't you?"

"The back stairs," Baines told him. "I found Miss Morse in the hall, sir."

"Was Foster with her?" O'Ryan questioned.

"No sir. I noticed Mr Foster running up the front stairs. We reached the hall at almost the same minute, sir."

O'Ryan's vigorous snort might have meant almost anything. "How long were you in the kitchen tonight, Baines?"

"All evening, sir."

"All evening? Didn't you see Morse any time tonight?"

"No sir. Some time before nine o'clock I went upstairs, but I did not see Mr Morse then."

The doorbell rang again. Sullivan's voice sounded from below and another voice which O'Ryan recognized at once. "Johnny Mack!" he roared delightedly.

Lieutenant John Mack of the homicide section walked into Sylvia's bedroom a few seconds later. I examined him closely, impressed by the deference which had obviously been in O'Ryan's voice. He was about forty, of medium height and build, and he was almost dapper, being immaculately dressed in a dark-blue overcoat, white silk scarf, derby hat and tan gloves. His first act was to remove his overcoat and fold it carefully upon a chair, putting the derby hat and the gloves on top of it. But, although he was apparently absorbed in these details, his eyes weren't missing an item of the scene in front of them. They were restless eyes—keen and alert as those of a lynx.

So intently had I been staring at Mack that I had paid little attention to the inconspicuous little man who had followed him inside.

"How are ya, Terry?" Mack greeted. "Remember Westborough? I promised to give him a break on the next big case, and this may be it."

"Captain O'Ryan, it is a great pleasure to renew our acquaintance," the little man declared earnestly. O'Ryan laughed and clapped him on the shoulder—so hard that the little fellow was very nearly bowled over.

"Theocritus Lucius Westborough! Good Lord, yes! Haven't you had enough of murder cases yet?"

"I fear," said the little man apologetically, "that an unsolved mystery will always exercise a peculiar fascination for me."

He was standing there a little shyly, twisting his black Homburg in his hand. Not much of a man as far as size went was Theocritus Lucius Westborough—if that incredible name could really be pinned upon him. He couldn't have been much over five feet six, and he was narrow-shouldered, flat-chested and scrawny-necked. His hair was sparse and silvery; his features showed that he must have been very close to seventy. His face was triangular: the forehead was both high and wide, but his cheeks narrowed down to a small, pointed chin. And, on top of everything else, his eyes peeked from behind a pair of gold-rimmed bifocals in a manner that reminded me of an owl blinking at a bright light.

Yet, oddly enough, this unprepossessing person was sponsored by a detective lieutenant. Not until later did I learn that this old man's brilliant chain of reasoning had solved for Mack a perplexing problem with regard to the killing of an unpleasant fat man named Elmo Swink.[*]

Westborough and the police lieutenant had been firm friends ever since the Swink incident. It was a good thing for me that they were—but I am getting ahead of myself.

"Nice mess you got!" Mack grunted. "So Morse did himself in? Or did he?"

O'Ryan shrugged his broad shoulders. "I haven't had time to get very far into things. Miss Morse—his granddaughter—was the one who found him."

"Who are these two fellows?" Mack asked. O'Ryan made belated introductions.

"Foster was Morse's attorney, and Baines was his butler."

"Dear, dear, but this is very interesting," exclaimed Mr Westborough. He had at last ventured to remove his overcoat.

"It's his right hand holding the knife," Mack mused. "Was Morse right-handed?"

"He was, sir," Baines informed.

"The knife is driven inward very deeply," said Mr Westborough softly, as though to himself. "Undoubtedly it was inserted with great force."

"Blood's all right here by the desk," Mack declared. "It happened while he was in this chair—whether he did it or somebody else did it."

"One would not think that a seated man would have the leverage necessary for so powerful a blow," reflected Mr Westborough.

Mack went to the windows and inspected the catches. One was unlocked—the window near the west wall—I noticed for the first time. Mack returned to the closed door leading to the hall.

"This is locked—locked from the inside."

"Yes," O'Ryan confirmed. "Foster found it that way."

Mack turned to the butler. "Were you here when Foster tried the door?"

"I was, sir."

"Did you try to open the door yourself?"

"I did, sir."

"And it was locked?"

"It was locked," Baines repeated with positive conviction.

"Key's still in the lock," Mack pondered. "Not that that necessarily means anything. What about this other door, Foster?"

"It was open when I found it."

"Open or unlocked?" Mack asked.

"Open."

"The hall door is the natural entrance to this room," Mack declared. He seemed to be thinking out loud. "This other door—" He wheeled abruptly upon Baines. "Whose bedroom is this?"

"Miss Morse's, sir."

"Why should this door be open when the hall door's locked?" Mack inquired.

"An odd circumstance," observed Mr Westborough. He seemed to be making a sort of inventory of the articles on the top of the desk, and I began to note them myself. There was the olive-green steel cabinet which contained the card index to the library. Then there was an open book—I was standing too far away to read its title—a pile of typewritten pages and an onyx desk pen set. One of its two pens had been taken from the stand and was lying, half submerged in blood, just before Morse's body. The typewritten sheets were drenched in blood, too. The book, however, was lying farther away and appeared to have escaped the red deluge.

Baines, who was also examining the desk, suddenly bent down to peer into the open drawer.

"Don't touch anything," Mack snapped.

"Oh, no sir. I was not going to, but—"

"Well, what's the matter with you? Anything missing there?"

"I'm not sure, sir," Baines faltered. "But Mr Morse always kept his purple parrot in that drawer, and I do not see—"

"Purple parrot?" Mack repeated in a puzzled manner. "Are you crazy?"

A faint hint of a smile crossed the butler's solemn face. "A terra-cotta statuette about six inches high," he explained. "Of a purple color, sir, with red glass eyes. Mr Morse, I believe, once referred to it as a kakapo, which I understand is a New Zealand ground parrot."

"A New Zealand parrot?"

"New Zealand was his birthplace, sir."

"This statue worth anything?" Mack asked.

Baines shook his head. "From other than a sentimental standpoint, sir, it was very nearly worthless."

"Well, it must be in some other drawer," Mack grumbled.

But it was not.

III

The doorbell clanged again, just as we completed our hurried inspection of the desk. "We'll have to talk over this business later," Mack growled. "The Identification Bureau fellows must be here now."

Several newcomers crowded into the room. The only one whose face I can remember was a spectacled young man carrying a tripod and camera. Greeting this youth as Jimmy Selzer Mack directed curtly:

"Shoot all the prints you find, but don't monkey with the body until after Doc Hildreth gets here. Better not touch the knife, either. And get some good pix from several angles—you know what we want. And be sure to get some shots of this mess on the desk; that's evidence."

The spectacled youth nodded in a bored manner as he unpacked his camera.

Meanwhile, O'Ryan was telling his two patrolmen:

"I want you to go over the whole house. Start at the top and work your way down. Look for any traces of a fellow hiding and any signs of blood. If you find either of 'em, report at once."

Phelan, a red-cheeked young man, nodded and was out of the door as eager as a hound upon the scent. His colleague, McCarter, a grizzled veteran of many years' service, followed at a more leisurely pace.

O'Ryan marshalled Baines and myself from the study in order to leave the room to the ministrations of the fingerprint men. Little Mr Westborough wrenched himself from the bookcases with palpable regret. Mack followed and closed the door behind him.

"Did you get Foster's story, Terry?"

"Only part of it," said the giant O'Ryan. "He was downstairs when Miss Morse found her grandfather."

I added hastily, "She had left me only a few minutes before. We were out of the house all evening and didn't return until midnight."

"Why were you downstairs?" Mack asked bluntly. "Why didn't you go home?"

I hesitated, not quite sure how to word my answer. Baines coughed discreetly.

"Beg pardon, sir, but do you wish anything further of me?"

"No, go on downstairs," Mack told him.

"Let's all go downstairs," O'Ryan suggested.

"Good idea," Mack concurred. "It's time to see what the Morse girl has to say."

We descended the stairs in pairs. Mack and O'Ryan were ahead, and Mr Westborough and I brought up the rear. The little man said to me:

"Mr Morse, judging from the manuscript upon his desk, appears to have been engaged upon some literary pursuit."

"Yes, he was writing a book," I confirmed. "He had a secretary come in every day and dictated it to her."

"Although most of the manuscript is at present unreadable I discovered that he had apparently been engaged in verifying a quotation from Burton's *Anatomy of Melancholy*. A first edition of that work was open upon the desk."

Seeing that he was upon such good terms with the police, I risked putting a question to him.

"Do they think this is suicide?"

"Dear me, I really cannot say. Certainly it is obvious that Mr Morse died in the chair in which he was found, but further than that I do not believe Lieutenant Mack will go without additional evidence. He is not the man to jump at unjustified conclusions."

"You mentioned," I continued, "that a powerful blow was necessary to drive the knife in as far as it went."

"In my opinion, decidedly."

"Morse was a powerful man physically. Do you see any reason why he could not have stabbed himself?"

"I do not know," he returned slowly. "That question must be determined by the medical examiner."

But if Hezekiah Morse had not taken his own life, I was thinking, who else could possibly have done so? Baines had not seen Morse since nine o'clock. Could my erstwhile client have been dead as long as three hours before we found him?

I knew in a vague sort of way that the medical examiner would be able to fix the time of death within very close limits—although the processes used were totally unfamiliar to me. But there was nothing at all to be alarmed about, I told myself. The murder—if it were a murder—had undoubtedly been committed some time before Sylvia and I had reached the house, and we could easily prove our whereabouts right up to the last moment if I could find the taxi driver again. No, there was nothing that need cause us the slightest worry. And yet, so inconsistent is the human mind, I was beginning to worry by the time we went into the living room.

Sylvia was seated in a big lounge chair facing the window. A tiny white handkerchief was clenched tightly in her hand, and she had been crying. One look at her grief-stricken face told me that.

O'Ryan began almost apologetically.

"Sorry, Miss Morse, but we have to ask you a few questions."

"Naturally," she agreed. There was something imperious about Sylvia's manner—something that persisted in spite of this shock—perhaps a touch of old Hezekiah Morse. Or perhaps merely a slight reserve that came from living too long in a lonely house with a domineering old man for guardian.

"This ain't no third degree," O'Ryan said good-humoredly. "Let's all sit down and be comfortable."

He seated himself upon a sofa and crossed his huge legs while he was talking. Somehow I was reminded of a big, good-natured mastiff.

But if O'Ryan were a mastiff, Mack was a greyhound hot on the chase. His lynx eyes never left Sylvia's face. And as for Mr Westborough, who was completely dwarfed upon the sofa beside the big O'Ryan—well, he was a silent little man, content to be a mere spectator and not an actor in the drama. Or so I thought then.

It was Mack who did most of the questioning.

"Where were you this evening, Miss Morse?"

"With Mr Foster." Her voice was steady, but there was a sudden rush of color to her cheeks. "He took me to dinner, and we stayed for the floor show. However, we were home by midnight."

"Not before?"

"Perhaps a minute or two earlier." She pointed through the open door to the hall. "That clock struck while we were talking."

Mack rose to his feet and walked to the hall, comparing the time indicated by the tall Jacobean-cased clock with his own watch.

"Okay, you were here at twelve. But Foster didn't give the alarm until twelve-ten."

"We didn't know till then," I broke in angrily. "I phoned as soon as—"

"I'm doing the talking," Mack reminded curtly. "Miss Morse, why was Mr Foster downstairs? Why hadn't he gone home after you left him?"

"I—I had agreed to rejoin him in a few minutes."

"You went upstairs to get rid of your wrap?" Mack suggested.

Sylvia scorned the subterfuge. "I went upstairs to speak to grandfather."

"What about?"

"A personal matter."

"That's no answer. You can tell us more than that."

She hesitated. "Why did you go upstairs to see your grandfather?" Mack persisted.

"Miss Morse is under no legal obligation to answer that question or any other," I informed. "You understand that every answer she makes is made voluntarily and of her own free will?"

"Sure," Mack growled. "Miss Morse, do you refuse to answer the question?"

"She does," I snapped.

Sylvia nodded her confirmation, and Mack passed to the next subject.

"What time was it when you went upstairs?"

"Didn't I tell you?"

"No."

"I'm almost sure I did."

"You told us the time when you and Mr Foster were talking in the hall."

"Well, I left him just as the clock had stopped striking."

Truthful Sylvia! I admired her, even while regretting that she had been quite so explicit. True, we had been separated not quite ten minutes, but in that time—

O'Ryan said:

"She screamed, and then Foster ran upstairs. I got that from the butler."

"What time was it when you screamed?" Mack asked.

"I—I don't know," she faltered.

"Do you know, Foster?"

"It was nine minutes after twelve," I said truthfully.

"You sure of that?"

"Yes," I replied, volunteering no further explanation.

Mack produced a cigar, bit off the end and spat it into the fireplace. "Your story doesn't hang together, Miss Morse. After leaving Foster in order to speak to your grandfather, you waited nearly ten minutes before you went into his room. Assuming, of course, that you didn't see him before the time you screamed."

Her hand tightened slightly about the arm of the chair; otherwise she displayed no signs of undue anxiety. "You are correct in that assumption."

"Very well, Miss Morse." Mack's face was that of a seasoned poker player. "Why did you wait ten minutes before going in to see your grandfather?"

"It's not necessary to answer that question, Sylvia."

"But I will answer it, Barry. You know how grandfather detested rouge and mascara. I sat down at the dressing table to remove my evening makeup."

"Humph!" Mack grunted. "That take ten minutes?"

"The operation frequently requires an even longer period, I believe," said Mr Westborough from the sofa.

Mack started his investigation in a new direction.

"When you came into your room, Miss Morse, did you notice the door which opens into your grandfather's room?"

"It was closed," she returned promptly.

Mack asked, with pretended casualness, "What was this matter you were going to talk over with your grandfather? Did it concern Foster?"

"I have already refused to discuss it," Sylvia said regally. Her dark curls made a stunning picture against the tapestried back of the chair.

"Sure it concerned Foster," O'Ryan contributed jocosely. "He wouldn't have waited for her downstairs if it hadn't."

"A non sequitur," murmured Mr Westborough. "The inference does not necessarily follow, Captain O'Ryan."

Mack was chewing on his cigar with a sullen ferocity. "Miss Morse, what was the first thing you saw when you opened the door to the library?"

Her face was ash-white. "Grandfather," she said in a low voice, her hand pressing convulsively against the chair arm.

Brutally, Mack asked: "Was that knife in his chest?"

Her lips barely breathed the affirmative.

"And then you screamed?"

"I—I don't remember screaming. The next thing I can recall is seeing Barry in the hall."

"Was the door from the library to the hall locked?"

"I didn't notice."

"Didn't you try it to see?"

"I don't remember."

"No?" Mack's tone was edged. "Well, please try and remember this: How'd that blood get on your dress?"

Glancing downward she shivered. Was she seeing that stain for the first time? I wondered.

"I'm afraid I can't tell you."

"Did you go near the desk?"

"I don't know," Sylvia said helplessly. Once more her eyes strayed to the hem of her dress. "Evidently, I must have. But it is all a blank until I saw Barry."

"Not very helpful are you, Miss Morse?" Mack observed sarcastically.

I jumped angrily to my feet.

"As Miss Morse's attorney I demand that you stop this at once. You've no right at all to subject her to this sort of thing."

Mack met my glare with one of his own. "You're not in a courtroom, Foster. Not yet."

Before I could reply the camera expert, Jimmy Selzer, ran into the room, sputtering like a bomb about to go off.

"Take a look at this key, will you?"

"Hall-door key?" Mack asked.

Selzer nodded. "No prints on it. Handle it if you want to."

Mack took the key, and I moved close to get a better look. It was a round key with a solid, tubular shank—the kind that is used in interior locks everywhere. Nothing at all out of the ordinary except for one thing.

The single drop of dried blood on its bow!

"Dear me!" exclaimed Mr Westborough. "This is very important evidence, indeed."

IV

Patrolmen Phelan and McCarter entered the living room, the red-cheeked Phelan acting as spokesman.

"Chief, there's no one hiding in the house. We've been over the whole place from top to bottom, and we didn't even skip a mousehole. And there weren't any bloodstains, either."

"How about the windows?" O'Ryan asked.

"All those on the first floor were locked from the inside. And so were most of 'em on the second floor. What's next, Chief?"

"You can look for a bloodstained glove," Mack ordered.

Mr Westborough nodded approvingly. "Excellently reasoned. It is obvious that there must be one." He paused briefly. "Although it might be a handkerchief or any other similar article."

"Yes, it might be a handkerchief," Mack concurred.

"Where should we look?" Phelan wanted to know.

"Come out in the hall, and I'll tell you," Mack said.

He returned alone a few seconds later. Jimmy Selzer completed his report.

"There're plenty of prints on the telephone and on the two doorknobs—most of 'em are badly blurred. We're about ready to call it a day if you want back up there."

"All right," Mack agreed. "Tell the fellows we'll come up in a few minutes." He scratched a match to relight his cigar as Selzer was leaving the room. "What's your slant on this now, Terry?"

The big Irishman was staring at Sylvia. "Murder," he said guardedly.

"Murder!" Sylvia echoed, springing to her feet in alarm. "You mean that grandfather—"

"Just that," Mack said curtly. "As I dope it out, he was stabbed by someone standing behind him. Whoever he was, he locked the study door for some reason and went out through your room, Miss Morse. We won't know when it happened until Doc Hildreth gets here."

"The butler'd know if Morse had had any visitors," O'Ryan suggested. Striding toward the dining room he bellowed "Baines!" in a voice that a bull would have had difficulty in emulating. Baines appeared from the direction of the kitchen.

"Do you wish anything, sir?"

"Anyone here to see Morse tonight?"

"One gentleman, sir. He gave the name of Mr Wells."

"Gave the name?" O'Ryan repeated in a puzzled manner. "What do you mean by that crack? Wasn't his name Wells?"

"I do not know, sir. He was a stranger to me."

"Can you describe him?"

"I can try, sir. He was wearing a dark overcoat and a derby."

"So were a million other fellows," Mack exclaimed disgustedly. "What did the man look like?"

"A rather small man, sir. About the build of this gentleman."

"You mean Mr Westborough?"

"Yes sir."

"Would you recognize him again?"

"Oh yes, sir. His beard was unmistakable."

"Beard!" Mack shouted. "That's something. What sort of beard was it?"

"A gray Vandyke, sir."

"Gray, huh? Was he an old man, then?"

"About the age of this gentleman, sir."

Further questioning revealed that Baines had noticed nothing else about the un-known Mr Wells except that he had insisted upon keeping on his overcoat when Baines had escorted him upstairs to the study.

"What about his hat?" Mack asked.

"I deposited that upon the table by the stairs, sir."

"Did he have a card?" O'Ryan inquired.

"He did not offer one, sir."

"What was his first name?"

"He did not inform me, sir."

"Do you know what time he came?"

"Yes. It was some time before nine, sir. Perhaps even as early as eight-thirty."

"And when did he leave?"

"I am unable to say. From the kitchen I could not have heard the front door close, sir."

"Did you see Morse when you took Wells upstairs?"

"No sir. The door to the study was closed, and I conversed with him from the hall."

"You didn't see Wells go inside?"

"No sir. I left Mr Wells at the study door and descended the back stairs to the kitchen."

"His story," O'Ryan broke in, "is that he was there all evening with the cook. That hasn't been checked yet. Baines, tell Miss What's-her-name we want to see her."

Baines bowed with imperturbable dignity. "The name is Sampson, sir."

Matilda Sampson had eyes at first only for Sylvia. She was a short, pudgy woman of middle age, and she was wearing a pair of tortoiseshell rimmed spectacles.

"Miss Morse, you poor lamb! I'd have come in here before to tell you how sorry I was, but that fat cop in the kitchen wouldn't let me."

Rising from her chair Sylvia patted the older woman's shoulder.

"Thank you, Matilda. I know you would."

"What have these men been saying to you?" the cook demanded. Standing with arms akimbo she glared furiously at all of us. "I'm a respectable woman, not used to killings and such. And I've always worked for respectable people, not that that doesn't include Miss Morse, the poor lamb!"

Sylvia suggested gently, "I believe that they wish to ask you some questions."

"Questions!" Matilda exclaimed angrily. "I'll question them! That cop has left his dirty feetprints all over my floor. I scrub and scrub, and you can just tell him he's got to clean it up before he goes."

"Never mind that," O'Ryan said gruffly. "Just tell us where you spent the evening."

"Right here in this house. In my kitchen."

"Alone?"

"No, Baines was with me from dinnertime on. We was playing cribbage — just like we do every night. Now what are you going to do about that mess in my clean kitchen?"

"You can give Murphy a mop and tell him I said to scrub the floor," O'Ryan told her. He chuckled as Matilda flounced from the room. "That 'll keep him out of mischief, I guess."

The doorbell pealed again — I had lost count of how many times it had rung since I had first seen old Hezekiah in the study. This time it was the coroner's physician, Dr Basil Hildreth, who was a short, rotund individual of forty-five to fifty. He carried a worn black bag, and a stethoscope protruded from his coat pocket.

"Johnny Mack and Terry O'Ryan!" he exclaimed the moment he had set foot inside the hall. "Hello, I've seen this little fellow somewhere before."

Mr Westborough extended his hand. "At the Hotel Equable, I believe. Dr Hildreth, do you remember the body of a certain Elmo Swink?"

"Good Lord, yes!" the doctor exclaimed. He wrung Westborough's hand so heartily that the little man winced. "So you're working with the police again, eh?"

"You honor me too much," Mr Westborough murmured. "This time I am a mere spectator."

I glanced back at the living room, where Sylvia had resumed her chair by the fireplace. If there was any way in which she could be shielded from the details of this sordid business! But I could think of none.

"So it's Hezekiah Morse, is it?" the doctor was saying. "Met the old coot once several years ago. Where do we go from here, Terry?"

O'Ryan led the way upstairs. I trailed along with them. I didn't like to leave Sylvia alone, but the servants were in call and I felt that I had to know the doctor's verdict.

The hall door was now unlocked and stood open. The fingerprint men had finished with the room, but they had left it much the same as when I had first seen it. Hezekiah Morse was still slumped over the desk, his eyes wide and glassy. Dr Hildreth, however, appeared to be most interested in the dagger.

"Knife got the heart, all right. Musta nicked the aorta, or there wouldn't be so much blood here. I can remember a stabbing case where the chest cavity and the heart chambers were filled, but there wasn't as much blood on the surface as you'd get cutting your face shaving. Yet the knife had penetrated the back between the fourth and fifth ribs, and the man was deader 'n a mackerel before he had time to know what it was all about."

Dr Hildreth, it didn't take me long to discover, was an exception to the usual taciturnity of the medical profession. He seemed to enjoy talking, and he kept up a brisk rapid fire of patter all the time he was making his examination.

"You can skip the ancient history, Doc," Mack advised. "What's the dope on Morse? When was he stabbed, and did it happen here, and could he have done it himself?"

"Of course it was done here," the doctor snapped. "You don't see any blood around the room, do you? He was probably killed right away, although that doesn't always happen. The coroner's office has a record of a Mexican who'd been stabbed in the right ventricle—he ran twenty yards before he dropped." He started to touch the knife, then stopped hastily. "This been checked for prints yet?"

"Hasn't been touched, Doc. I told 'em to leave it just as it was."

"All right, I'll be careful. This looks the right size, and it's certainly sharp enough to make the puncture." Taking a small pair of scissors from his bag he cut away Morse's clothing. "Blade's double-edged, about three quarters of an inch wide, under a sixteenth inch thick. Wound's larger—looks like the knife handle had hit against the desk when he fell forward."

"That's the knife, though?" Mack queried.

"If it isn't I'll never do another job for the coroner," the doctor said cheerfully. "No signs at all of rigor. Say, how long ago did they find this fellow?"

"An hour and a quarter," said Mack after he had referred to his watch.

"Well, I want to talk to the first person who—"

"That was Miss Morse. We'll have her—"

"Maybe I can answer your questions," I broke in. "I was here almost at once."

"Who 're you?" the doctor asked bluntly.

"He's Morse's attorney," Mack informed. "Name's Foster."

"Well, Foster, I hope you kept your eyes open. Most people don't. See this pool of blood?"

I wasn't likely to overlook that sight.

"Sorta thick, isn't it?" the doctor went on. "Something like jelly? Was it that way when you first saw it?"

"It was not," I said.

"It hadn't begun to thicken?" the doctor questioned.

"No, it was a thin red liquid."

Dr Hildreth whistled. "Well, that fixes your time of death for you. Blood coagulates in from five to ten minutes. If it hadn't started to coagulate when Foster first saw it Morse couldn't have been stabbed longer than ten minutes from that time."

The full import of his words swept over me in a sudden damning flood. That would put the stabbing no earlier than midnight—but God in heaven how impossible that was!

Because there hadn't been anyone in the house at that time but Sylvia, myself, Baines and Matilda. I was downstairs; the two servants were together in the kitchen. That left only Sylvia . . .

V

This case was fast assuming the aspects of a gigantic nightmare to me. If Doctor Hildreth was right concerning the time of death he had proved the impossible, *because no one had left the house after Sylvia and I had entered.* That was self-evident: From my chair in the living room I could have seen anyone approaching the front door; the back door opened from the kitchen, where the two servants had kept each other company; nearly all the windows (except the one in the study) had been found locked from the inside.

And Morse's murderer was not lurking within the house; no, it had been thoroughly searched. Unless—"

But reason itself recoiled from a supposition so hideous. There must be some other explanation; perhaps it was suicide after all—in spite of that drop of blood upon the study door key.

There must be some logical way in which to account for that. If there were traces of blood between the door and the body of Hezekiah Morse I could advance the theory that Morse himself had locked the door *after he had stabbed himself.* Why not? Dr Hildreth had just mentioned the case of the Mexican who ran twenty yards after receiving a knife thrust in the heart. It was a pretty theory, but it didn't fit the facts. Scan the rich blue Chinese rug as closely as I might, I couldn't find a sign that even a single bloody drop had fallen there.

Well, then, Dr Hildreth must be mistaken about the time of death. Or I had been wrong about the condition of the blood when I first viewed it. But I couldn't convince myself of that; the picture was etched upon my brain in a manner that couldn't be erased.

Besides the globular doctor had not yet finished. He was now taking a reading from a thermometer.

"The loss of body heat gives another check on the time. The temperature of the body drops about 1.6 degrees an hour on an average. It takes about twenty-four to thirty hours for the body to cool completely. That's normal for a clothed body. A naked one cools faster for obvious reasons. And a fat one will usually hold its heat longer than a thin one."

"That is a very interesting piece of information," chimed in Mr Westborough. His eyes, peering behind the bifocals, hadn't left the doctor for several minutes. "If I mistake not the temperature of the body should enable you to fix the time of death with reasonable precision, thus confirming the evidence of blood coagulation, which alone might not be conclusive."

"It *is* conclusive," the doctor snapped.

"Dear, dear! I was referring to"—he looked squarely at me—"the uncertain human element."

"Oh, I see what you're driving at," the doctor nodded. "Well, the loss of body heat gives just a good rough approximation. There's so many things to be taken into consideration. A hemorrhage like this quickens the cooling, for instance. And the temperature of the air makes a difference, too. Have these windows been opened since you came?"

"They were closed when we got here," O'Ryan informed. "We haven't opened 'em."

"Well, you take two objects at different temperatures: say the stiff here and the air in the room. The bigger the temperature difference between them, the faster the—"

"Yeah! We get it!" Mack acknowledged. "Even dumb cops like us ought to know a stiff is going to cool off quicker in a cold room than in a warm one. What's the dope from your little thermometer?"

"As nearly as I can tell the body temperature confirms the evidence of blood coagulation."

Mack glanced sharply at me. "So Foster was telling the truth about the state of the blood when he first saw it?"

"I see no reason whatever to doubt his word."

"I don't either. Not about that point anyway," he emphasized meaningly. "Well then, Doc, you'd say that Morse was killed at midnight?"

"Certainly no earlier, if Foster's watch is right!"

It was. Mack and O'Ryan had already checked it.

"Okay, Doc, now tell us whether it was murder or suicide."

"Expect the coroner's office to do all the brainwork?" the doctor grumbled. "You ought to have sense enough to dope that out for yourself."

"Maybe I did," Mack grinned. "Maybe I just want to find out how dumb you are."

The doctor snorted. "Maybe I'm a green-eyed hippopotamus! I can give you half-a-dozen good reasons why it wasn't suicide!"

"Shoot!"

"In the first place the direction of the wound is obliquely downward—the edges of the incision are unequal and that indicates the knife went in obliquely. A fellow going to stab himself in the heart would stick the knife in horizontally nine times out of ten.

Then the wound would be straight from front to back and not right to left, as it is. Suicides rarely stab downward at the heart—you get more force pushing it straight in."

"Anything else?"

The doctor pointed to the clothing he had cut away from the wound.

"Just look at the work this knife had to do! First it went through his coat, then his vest, then a heavy Oxford cloth shirt, then his underclothing—all before it penetrated his body. Now a man sitting down and stabbing himself would have one hell of a time getting the knife through all that—it could hardly be done except by a man standing and coming down from behind with a powerful swing. Morse's Oxford cloth shirt alone might deflect the knife unless it traveled with considerable force."

He pointed to the incision.

"Now look at this bit of cloth from Morse's underwear—driven into the wound! That 'll give you an idea of the power with which the blade went in."

So Mr Westborough had been right! The little man had been a shrewder observer than I had supposed.

"Yeh, you've made a pretty good case for homicide," Mack conceded. "Now what kind of fellow did it?"

"What the devil does the city pay you for?" the doctor demanded. "Well, I'd say the murderer had to be quick—and pretty strong. He was standing behind Morse's chair and came down with the knife through the chest and into the heart—from the position of the wound I'm not so sure but what the blade didn't nick a rib! That help any?"

"Some!" Mack grunted. "Think it could be a woman's job?"

I had been dreading this question—even though I sensed its inevitability.

"Maybe. Let's see: Morse is seated in a low chair—that would help to make up for the difference in height—well, I'd say your woman couldn't be any shorter than five feet six or seven inches. And she'd have to have strong wrists—probably used to playing lots of golf or tennis."

Strong wrists? Well, Sylvia fenced, I was thinking. And I had talked to her fencing master, a lively little Frenchman. What had he said? "Ah, monsieur, nothing in the world will so strengthen the wrist muscles. *Nom d'un nom*, nothing!"

I had fenced with Sylvia myself; I knew only too well the supple strength of those wrists, the strength which had been able to parry so easily my most powerful thrusts, while her darting ripostes touched just above my heart. Sylvia's hand was used to grasping the hilt of a foil . . . a foil and a dagger! One blunt, the other sharp, but was there not a certain psychological association . . .?

I broke off this trend of thought abruptly. I didn't have the courage to follow further on that path. But, in spite of everything, I remembered that Sylvia was tall. She was nearly five feet eight!

VI

Have I mentioned reporters? A whole clanjamfrie of them descended upon the house shortly after Dr Hildreth's departure. O'Ryan left the study to handle these genial ghouls of the press, and, thinking of Sylvia, I went with him. I was just in time. Three or four of them were grouped about her, all firing questions at once, but they deserted her without a qualm the instant O'Ryan appeared on the scene.

O'Ryan gave them some information — not too much — and allowed them to ascend to Hezekiah Morse's study. Useless for me to attempt a protest against the invasion! Moreover — the thought came to me with sickening suddenness — to antagonize the press at this juncture would be about the most stupid move possible to make.

However, I was thankful to get rid of them so easily, because at that instant what I wanted above everything else in the world was a chance to talk to Sylvia alone.

Strictly speaking we were not alone. The cop by the front door, a beefy, red-faced patrolman who had relieved Sullivan, could see us, but he was too far away to overhear if we spoke in low tones. And besides he wasn't even looking our way now — he had tilted his chair at a precarious angle off the floor and seemed to be entirely absorbed in his thoughts — whatever they might be.

After the last reporter had filed from the room I stood without speaking for perhaps half a minute. Sylvia was seated in a lounge chair; her back was toward me; I couldn't see her face at that moment, but I could read only too plainly the grief expressed by the dejected droop of her shoulders.

"Sylvia," I began, with as much hesitancy as little Mr Westborough. "Sylvia, dear!"

She turned her head; her deep blue eyes were misty, and her mouth quivered slightly. "Yes, Barry?"

Minutes were flying, minutes that were more precious than emeralds. And still I couldn't tell her. Couldn't say, boldly and brutally as I must, "Your grandfather was murdered — at twelve o'clock — while you were upstairs. As your attorney it is my duty to caution . . ."

No, I couldn't say it, but Sylvia was braver than I.

"Barry, is it true — what that detective said a little while ago? That grandfather was — "

She shrank from the word; I could sense her inward shrinking. Desperately I blurted out, "It happened at midnight — while we were in the house."

She sprang from her chair, her face suddenly as white as her gown. "Barry, he was killed? Killed at midnight, you say?"

I nodded. Somewhere, no doubt, there were words adequate to explain, but I could think of none of them. I couldn't even look her in the eyes. Instead I gazed at the ring on her fourth finger, and I noticed, dully as one does notice such trivialities at such times, that the stone was glowing a dull raspberry red. Outside in the daytime it would be as green as spring leaves. A peculiar rare stone, alexandrite, I believe. The ring had been a present from her grandfather, I could recall her telling me. From old Hezekiah who—

Sylvia's clutch on my arm brought me sharply back to my senses. There was strength in those slender white fingers.

"Barry, what are you saying! You know that couldn't be possible."

"But the medical examiner—" I began uncertainly. She scarcely seemed to hear me.

"He was locked in his study. The only way in was through my room. And nobody left the house."

I groped for words. "But the medical examiner swears he was killed no earlier than midnight. Something about the blood . . . oh, Sylvia!"

Fool! I was thinking. Barry, you damned fool! You were the one who told them about the blood. Couldn't you have known something was wrong when you first saw it? Couldn't you have lied to them—lied for her?

Sylvia grasped intuitively what it had taken me several moments to reason out—too late.

"If that's true, Barry, if the medical examiner is right—"

"They usually are," I said inanely.

Her voice didn't falter. "Then the police will say that I killed grandfather?"

I hung my head in mute acquiescence. I would rather have faced a firing squad than her eyes.

"But I didn't kill him, Barry," she said simply.

I didn't have a chance to answer her. Looking back at it all now I often wonder what I would have said if the cop at the front door hadn't interrupted us. He carried his chair from the hallway to the living room door and set it down with a loud thump.

"Captain's orders, Miss. You're not to talk with him alone. I've heard what you've been saying so far, and I have to hear the rest of it."

I glared—somehow it relieved me just to find an object at which I could glare.

"Miss Morse is not under arrest, and even if she were she has the right to talk privately with her attorney. You're exceeding your authority, my man."

He didn't like my tone—I hadn't intended that he should. I was rapidly losing control of my temper, which was a mistake because the police aren't to be bullied.

"Anything you have to say to her, you'll say in front of me. If you don't like it, tell the captain." He sat down with a decisive grunt by way of a period to the sentence.

I made the best of it. "All right, then, have a cigarette?"

He shook his head. "Never smoke 'em. Now if it was a cigar—"

Heavy feet sounded on the stairs. They were coming for Sylvia now, coming to put on the thumbscrews of third degree, to force her to confess— But it was not that.

No—it was a wicker basket which was being carried down the stairs. A wicker basket six feet long! Hezekiah Morse's farewell to this old house on Division Street! Before I could make any move to shield her Sylvia had seen it, too.

If she had cried it would have been easier. Tears would not have unnerved me as much as that deathlike rigidity with which she stood. I put my arm around her and led her to a chair.

"Would you like a glass of water?" I asked. It was an asinine question but it was the only thing that popped into my mind, and I had to say something. Comfort her? As if I could!

"No, I'm all right now, Barry, honestly! It's just that — well, it was sudden . . ."

The cop was pretending not to notice us; not a bad fellow after all.

"Barry, they will question me, won't they? What shall I answer?"

"Nothing at all. You're not obligated to tell them anything. Even in court a person doesn't have to answer questions when he might incrimi —"

I stopped. It sounded too much as though I already believed in her guilt, and I didn't! Or rather I couldn't be sure of anything. Feelings were mixed up with facts in a queer sort of hodgepodge in my brain. But Sylvia's voice was not the voice of a guilty person.

"If I told them the truth, Barry, just the plain, simple truth, no more and no less, could they twist and turn it around so that it would all sound like lies?"

"Absolutely not," I returned promptly. Hope was pushing its way forward in my mind, hope growing like a lily from an oozy black mire. "Only stick to the truth, and they can't make you contradict yourself. Third degree, all kinds of cross-examination are helpless against the truth. It's the shining armor which —"

How much more I would have said in this vein I don't know, but Sylvia interrupted me. There was a look on her face which meant — well, everything in the world to me.

"Thank you, Barry. I shall tell them the truth. The truth, the whole truth, and —"

"A very wise decision indeed, Miss Morse," said a voice behind me. I turned. Little Mr Westborough was standing, a trifle self-consciously, in the hall.

VII

Whatever the connection of this odd little man with the Chicago Police Department, he was not at all unfriendly. I sensed that in his shy manner as he waited in the hallway.

"You will pardon the intrusion, Miss Morse?" He made no attempt to enter the living room uninvited. "Lieutenant Mack wishes to ask a few questions of Mr Foster."

"Won't you have a chair, Mr Westborough?" Sylvia invited.

"Thank you, I shall." He selected a large wing chair which almost totally eclipsed him from view. "Do not hurry yourself, Mr Foster. No hurry at all. Dear me, there is at present a veritable bedlam upstairs, if you will forgive my mentioning it, Miss Morse. The ingenuity displayed by four reporters in the fabrication of questions is almost unbelievable."

Sylvia tried to repress a shudder. "It will be a front-page sensation? In all the newspapers tomorrow?"

His grave voice was sympathetic. "I very much fear so."

O'Ryan's big voice boomed from upstairs, "You know as much as we do about it now, boys. Run on back and write your stories."

There were shouts of "Okay!", "So long" and "Sure you're not holding out on us, Cap?"; then they trooped down the stairs pell-mell. Rushing into the hall, I intercepted them at the foot of the staircase.

"I'm Miss Morse's attorney. It may endanger her health permanently if she has to talk any more tonight. I hope that you'll be decent enough to let up on her and put me through the works instead."

They were sporting enough to agree to this, and I spent a very busy five minutes answering (or evading) questions. Considering it was my first experience I don't believe I did so badly. At length even the most persistent of the four was willing to concede that I was a turnip from which all nourishment had been squeezed, and I was able to return to the living room, where I found Sylvia deep in conversation with Mr Westborough. Her manner was more relaxed than I had seen it since I had first waited at the bottom of the staircase.

She called to me, "Mr Westborough is quite an authority on Roman history, Barry."

"Dear me, no, I am a mere student of the subject," the little man disclaimed modestly.

"Anyway he is writing a monograph on Heliogabalus," Sylvia finished. "And he's already written a book about the Emperor Trajan. Isn't he a real celebrity?"

"He certainly is," I concurred. So the little man wasn't a detective at all, but a historian.

"And now, if you don't mind, shall we return upstairs? Lieutenant Mack will be growing impatient."

Hezekiah Morse's study was exactly the same; there was the same bloody smear upon the desk and the rug. But Hezekiah himself was gone, and the room seemed strangely empty, in spite of the fact that Mack, O'Ryan and the two patrolmen, Phelan and McCarter, were all present.

Or perhaps I must except Mack, who could hardly be called present. He had climbed out of the west window and was standing on the sill outside, a flashlight in his hand. "There's been no monkey business," I could hear him saying. "This window wasn't forced open, Terry."

He jumped back to the floor of the study. "Hello, Foster. Answer a question for me. Wasn't this window usually kept locked—like the other one is now?"

"I believe so," I assented. "Morse's books are valuable, and he took every precaution."

"Then why the hell do we find it unlocked?" Mack wanted to know. "No, I'm not saying anyone could've got in by it. There's no rain pipe or anything; only a human fly could 've crawled up that front wall. But why does this window happen to be unlocked just on this particular night at this particular time?"

"An odd circumstance indeed," contributed Mr Westborough. He leaned far forward out of the window which Mack had left wide open. "Lieutenant Mack, may I borrow your flashlight?"

"Sure," grinned Mack, handing it to him. "What's on your mind now?"

"Very little. I merely wished to see if the impression of a ladder could be discerned upon the turf below us, but I fear the distance is too great to—dear me, whatever are those?"

I followed Mack to the window, to tell the truth, well pleased at the turn the investigation had taken. If it could only be established that someone had left Hezekiah Morse's study by its one unlocked window! However, Mr Westborough had found nothing to confirm that supposition. What he pointed out was merely a series of small holes in the gray stone about a foot below the window ledge. The nearest was almost a foot and a half from the edge of the sill and there were others under the second window and also under the window of the adjoining house. All of them were in a straight horizontal line.

"Whatever can their purpose have been?" pondered Mr Westborough.

"Might 've been some ornamental ironwork hung there," Mack theorized.

O'Ryan nodded. "Might 've been at that. There used to be a lot of that old junk around these parts."

"Baines might be able to tell you something about it," I suggested.

O'Ryan bellowed for the butler, who was presently escorted upstairs. He looked sleepy—and a little scared. Neither he nor Matilda had been allowed to go to bed. They had been kept together in the kitchen with a patrolman to report every word they said to each other, I learned afterwards.

Bowing, Baines waited for O'Ryan to speak.

"What do you know about these holes under the windows?"

"There was at one time a small decorative balcony, sir. It was suspended not only from below these windows but also from under the windows of Mr Vail's house next door. But it was demolished several years ago since Mr Morse feared that this architectural adornment might facilitate the ingress of burglars. His collection of rare books is extremely valuable, sir."

"Well, it looks like your boss had shut out his second story men, all right," Mack conceded. "Nobody can climb up that wall without a rope or a ladder, or I'll eat my hat. But what did the fellow next door say when Morse started to haul down his ironwork?"

"Mr Vail had given his consent, sir."

"Vail?" Mack repeated. "Who is this Vail?"

O'Ryan interrupted before Baines could reply. His bulky body was stooped over the wastebasket by Morse's desk, and his big, clumsy hands were pawing through its contents.

"There's paper and a string here, Johnny! Paper and string!" He straightened up and turned sternly upon the butler. "Say, what time did you empty this wastebasket?"

"This morning, sir."

"Then Morse unwrapped some sort of parcel since then. Know what it was?"

"No sir."

"Morse go out today?"

"Only for a brief walk about four o'clock, sir."

"Was he carrying a package when he returned?"

"He was not, sir."

"You're sure of that?"

"Yes sir."

"Did any packages come for him today through the mail or from some store?"

"Nothing, sir."

"Anyone bring a package to him?"

"I believe Mr Wells, of whose visit I informed you a short time ago, sir, was carrying a package under his arm."

"Well, why the devil didn't you say so?" Mack demanded in an exasperated voice.

"You didn't ask me, sir."

"Say, who is this Wells, anyhow?"

"As I told you before, sir, I haven't the slightest idea."

"You went up with him to the study, didn't you?"

"Yes sir."

"Could you hear anything that Morse said to him?"

"I do not eavesdrop, sir."

"Well, slap my dirty face!" Mack exclaimed. "Baines, you win the jack pot. Who else besides Wells called on Morse today?"

"Only Mr Vail, sir."

"The fellow next door, huh? What did he want?"

"He was a very intimate friend of Mr Morse's," Baines informed reprovingly. "Mr Vail came about three this afternoon and stayed until shortly before Mr Morse went out for his walk."

"And those two were all the visitors Morse had today?"

"There was also his secretary, Miss Guild, but she can scarcely be placed in the category of visitor."

"Any telephone calls?"

"One while Mr Morse was at luncheon. About one-thirty, sir. A man's voice which I could not identify."

"Could you hear the conversation?"

"I did not remain in the room while Mr Morse was talking."

"Suppose that call was from Wells making an appointment for the evening," I cut in. "If you trace it, you—"

"Trace it," Mack cut in disgustedly. "How the hell can we trace a call from one dial phone to another? If it was made from a toll phone we might have better luck—they keep a record of those calls." He had several more pieces of information to add on this subject.

"Anything else, sir?" Baines inquired respectfully.

"No, run back to the pinochle game," Mack ordered, relighting his cigar and throwing the match on the rug.

"Cribbage, sir," Baines corrected as he left the room.

"Nuts!" O'Ryan glowered. "I'd like that guy a whole lot better if he'd forget to say 'sir' once in a while."

"Willing enough to talk, though," Mack commented. He looked at me sternly. "Hope I can say the same for you, Foster. You ought to know all about Morse's affairs."

"As far as I know his affairs were simple. He had been a client of my firm, Steelcraft, Cunningham and Swift for a number of years, but lately we have had very little to do for him."

(Leaving out those confounded wills, of course! But I wasn't going to bring up that subject!)

While Mack questioned me O'Ryan was rummaging through the drawers of Morse's desk, and Mr Westborough seemed very intent on the bloodstained papers upon its top. Those papers were innocuous; I knew that, but I felt a little uneasy at O'Ryan's investigations. No telling what might turn up in one of those capacious drawers.

"Oh, you didn't?" Mack went on. "How did Morse have his money invested?"

"The bulk of his fortune was largely in government bonds and other sound securities. He also owned some real estate, mostly apartment buildings."

"How much was he worth?"

"I couldn't say exactly. Two million dollars might be a close estimate. His holdings had shrunk considerably during the depres—"

Mack grinned. "Where have I heard that story before? But Morse had at least piled up enough dough so he didn't have to work. What'd he do with all his time? I'd go nuts just sitting around."

I waved my hand at the bookcases. "This collection kept him fairly well occupied. He was writing a book about them. A sort of glorified catalogue, you might call it."

"It was evidently the latest installment of this work he was perusing at the time of his death," Mr Westborough remarked. Thumbing through several sheets he read aloud:

" 'And for those other faults of barbarism, Doric dialect, extemporanean style, tautologies, apish imitation, a rhapsody of rags gathered together from several dunghills, excrements of authors, toys, and fopperies confusedly tumbled out, without art, invention, judgment, wit, learning, harsh, raw, rude, phantastical, absurd, insolent, indiscreet, ill-composed, indigested, vain, scurrile, idle, dull and dry; I confess all ('tis partly affected), thou canst not think worse of me than I do of myself.' "

"Say, that guy didn't have much of an opinion of himself!" O'Ryan exclaimed.

"What's it all about?" Mack wanted to know.

"It is from 'Democritus to the Reader', Burton's satirical preface to *The Anatomy of Melancholy*," Mr Westborough explained. "That is the book now lying upon Mr Morse's desk. Undoubtedly, he wished to verify the quotation, which he had cited in his own work."

"Well, I don't see much in that lead!" Mack uttered with the contempt of the thorough realist. "Books aren't going to get us anywhere on this case."

"I am not so sure," Mr Westborough demurred gently.

"Foster," Mack demanded peremptorily, "what do you know about Morse's will? He had made one, hadn't he?"

It had come at last—but I was calmer than I thought I would be!

"Yes, several of them."

"Several? Couldn't he decide who was to get—"

"It wasn't so much a question of who as of how."

"You'll have to explain that."

"As is common when disposing of large fortunes, the property wasn't willed outright, but was tied up in the form of a trust. Mr Morse kept changing the trust provisions—continually altering the power of the trustees."

"But the same people were to get the dough?"

"Yes, the beneficiaries, with very minor exceptions, remained unchanged."

"Sylvia Morse one of 'em?"

"Naturally. She was his granddaughter and his only living relative."

"Who were the other beneficiaries?"

"In the last will signed by Morse about two thirds of the estate was left in trust for Miss Morse and one third in trust for Vail. Baines and Matilda were to get five hundred dollars each and about half-a-dozen charities were mentioned."

"Vail, eh?" Mack perked up at the mention of this name. "Say, what sort of guy is he?"

O'Ryan, who had continued his search of the desk, interrupted before I could answer.

"Here's Morse's checkbook, Johnny, and you can take a look at this."

"This," I noticed as I leaned across the desk, was the stub of a check made out for one thousand dollars on the Continental Illinois National Bank and Trust Company. It was made out to cash, and the date indicated that Morse had signed it on the last day of his life.

VIII

"Was Morse in the habit of drawing large sums of money from the bank?" Mack asked Baines, who had been called in once more for consultation.

"No sir. He was not. Once a week he visited the bank and drew out enough cash to pay the household expenses, sir."

"When'd he do that?"

"Every Monday, sir."

"Hm! This is Wednesday—or rather Thursday morning. He went last Monday as usual, I suppose?"

"Yes sir."

"It's dated Wednesday," Mack speculated aloud. "Wonder where Morse cashed it if he didn't go out until four."

"Banks are closed then, and a grand is quite a sizable amount to get together on the spur of the moment," O'Ryan commented.

"What does that suggest to you, Terry?" Mack asked after Baines had again left the room.

"I'd say Morse had to have some cash pronto for something."

"Or somebody!"

"Blackmail, eh?"

"When a guy collects as much jack as Morse had he can expect to be shaken down for a little of it now and then."

I was able to confirm this, and I did.

"An attempt was made about four months ago to blackmail Mr Morse. A man by the name of Ernest Hands, ex-clerk in a broker's office, had collected what he thought was evidence implicating Morse in an off-color stock speculation. He wanted five thousand to keep quiet."

"He get it?"

"He got six months instead! Morse's skirts were legally clear on that deal—if it had smelled to the general public—and he could afford to be tough. He was!"

"What happened?"

"Morse played along with Hands, let him think he was scared to death and persuaded the fellow to come to his study. Hands was a rank amateur at the game and didn't have much sense at that. Morse led him along to spill the whole story, while I waited in the next room with a dictograph and a representative of the State's Attorney's office thrown in for good measure. Hands didn't have a Chinaman's chance when it came to court. He got the full sentence too—six months."

"What kind of fellow was Hands?"

"Little dried-up shrimp of a man with pale blue eyes and a drooping mustache."

"Hum," Mack grunted thoughtfully. "Is he still in the big house?"

"He was the last I heard."

O'Ryan had come to the wide, shallow top drawer of the desk. As he jerked it open, he let out a yell.

"Here's Morse's gat!"

Mack left me at once and dashed across the room. "Let's take a look at it, Terry." He handled it very carefully with his handkerchief, I noticed. "Smith and Wesson thirty-two." He broke it open and the cartridges popped out upon the glass top of the desk. There were six of them. "Chambers full," Mack observed, "and the barrel's clean, too. This didn't have any more to do with it than my Aunt Harriet up at Niles, Michigan."

But O'Ryan had found something else in the top drawer of Morse's desk—a number of typewritten sheets, which were bound together by brass fasteners within a blue manuscript cover. I glanced over his shoulder, and the minute my eyes fell upon the first two words, my heart traveled downward to the general vicinity of the patent-leather Oxfords I was wearing. Hezekiah Morse had made a carbon copy of the typewritten instructions he had given me. The instructions for his last, diabolically conceived will!

"It's Morse's will," O'Ryan roared. "And it's got a lot of dope here that Foster kept mum about. Baines was to get five thousand—not five hundred. And good God, what's this?"

"Let's see!" Mack shouted, snatching the document from O'Ryan's hands. He perused it rapidly, his eyes skipping over words but extracting the sense of the whole. "Listen to this, Westborough. Here's the motive for our case—and my God, what a motive!" He read aloud: " 'In the event my granddaughter, Sylvia, fails to comply with my wish to marry Vail I want it clearly expressed that she shall receive nothing upon my death but my purple parrot.' "

"The purple parrot!" Mr Westborough gasped. "Dear me, how very odd!"

Mack put down the manuscript the better to glare at me. "Why did you lie to me about Morse's will, Foster?"

"You asked me the terms of Mr Morse's will, and I told you," I returned. "What you have been reading are some notes concerning a will which never became effective."

O'Ryan turned back to the top sheet. "The date's a week old, Foster. Don't try to put anything over on us."

"Nevertheless," I persisted, "Morse had never signed the will."

"You drew it up for him, didn't you?" Mack demanded.

"Well, yes," I admitted.

"He was gonna sign it, wasn't he?"

I told the exact truth; they were bound to find out sooner or later. "So far as I know, Morse expected to come to the office today for that purpose."

"Was Mr Vail still to get his third share of the estate?" inquired Mr Westborough.

"Only the bequest relating to Baines had been changed," I returned. "Otherwise, the new draft merely alters some trust provisions with the exception of—"

"Of this clause relating to Sylvia Morse?" Mack finished. "Two thirds of two million dollars! Christ, what a motive! And the girl's in love with you, Foster. She wanted to marry you."

"No," I said. But my denial failed to carry conviction.

"That's what she had to tell the old man that was so important it couldn't wait until morning," O'Ryan contributed with a sudden flash of Celtic insight.

"Sure, it all hangs together," Mack agreed. "You and she were engaged, Foster.

Probably just got that way tonight. She wants to marry you; she goes up to tell the old man, and bingo the fireworks start!"

I found an unexpected ally in Mr Westborough.

"The deceased, I should judge from his face, was a gentleman of a somewhat irascible character, was he not, Mr Foster?"

"That's putting it mildly," I said with a wry face.

"De mortuis nil nisi bonum," he quoted softly. "What a pity that we shall have to break the tradition in this instance! And I should also judge that he possessed a very loud and carrying voice?"

"Like a bull's," I admitted. "That is, when he really got mad at someone."

"Excellent!" beamed Mr Westborough. "Now, Mr Foster, as a sensible gentleman, I trust you will see the folly of answering my next question other than truthfully. Did you or did you not hear voices from the study while you were waiting downstairs for Miss Morse?"

I started. This little fellow had an uncanny knack of hitting upon the truth. Why, it had struck me rather queer at the time, I remembered, how fantastically quiet the house had been!

"No," I said. "I give you my word that I heard no voices from upstairs."

"Well, what about it?" Mack asked, looking rather puzzled. "What 're you driving at, Westborough?"

"Dear me," smiled the little man. "The inference appears so obvious! Unless Mr Foster is lying (and if so he has not helped his fiancée as he will learn presently) *Miss Morse could not have apprised her grandfather of their engagement.*"

"Something in that," Mack mused thoughtfully. "The old boy would 've raised plenty of commotion if he'd heard *that* news."

"Yes indeed. If my judgment of physiognomy is at all accurate, his roars of rage would have shaken the house down—speaking figuratively, of course. Therefore, either Miss Morse's story of not going into her grandfather's room is entirely true, or—"

"Or what?" Mack demanded.

There was a peculiar expression on the little man's face. "If Miss Morse killed her grandfather she *killed him without warning.* Killed him in the midst of caresses, coaxings, blandishments—all maneuvers to get behind his chair where, unseen, she could seize the dagger. A terrible crime, gentlemen! A crime that could be conceived only by such a misshapen monster as Gloster. Gloster whose boast, if I recall my Henry VI aright, was 'Why, I can smile, and murder whiles I smile.' "

"Sylvia couldn't possibly have done that," I found myself saying.

Mack sniffed doubtfully. " 'Murder while I smile', eh, Westborough? Well, it's usually a woman's way of killing!"

"But," Mr Westborough objected, "in the event your hypothesis is true, how explain the disappearance of the purple parrot?"

"I don't," Mack admitted. "What difference does it make? It wasn't worth a damn."

"For that very reason it becomes of even greater significance," smiled Mr West-borough. "Were it of value one could conceive of innumerable reasons for its disappearance."

"I get it," Mack said, a little sheepishly. "That is something of a puzzler when you come to think of it!" His face brightened. "Hell, it isn't either! Miss Morse knows the old man was planning on booting her out with nothing but that damn parrot. She simply got mad and pitched the thing out the window. I can't say I'd blame her."

"Well, we can check up on that, and check up right away," O'Ryan cut in. He turned to the two patrolmen, who had been waiting patiently by the doorway. "Phelan, McCarter, go downstairs and look under all the windows—as far in any direction as a girl 'd be able to throw. See if you can find any pieces of a purple-clay parrot."

Mack added instructions of his own.

"And take a look at the turf under the study window—the one that was open. See if there 're any marks that look like someone had a ladder resting there."

The patrolmen nodded understandingly and were gone. "You were engaged to her?" Mack asked of me. There seemed to be little point in lying further about it.

"Yes, we were engaged."

"Happen tonight?"

I admitted that the assumption was correct.

"Well, tough luck that this had to come up," Mack said with a gruff sympathy. "Right now I'm kinda interested in the fellow who was to get a third of the estate, regardless of whether or not he married Sylvia Morse. What kind of fellow is this Vail?"

By all rules and regulations Sylvia should have preferred Tom Vail to Barry Foster! Even though she didn't I couldn't help being a little jealous of the man. However, I tried to be fair in my appraisal.

"He's rather slender, stands about five feet nine, has steel-blue eyes that can stare you out of countenance. Roman nose and long, thin hands. Talks with a slight drawl, and you think when you first meet him that he's affected, but there's nothing sissified about Vail. He's a fine boxer and a crack revolver shot—as a matter of fact he won several prizes shooting in tournaments. Well, that's about all I know, except that he was once in the diplomatic service."

"Related to Morse?"

"Not that I know of."

"Damn funny the old man should take such a big shine to him," Mack mused.

"Say, how'd Vail feel about marrying Sylvia Morse?" O'Ryan cut in.

The answer to that was easy—only too easy.

"He was in love with her," I said slowly.

"Well, that makes the cheese more binding," Mack exclaimed. He left me to stroll about the room, glancing at the bookcases, but I soon found that he was not looking at the titles of the volumes inside. "These are queer old houses, do you know it! Most of 'em were built two or three in a row with one wall between them. Architect's way of saving money, I guess. Not a very thick wall at that. Any carpenter could make a door between this house and the next. Is there one?"

"I never heard of it."

"Guess we'll have to have Baines up again."

The butler's legs must be getting tired of climbing the back stairs, I couldn't help thinking. However, it was difficult to visualize Baines complaining.

"Ever hear of a passage between this house and Vail's?" Mack asked.

"If there is such a thing, sir, it is quite unknown to me. I never heard Mr Morse speak of it."

"Did he ever tell you when he was going over to see Vail?"

"Frequently, sir."

"Well, did he go out the front door at those times?"

"Always, sir."

"Humph!" Mack muttered, still unconvinced. "I've heard of bookcases being built to hide a door—you worked a spring or pulled a lever and a whole section slid back—"

"Yeah," O'Ryan guffawed. "I've read them kind of yarns too. Be your age, Johnny! We know enough now to make the pinch."

"Got to check every angle," Mack retorted gruffly. He turned to the butler. "Suppose there was such a door. Where would it lead to, Baines?"

"Into Mr Vail's bedroom, sir."

Mack said with obvious excitement, "Do you hear that, Terry! We're going to have a couple of men in tomorrow to shift these bookcases and sound the walls."

O'Ryan grinned. "Waste of time, but if it 'll make you any happier—" Patrolman McCarter returned to the study before he could complete the sentence. "Well, did you find any signs of a ladder being used?" O'Ryan wanted to know.

McCarter shook his head. "Not on this job, Chief. It 'd have to rest on a plot of grass under the window. The turf is pretty hard, but it's not frozen, and if a ladder had been used there 'd be sure to be a couple of dents."

"Any footprints on the turf?" Mack asked.

"No," McCarter answered, "but they probably wouldn't show—ground's too hard—"

"If a guy dropped from this window his prints 'd show all right," Mack declared grimly.

"Never thought of that," McCarter exclaimed, his round and ruddy face puckered. "It 'd be considerable of a drop."

"It would," Mack agreed.

"Well, the turf's as smooth as a baby's hind end," McCarter informed.

"Now, what about that purple parrot?" O'Ryan demanded.

McCarter grinned. "Phelan's still looking for it. Persistent, that guy is! But we've gone all over the street and the sidewalk with flashlights—every place it could 've been thrown from an upstairs window. So far not even one dinky piece of the thing has turned up."

"Well, go on back and help Phelan look for it," O'Ryan directed. Followed closely by Baines, McCarter left the study. Mack wheeled on me abruptly:

"I want Miss Morse here for questioning."

"Here? In this room where her grandfather—"

"Yes, here," Mack growled. "Anything to say about it, Foster?"

I managed to curb the reply that sprang to my tongue.

"She told me only a short while ago that she intended to tell you the truth with no mental reservations. May I go down for her?"

"Yeh, if you don't take all night about it."

I found Sylvia abstractedly turning the pages of a magazine. She glanced up as I entered, a trembling ghost of a smile on her face.

"Barry, you look like the interne announcing that everything's ready in the operating room."

"It isn't that bad," I said consolingly. "You needn't talk to them at all if you don't want to."

"But I do want to. I want them to know the truth."

The truth? Yes, I thought so. But would Mack and O'Ryan? I wondered. It was plain enough to me that they were convinced that they had a case. And it looked like an almost airtight one, I was forced to admit. For no particular reason I thought of little Mr Westborough, and, oddly enough, the thought proved to be comforting.

Mack began in an almost jovial fashion as we entered the study, "Well, Miss Morse, feel like answering a question or two?"

She nodded, her eyes deliberately averted from the desk.

"All right," said Mack, "have a chair."

He was seated at Morse's desk, and the place he had prepared for Sylvia was directly in front of him. I hurriedly interposed.

"Miss Morse will sit here," I said, indicating the chair by the small typewriter desk, which was used by Morse's secretary in the daytime.

Her look was ample thanks. Poor Sylvia! Looking back at it now, it seems that there was so little I was able to do to make her lot easier.

There was a goosenecked lamp with a green shade upon the typewriter desk, and O'Ryan was fixing the shade so that the light would shine upon Sylvia's face. I twisted the shade the other way.

"The light is bothering Miss Morse's eyes, Captain O'Ryan."

He glared at me in discomfiture. "See here, Foster—"

"Let it go, Terry," Mack interrupted. Behind the big glass-topped desk he had assumed almost a judicial aspect—an effect slightly marred, however, by the cigar which was bobbing in the side of his mouth.

"Miss Morse, you told us you came to your room at twelve o'clock?"

"Yes," Sylvia confirmed. Her voice was steady, but her hands, crossed upon her lap, were trembling the barest trifle.

"Did you close the door from your room into the hall?"

"I think I did. I'm not quite sure."

"No?" Mack questioned sarcastically.

"I'm not sure of anything tonight," she admitted faintly.

Mack declaimed with easy assurance, "The door might have been open, then, Miss Morse?"

"It might have been," she agreed.

"At that time did you hear the noise of a person moving? Either from the next room or from the hall?"

"No," she returned promptly.

"Then there was no one on this floor but yourself and your grandfather?"

I couldn't stand for that. "That's not a fair question. You've no right to ask what Miss Morse thought."

"Speak when you're spoken to," Mack snapped irritably. "This isn't a court, Foster, and I'd advise you to pipe down if you want to stick around. Well, Miss Morse, what about it?"

"How could I know whether anybody else was on the floor or not?" Sylvia asked.

"If anyone had been, you'd have heard him fast enough," Mack declared positively. "These floors creak to high heaven when a fellow takes a step. You couldn't miss a noise like that, Miss Morse. Not unless you wanted to."

She faltered, "I don't know whether I could or not."

"Don't know, eh? Well, you do know this. You were going in to ask your grandfather's consent to marry Foster."

She started—and I thought of a bird inadvertently blundering near a crouching cat.

"Do you admit that's true?" Mack demanded.

"Yes," she said softly. "It's true. But that doesn't have anything to do—"

"It has everything to do with it," Mack cut in peremptorily. "Your grandfather wouldn't allow you to marry anyone but Vail. He was going to disinherit you if—"

"I don't know how you—"

"Never mind how we found out. We did, and that's all that concerns you. Miss Morse, do you play much golf or tennis?"

"A good deal of tennis." Her face was plainly puzzled. "Why?"

Mack blandly ignored her question. "I had you doped out as a tennis player. Good strong wrist muscles. Firm fingers. Fingers that can hold—"

I couldn't put up with any more of it. No man could.

"Miss Morse's tennis hasn't a thing to do with this. Please confine your questions to the actual matter in hand."

"Have it your way," Mack said with pretended joviality. He winked at O'Ryan, standing across the room. "Funny, Terry, that Miss Morse should spend nearly ten minutes just sitting at her dressing table."

O'Ryan returned the shuttlecock with a chuckle. "If it had been me, I'd have been right anxious to find out what granddaddy was going to say to me."

"You'd think she would," Mack grunted. "And instead she spent the entire time just fixing her face."

I motioned to Sylvia to make no comment upon this badinage, but she failed to see my signal. "A woman's way of procrastination, Lieutenant. You see I was frightfully nervous, and—"

Mack was across the room in one spring—the cat claiming its victim.

"You're lying, Sylvia Morse. We know you're lying. You went into your grandfather's room right after twelve o'clock, and you didn't dare tell him about Foster. You walked around the desk behind him and saw that knife. You reached out a hand for it—he didn't even look up. You grabbed it and—don't lie, Sylvia Morse! Lying isn't going to help you. I'm right, and you know it. Just look at your dress! His blood spattered on it when—"

"Dear me," interrupted Mr Westborough. "But in that event why is the *hem* of Miss Morse's gown stained and the hem alone?"

IX

Mack's last statement had been pure rhetoric, it was at once evident. However, the detective was a big enough man to admit when he was in the wrong.

"You're right, Westborough. She must 've brushed against the edge somehow." Rising from the chair, he stooped to make an examination. "Yeh, there's a sort of smudge here."

"Therefore, it is necessary to consider the time factor," Westborough resumed. "Miss Morse, you will pardon my somewhat gruesome allusions? The blood did not reach the side of the desk instantly. The large pool must first have formed upon the top before the overflow was able to trickle down the side. A considerable interval— perhaps one as long as several minutes—is indicated. Is it reasonable to suppose that Miss Morse remains all this while behind her grandfather's chair?"

"Why not?" Mack asked grimly. "She had to fix his fingers around the knife handle."

"But I didn't!" Sylvia exclaimed piteously. "I didn't do anything of the kind."

I broke in angrily:

"Unfounded accusations before witnesses are slanderous if I know anything about the law. Miss Morse has grounds right now for an action."

"Nuts!" Mack ejaculated. "I don't bluff worth a damn, Foster. You've got to ex- plain just how her dress did get bloodstained."

But Sylvia still insisted that she didn't remember going near the desk.

"I saw him sitting there—saw that awful knife! Then it's all a complete blank until I met Barry—Mr Foster—in the hall."

"Quite understandable," breathed Mr Westborough. He was on our side; I no longer had any doubts of it. "Such an intense shock—I believe that any psychiatrist will confirm this—might well account for the hiatus in Miss Morse's memory."

Sylvia's head was poised high, and there was more than a trace of her grandfather in her voice.

"If I were lying to you, lying about anything, you understand, it would be easiest of all to lie about that. But I'm telling you the exact truth. I can't remember going near the desk. I can't even remember screaming."

"I wonder if you are telling the truth?" Mack said sternly.

"Try me," she urged. "Ask any question you want."

"No," I shouted. "I'm not going to let you take advantage of her. Mack, I'm telling you once and for all that Miss Morse cannot be compelled to incriminate herself."

"No?" Mack drawled. He was smiling—hatefully. "Even for a lawyer, Foster, you're all-fired anxious to cover up. You're not worrying over her nearly as much as you pretend. What you're really afraid of is that she'll incriminate you."

"That's a lie," Sylvia flashed. "Mr Foster couldn't have had anything to do with it. He was downstairs the entire time."

So I was forced to hide behind a girl's skirts! I didn't like it—no man would—but I didn't see anything I could say that wouldn't make the position even worse.

"Miss Morse can scarcely confirm my whereabouts." I was hoping that they'd be dumb enough to take that for a confession.

They weren't.

"She doesn't need to," Mack said. "You're cleared if she says she didn't see you come out of this room."

"I didn't," Sylvia returned at once. "I'll sign a statement or swear it or do anything else that—"

"Nothing else is needed," Mack cut in, his eyes narrowing shrewdly. "Miss Morse, were you sitting in such a way that you'd have been sure to see Foster if he had come out?"

"Don't answer!" I cried. "Sylvia, don't an—"

But she had answered.

"Yes. I was seated almost directly facing the door. I couldn't have helped seeing him."

That did it! In spite of myself, I couldn't help yielding a grudging admiration to the cunning manner in which Mack had spun this web. For if Sylvia had been able to see me leaving the study certainly she would have been able to see anyone else performing the same act. *And there was no other way out than through her room.*

"That's all I wanted to know," Mack crowed jubilantly. "You could see *anyone* who came out of the study, Miss Morse. And no one did come out for the simple reason that no one was there. Miss Morse, you killed your grandfather."

I clutched at straws. "Perhaps Morse was killed earlier."

"I'll take Doc Hildreth's word on that any day against yours."

"I don't mean the doctor's wrong, but after all he does allow some leeway. He didn't say that Morse couldn't have been killed a few seconds or maybe a minute before Miss Morse reached her room."

"Where does that get you?" Mack snapped. "The killer's got to go some place, hasn't he? He can't disappear into thin air. You'd have spotted him if he went down the front stairs. If he ran down the back stairs he'd have gone into the kitchen where two independent witnesses were sitting. What's left? He isn't in the house—Phelan and McCarter didn't overlook a place where even a mouse could hide, they say. And the windows were locked from the inside."

"One window in this study wasn't locked," I reminded.

"Hell's bells!" Mack exclaimed. "Are you trying to tell me he turned into a bat and flew away?"

Phelan and McCarter entered the room at that moment. Phelan looked noticeably crestfallen.

"Chief, if that purple parrot was thrown from a window of this house, I'll eat the thing myself."

"Purple parrot?" Sylvia echoed. "You mean grandfather's?"

"We do," Mack said grimly. "Of course you don't know it's gone?"

"No," she answered, ignoring his tone. "Is it?"

"It is," Mack said firmly. "When did you see it last, Miss Morse?"

"I can't say definitely."

"When was the last time you were in here, Miss Morse?"

"You mean before I returned this evening with Mr Foster?"

Mack grunted affirmatively.

"This afternoon, somewhere around four. I came to put back a book."

"A book?" questioned Mr Westborough. "May I ask the name of it, Miss Morse?"

"The first volume of Browning's *Men and Women*."

"Indeed?" smiled Mr Westborough. "Dear me, I thought that only such old fogies as myself ever read Robert Browning."

"He isn't my favorite poet," Sylvia admitted. "However, there was a certain quotation running through my mind, and it seemed to be just the sort of thing that Browning would have written. I had to make sure."

"Indeed, yes," Mr Westborough beamed. "I have often experienced the identical sensation. Did you succeed in verifying your conjecture?"

"Oh yes. I already had half an idea where to look for it. You know the stanza that begins: ''Tis an awkward thing to play with souls'?"

" 'And matter enough to save one's own,' " Westborough finished.

Her glance was admiring. "You *do* know your Browning."

"Mr Browning and I have had some very pleasant hours together," the little man said with a pleased chuckle. "Your grandfather owned so many rare and valuable books, Miss Morse. Is it possible that this volume is a first edition?"

"I think it is."

The light of the genuine booklover was gleaming in his eyes. "May I have your permission to examine it, Miss Morse? Although I have lived nearly seventy years I have never been fortunate enough to see a first edition of *Men and Women*."

"It's in there," Sylvia said, pointing to one of the bookcases.

"The books are arranged alphabetically by authors?" Westborough inquired.

"Yes, except for the folio editions. They are segregated along the west wall in those bookcases with the deep shelves."

"Naturally those giant tomes would require specially built cases," Westborough agreed. "But *Men and Women* is not of their number, for I see that very work now." Lifting up the sliding glass door, he took out a volume bound in faded green cloth. His eyes traveled caressingly over the title page. "London: Chapman and Hall, 193, Piccadilly. 1855," he read aloud. "Yes, this is a first edition, Miss Morse, and it is in exceedingly fine condition." Regretfully, he restored it to the shelf. As he did so, I could see him give a slight start. "Is there by any chance an index to your grandfather's library, Miss Morse?"

"That olive-green cabinet on the desk. Grandfather made out every card in it himself."

Measuring about a foot square by a foot and a half deep, the cabinet contained four drawers, each of which held about a thousand cards. Mr Westborough jerked out a top drawer.

"They are indexed by titles, I see."

"And by authors, too, in the two lower drawers," Sylvia informed.

Mr Westborough had withdrawn two cards and was comparing them meticulously. "All of these cards, you say, are in Mr Morse's handwriting? It is rather odd that he should undertake such a tedious clerical chore."

"He didn't think it tedious," Sylvia said. Her eyes were moist. "Grandfather loved these books, Mr Westborough. No detail in connection with them was ever too much trouble for him."

"A true bibliophile indeed," Westborough declared. Replacing the cards he opened a lower drawer and withdrew two more. These also he returned to their proper position. "It is the same. Exactly the same."

"What's eating you?" Mack wanted to know.

"It is the merest triviality," said Mr Westborough. "Not worth mentioning, I assure you."

Nevertheless, even Mr Westborough could be mistaken. Although, looking back upon it now, I don't see how any man on earth could have guessed the astounding secret of those index cards.

X

"Let's get back to the purple parrot," Mack suggested. "Was it worth very much, Miss Morse?"

"A terra-cotta statuette? And not even particularly well done? I'd say it would be overpriced at a dollar and a half. Grandfather was attached to it because it was a New Zealand parrot. He was born in Dunedin, you know."

"We're wasting time," O'Ryan interrupted gruffly. "Phelan, take Miss Morse to the living room. She isn't under arrest—*yet*, but you're not to let her out of your sight."

"I'm coming with you," I said. "Sylvia, dear—"

Mack's voice cut curtly across mine. "I want you to go next door with me, Foster, to rout out Vail."

"Vail!" O'Ryan exclaimed. "What's he got to do with it? We've got our case already solved."

"Not until all the loose ends are tied up," Mack maintained firmly. "Vail is going to get a third of two million dollars, isn't he? That's motive enough for half-a-dozen murders."

He was silent on our way downstairs, and I was completely absorbed in thoughts of Sylvia. "Not under arrest—yet!" O'Ryan had said. I hadn't liked the way in which he had emphasized that little word "yet."

But, in strict justice, I was compelled to admit that the police attitude was not altogether unreasonable.

After we had walked the few steps to the adjacent house Mack pressed his finger against the bell and held it there. Presently we heard advancing footsteps from within, and then Vail's servant, Hudson, opened the door a few inches and stared at us suspiciously through the crack. He was a portly individual of about forty-five, and he was clad in slippers and a dressing gown.

"Mr Foster!" Hudson exclaimed. His memory was remarkable, because he had seen me but once before in his life. "I'm sorry, but Mr Vail has been in bed for nearly two hours."

"Well, that's just too bad," Mack jeered. He threw back his coat lapel to display his shield.

"The police!" gasped the thoroughly frightened Hudson.

"Right the first time, Fatty," Mack exclaimed. "Open up there."

Hudson reluctantly complied. "I shouldn't like to waken Mr Vail," he said hesitantly.

"Well, you better do it anyway," Mack advised peremptorily.

Hudson ushered us into the living room and withdrew. As Morse's and Vail's homes were almost exact duplicates on the outside, a stranger could not be prepared for the startling difference in the two interiors. Stepping through Vail's door seemed to bring us right into the heart of old Spain.

The rough white plaster walls and the soft red floors (covered only by occasional small rugs) seemed to impart a certain brightness to the rooms that was lacking in the murky gloom of Hezekiah Morse's dwelling. Spanish chairs, upholstered in rich velvet, flanked a curious sort of cabinet beautifully inlaid with ivory scrolls—a cabinet that had a drop front like a writing desk and was mounted on a stand with turned uprights and an elaborate arcaded base.

"A vargueño," informed Mr Westborough, who had accompanied us from the other house. "Authentically Spanish."

Mack was regarding one of the huge chairs doubtfully. With its red upholstering fringed with gold, it was a magnificent article of furniture — far too magnificent for everyday use. "Some dump!" Mack exclaimed. He sat down, somewhat gingerly, on the velvet chair and ejaculated, "See the swell looking dame over the fireplace, will you?"

I had seen the portrait upon my previous visit; in fact, it was impossible not to notice it, so completely did it dominate the entire room. The full-length figure enclosed within the huge gold frame was life-size or larger. It was a portrait of a woman, seated in just such a chair as Mack was now occupying and toying with an ivory fan. A lovely, vivacious face with steady gray eyes and sensitive nostrils, a face that seemed (so skillfully had the artist preserved his illusion) to be glowing with the breath of life itself! Her light chestnut hair was partially covered by a characteristically Spanish headdress, which tumbled in a lacy black cloud about the gleaming whiteness of her shoulders.

Mr Westborough observed, a trifle self-consciously, "Gautier made the statement that a woman in a mantilla must be as ugly as the three cardinal virtues in order not to look pretty."

Mack laughed. "Well, this dame's not even as ugly as one of 'em. She's a honey, that baby. But she's a blonde, and I thought all these Spanish janes had black hair and black eyes."

"It is difficult to generalize with any degree of exactitude concerning the women of Spain," Westborough informed. "The fair type predominates among the Catalans, and I have little doubt but that this woman is of that people. Her skin is a pure white, not of that delicate bronze shade of the women of Andalusia and Castile, while her face, mobile and expressive, lacks the impassive serenity so common among the women of southern Spain."

"Yeh?" Mack commented. He rose from the velvet chair to fling his cigar butt into the fireplace. "Wonder how long this guy Vail expects us to wait here, anyway?"

Hudson returned, alarm written upon his round full moon of a face. "I have not been able to wake Mr Vail." He paused uncertainly. "The truth of the matter is that he came home intoxicated. I'm afraid that it will take several hours for him to sleep it off."

"Well, we're not going to wait that long," Mack informed, striding toward the stairs. "Put some coffee on the stove and we'll see he gets up to drink it, all right. Where's his bedroom?"

"First room on your left."

Mack paused, his hand on the wrought-iron rail of the staircase.

"Say, Fatty! What time 'd you say your boss got in tonight?"

"I didn't say," Hudson evaded.

"Well, what time did he get in?"

"Very close to one o'clock."

"Don't forget about that coffee," Mack reminded as he reached the landing.

Hudson had not exaggerated Vail's condition. We found him lying, very drunk and snoring, in a huge bed, which had an unusually high carved headboard painted in yellows and blues. His clothes were strewn on several chairs—Spanish chairs with turned legs—and his hat was perched grotesquely on one of the tall candlesticks at either end of an enormous bureau.

"Stewed is right!" Mack exclaimed with a derisive sniff. His glance left the occupant of the bed to traverse the east wall—the wall which partitioned this room from Hezekiah Morse's study—and his face brightened as his eyes rested upon the huge tapestry which hung there. He strode across the room and lifted the tapestry high, allowing it to fall with a chagrined expression as he uncovered nothing but a plain blank wall.

He recrossed the room and shook the sleeping man's shoulder. "Wake up, there!" Vail grunted, turned over on his other side, and fell fast asleep again. "I'll fix him," Mack observed. He went into the adjoining bathroom and came out with a full glass of water, which he splashed into Vail's face. The latter sat up, his blue-striped silk pajamas drenched.

"What the hell! Who the devil are you?"

"Police," Mack said succinctly and showed his shield.

"Well, what you doing here? Get out."

"Vail," I asked. "Do you remember me? Foster?"

"Don't know you from Adam," said Vail, and turned his back. "Gotta go to sleep."

I grasped his shoulder and shook hard. "Vail, wake up. Mr Morse's been murdered!"

"Eh?" In Vail's befuddled condition words required a considerable interval to reach his consciousness. "Foster!" he exclaimed. "Uncle Hezekiah's lawyer. You say someone's been murdered?"

"Mr Morse!" I shouted in exasperation.

Vail jerked bolt upright; the idea had at last penetrated. "Uncle Hezekiah killed! Oh my God!"

"Come on, let's get going," Mack said gruffly. "Stick your head under the shower and put on some clothes. Your man has some hot coffee downstairs."

Vail staggered from his bed and into the shower. After his douche in cold water he began to show more animation, but I had to help him dress.

"Come on, hurry up there," Mack directed. Vail was unsteady on his feet, but we steered him downstairs to the living room, where Hudson was waiting with a tray. Pouring a cup of piping hot coffee from a big silver pot he handed it to his employer.

"No cream or sugar in it," Mack ordered sternly. "And drink it right down."

Vail swallowed as much of the hot coffee as his throat would stand, set the cup on the table and rose to his feet. "Did you actually say that Uncle Hezekiah has been killed?"

"Murdered," Mack confirmed callously. "We want you over there now."

"You don't know who did it?"

Mack's look was long and searching. "We think maybe you can help us find that out."

We returned next door to the study, where O'Ryan was waiting. Seating himself at Morse's desk Mack began his interrogation.

"Vail, you referred to the deceased as 'Uncle Hezekiah.' Is he any relation of yours?"

"No."

"If he wasn't related to you why were you to inherit a third of his property?"

"That's a long story," Vail answered. "I'm not sure I care to tell it beyond saying that Mr Morse had been a close friend of my parents long before I was born."

"He wanted you to marry his granddaughter?"

Vail stiffened immediately. "I'd rather not discuss that."

"But you will discuss it," Mack insisted.

Vail took a silver cigarette case from his pocket. "See here, Lieutenant What-ever-your-name-is! I don't think that Morse's private business has anything at all to do with his death."

"That's for us to decide. And my name is Mack. Lieutenant John Mack of the homicide section." He chewed savagely on his cigar. "If you know what's healthy you'll answer questions. Did Morse have any enemies?"

"Of course he had enemies," Vail replied without hesitation. "What man with two million dollars hasn't?"

"Well, do you know anyone that might 've killed him?"

"No."

"What about Wells?"

"Wells?" Vail repeated.

"Yeh, know anyone of that name?"

"Several people, I should imagine. It's not an uncommon name."

"Don't try to be funny. Baines claims that a guy by the name of Wells, no first name known, dropped in some time before nine in the evening."

"Well?"

"No, Wells," Mack yelled in vexation. "Have any idea who he could be?"

Vail shook his head. "I don't know any Wells with whom Morse had dealings."

"How long has Baines been with Morse?" Mack inquired.

"At least twenty years."

"Did they get along all right?"

"Doesn't twenty years' service speak for that?"

"When I ask you a question, answer it! I don't want any riddles."

"And I don't need any insolence. Modify your tone if you want information from me."

"Listen, you, I'm not asking questions because I like to hear you talk," Mack roared angrily. "You may have been Morse's pet, but you're no more than a pain in the neck to me."

O'Ryan added threateningly, "You aren't doing yourself any good this way, Vail."

Leaning languidly against the back of his chair Vail surveyed the two officers with a thinly veiled contempt.

"May I ask just what you would like to know—gentlemen?"

His sarcastic inflection of the last word passed unheeded, although I could sense that Mack was inwardly boiling.

"I asked, did Morse get along all right with Baines?"

"As far as I know, Morse valued Baines highly."

"How long has the cook, Matilda, been here?"

"Morse hired her when he first moved into this house four years ago."

"He only had two servants?"

"How many did you expect him to have in a house this size? I only have Hudson."

"Didn't Morse even have a chauffeur?"

"No, he didn't own a car."

"Two million bucks and didn't own a car!" Mack exclaimed wonderingly. "What in hell 'd he get out of life?"

"It would be useless for me to attempt to explain," Vail said patronizingly. With a visible effort Mack controlled his temper.

"Is there a secret doorway between your house and this one?" he asked.

Vail's eyebrows lifted. "Aren't you a bit melodramatic?"

Mack's annoyance was evident; no doubt this secret-door business was one of his prize pumpkins.

"That idea's not so damn farfetched as you seem to think, Vail. It wouldn't be much of a job for a carpenter to cut through the wall between these two houses."

"I agree," Vail assented in a bored manner, "but why go to all the bother?"

"Well, we'll know tomorrow if you're lying about it," Mack informed. "Every inch of this wall is going to be sounded."

Vail's face was unperturbed. "A harmless way of amusing yourselves, I suppose."

Mack ignored the gibe. "When was the last time you saw Morse alive?"

"This—yesterday afternoon."

"What time?"

"Between three and four."

"Here?"

"No, I didn't come up here. His secretary was typing so we talked downstairs."

"What about?"

Vail shrugged his shoulders eloquently. "Another matter I don't care to discuss."

"Wise guy," Mack sneered. "Well, tell me if Morse wanted you to marry his grand-daughter."

Vail hesitated. "It's a matter of record, as Foster would probably say, so I don't mind telling you that he did desire such a marriage."

"And how 'd you feel about tying up with Sylvia Morse?"

"I prefer not to discuss it," Vail answered coldly.

Mack growled, "Did you know Foster had drawn up a will disinheriting Miss Morse if she refused to marry you?"

Vail deliberated for several seconds. "Yes, I was aware that Morse wanted such a will."

"And you knew he hadn't signed it?"

Vail nodded. "And thank God for it!" he added hotly.

"So you didn't want to marry the Morse girl, huh?" Mack's glance was shrewdly penetrating.

"Once and for all I'm telling you that my relations with regard to Miss Morse are strictly private," Vail said angrily.

"Spanish pride is proverbial," Westborough interposed gently. Seated in an inconspicuous corner of the room he had hitherto taken no part in the conversation. "And the Catalans, although the least Spanish, are not the least proud of all Spanish people."

"What the devil!" Vail exclaimed. "I never saw you before in my life. How do you happen to know my mother was a Catalan?"

"A mere surmise against long odds," Westborough smiled. "The large portrait in your living room is obviously of a Catalan beauty. But the mantilla is now rarely worn in Catalonia—either the portrait was painted years ago or the mantilla assumed by the sitter for effect. An inspection of the paint and canvas inclined me to the former view. The portrait could, of course, be a mere decorative adjunct to your attractively furnished drawing room, but in that event why not a more conventional Spanish type? I conjectured that the subject held a sentimental association for you, and your mother appeared to be the most logical possibility."

"Well, you're right," Vail admitted grudgingly.

"Yeh, but that portrait's got as much to do with this case as my Aunt Harriet up at Niles, Michigan," Mack declared. "Vail, did you know that Sylvia Morse is engaged to Foster?"

Vail's start was genuine. "No, I didn't know that," he admitted slowly. "Accept my congratulations, Foster."

"Thanks—" I was beginning when Mack's voice cut in sharply.

"Never mind that now. Vail, what time 'd you get home this evening?"

Vail's shoulders shrugged once more. "I haven't the slightest idea; you'll have to ask Hudson."

"We did," Mack told him. "You got in around one o'clock."

"Then why ask me?"

"Because," Mack emphasized the words significantly, "Hezekiah Morse was shot at twelve o'clock."

"Shot?" Vail asked. "I thought—"

"You thought what?"

"Well, judging from the look of things, there seems to have been an unusual amount of blood. It would suggest the severing of one of the great arteries."

Mack stared with undisguised suspicion. "Vail, you know something about this business. You know that he was stabbed and not shot."

"I tell you I didn't know. That was nothing but a guess."

"Well, if you're innocent, it'll be easy enough to prove it. Can you tell us where you were at twelve o'clock."

"Certainly," Vail responded, "I was with—" He stopped abruptly. "That is, I was visiting a friend."

"What's his name and address?"

Vail shook his head. "I can't tell you."

"The hell you can't! Let's have the name."

"I don't choose to have her name dragged through the newspapers."

"Calling on a lady, eh?" Mack grinned insinuatingly. "Well, you can forget the movie stuff. Let's have her name, or—"

"Is that a threat?" Vail asked with apparent carelessness. But I was watching his fingers clench, and I remembered that the man had been rather noted as an amateur boxer.

"It's anything you want to make it!" Mack shouted. He controlled himself by a prodigious effort. "Vail, if you have a genuine alibi for twelve o'clock, for God's sake give it to us. Or else we'll have to draw our own conclusions."

"Draw them," was Vail's retort. His jaw had set at an obstinate angle. Rising from the desk Mack stamped out his cigar; the ashes left an ugly gray smear on Morse's Chinese rug.

"All right, you'll have to take the consequences. You had a good motive for killing Morse, and you refuse to tell us where you were at the time he was killed. This job lies between you and Miss Morse if you want the plain truth."

"Miss Morse!" Vail exclaimed with patent anxiety. "It's unthinkable that she could be involved."

I shook my head. "Unfortunately, Vail, Sylvia happened to be in her room alone from twelve until about ten minutes past. And the medical examiner insists that Morse was stabbed no earlier than twelve."

"And they suspect Sylvia!" Vail scoffed. He strode across the room and banged his fist on the glass top of the desk. "By God, if brains were little drops of water, the police department would be the Sahara Desert!"

O'Ryan's face reddened. "I don't like that crack, Vail. One more like it and we'll have to stick you in the lockup."

Vail glanced across the room at Westborough in his obscure corner. "As a person of some intelligence it must amuse you to observe how these brilliant minds function."

"Your manner is undeniably provocative, Mr Vail," the little man scolded gently.

Vail, perversely set on infuriating the two officers, continued, "Obviously the problem is too much for their limited powers of reasoning."

O'Ryan's hamlike hand came down—none too gently—upon Vail's shoulder. "Either you shut up, or—"

"Take your damn hands off me!" Vail shouted. Eluding O'Ryan's grasp he swung, but, in spite of his size, O'Ryan was quicker. His big fist caught Vail squarely on the chin, and the latter flopped to the floor without a sound.

"Hell!" O'Ryan exclaimed in genuine consternation. "I didn't mean to knock the guy cold!"

XI

I shall deal briefly with the remaining events of that night. Vail was revived and hustled down to a waiting patrol wagon. He had deliberately done his best to antagonize the police, and it was little wonder they regarded him with suspicion. But as for Sylvia—well, not until the patrol wagon had actually driven away could I fully realize that she, too, had been arrested. Standing at the threshold of the now darkened house I felt that I could never again believe in the existence of human sanity.

Before climbing into his car parked before the house Mack growled a few words of caution. "We've got nothing on you, Foster—so far. But I'd advise you not to try to leave town."

As if anything could be farther from my thoughts! Mack drove away, and I began to walk west on Division Street toward my hotel. Nothing could be done about securing Sylvia's release that night, I pondered. Moreover, it was rather doubtful if we could succeed in getting a writ of habeas corpus even in the morning. And any premature attempt must inevitably have a damaging reaction when the case finally came to trial. At this point, I remembered gloomily that I was out of my element in matters of criminal law; my firm confined itself solely to civil cases. But if energy could make up for experience—

A voice hailed me, and I turned to see Mr Westborough hurrying behind me. Rather strange that he should be there because I had heard Mack offer to drive him home. "I believe that we are going in the same direction, Mr Foster?"

I slowed my pace. "Nippy weather," I remarked asininely.

He was breathing hard, as though he had been running for some time. "A decided chill," he gasped. "Mr Foster, I have been at some pains to overtake you because I should like to offer a suggestion."

I said ungraciously, "All I want is to clear Sylvia Morse of this unspeakable charge your friends, the police, have hung on her."

"From their own viewpoint, Mr Foster, they are right—indeed, they would be lax in their duty to act otherwise. But there are elements in this problem that are far from superficial. My hotel is no more than a few blocks away. I suggest that you accompany me there, and that together we endeavor to arrange the night's events into some semblance of logical continuity."

"It's after three," I demurred.

"Dear me, so it is! But, unless I err greatly in my estimate of you, you will scarcely be able to sleep soundly tonight."

"You've said it," I agreed. "But, before I go with you, I want to know the answer to one question. Do you believe that Sylvia Morse is innocent or guilty?"

"It is my belief that the truth may be ascertained by applying rational methods of investigation. Further than that, I cannot say."

His words reassured me; somehow more than if he had said glibly that he believed in Sylvia's entire innocence. "All right, I'll go with you," I agreed. Rather providentially a cab whizzed by on North State Street, and I succeeded in calling it back. Mr Westborough gave the address—the Hotel Equable, which proved to be a good-sized residential hotel a few blocks away.

After receiving the key from the night clerk, a blond Scandinavian, whom Mr Westborough addressed informally as Chris, we took the elevator to the third floor and strolled down a long corridor to Mr Westborough's room. The little man scurried about hospitably as soon as we were inside the door. "Pray allow me to relieve you of your hat and overcoat, Mr Foster. And I can quite conscientiously recommend that large chair."

Rummaging through the drawer of his writing desk Mr Westborough produced a pad of scratch paper and two pencils. He divided the pad into two sections and presented me with one of them and with a pencil.

"No doubt you will wish to jot down various impressions of this discussion. Nothing is more fleeting than an unrecorded idea—as I have learned from sad experience."

I humored him by accepting the pad, but I rather doubted that any ideas I might have that night would be worth recording. I could think of nothing except the hard and bitter fact that Sylvia had been arrested.

"Contrary to the general belief," Mr Westborough told me, "ideas rarely spring spontaneously into existence but must come from specially prepared soil. Although it may strike you as a ridiculous waste of time let us lay the foundation for our edifice of thought by a discussion of the Morse house itself. Suppose that you tell me everything that you can remember of it."

"As you know, it's a three-story residence located on the south side of the street," I began. "Externally an exact duplicate of Vail's house, and there's a party wall between them. The servants' quarters are on the third floor, but I've never been up there so I can't tell you a thing about them. And on the second floor—"

"Just a minute, Mr Foster. I believe that in the course of the conversation tonight someone mentioned that Mr Morse had owned the dwelling but four years?"

I nodded. "He bought it from a man named Jonas Spendall."

"It is a rather small house and does not appear particularly desirable for a wealthy man. Have you any idea why he should desire to purchase such a dwelling?"

"There's only one reason that I can think of, and that is its location next door to Vail's house."

Mr Westborough nodded sagely. "Pray proceed."

"There are only four rooms on the second floor—but why do we have to go into all this?"

He ignored my objection. "Morse's study, Miss Morse's bedroom and two additional bedrooms across the hall. The front bedroom upon the other side of the hall was Morse's, I presume?"

I nodded.

"Now, let us return to the study. The windows are ordinary sash-type windows. Both of these were found closed, but only one locked, a fact which may be of some significance when it is considered that Morse appeared to display some degree of apprehension with regard to the safety of his book collection."

"But that smooth wall?" I objected.

He waved assent. "Entirely right. I am not suggesting, merely enumerating. Outside of his books, Morse kept no valuables in his house of which you are aware?"

"No, he had a safety deposit box. Of course, he had one or two pieces of good furniture, but that's a little bulky to attract burglars. Come to think of it, the things he seemed to value most, after his books, were his iron candlesticks."

"I believe that I noticed the pair to which you refer. They seemed to me to be authentic colonial—probably dating at least as far back as the Revolutionary War period."

"Not much to look at."

"Severely plain," he agreed, "but iron candlesticks in general are earlier than brass and consequently harder to obtain."

"Well, I don't think these were so terribly valuable. Although," I admitted, "they were made in a rather clever way. There's an iron top, which you unscrew to put in the candle. The candle rests on a spring at the bottom of the holder, and the pressure of the spring keeps the wick at a constant height."

"Most ingenious," he agreed. "Somewhat reminiscent of the celebrated Carcel lamp of the same period, in which a clockwork mechanism was used to force a steady supply of fuel to the wick. However, we deviate from our course. An object of even less value than the candlesticks may have been removed by the thief who entered Morse's study, if thief there were."

"You mean the purple parrot?"

"Its color is not the least of the mysteries confronting us," he said slowly.

I disagreed violently. It was—the very least—as far as I was concerned.

"Suppose that we temporarily table the question of the purple parrot?" he suggested. "Before Miss Morse's innocence can be either proved or disproved a number of other questions require an answer."

"I can think of one. Why was the study door locked from the inside?"

"That is a vexatious problem," he admitted. "If an attempt to simulate suicide, it failed completely, for the very first clue to explode the suicide theory was the blood-stained door key. Perhaps the action was an attempt to implicate Miss Morse—"

"In which event, it succeeded diabolically," I interrupted.

"But such an attempt would suggest a certain familiarity with the time of Miss Morse's homecoming. That event was not prearranged, but occurred solely by chance, did it not, Mr Foster?"

I admitted that we had had no definite intention of returning at any stated hour when we left the house. "But," I added (something in this little man's quiet way of thinking aloud had stimulated my own cerebral activity), "if we grant for the sake of argument that Sylvia did kill her grandfather, why should she lock the door to the hall while leaving the door to her own room unlocked?"

"Excellently reasoned, Mr Foster. Certainly the common-sense procedure would be diametrically the opposite."

"It was fixed to look like a suicide," I continued. "Morse's fingers being around the knife handle and so on. But the murderer might have known all the time that the police would soon find out it wasn't suicide. That's why he locked the study door from the inside. It's all a deliberate plot to involve Sylvia!"

But he was not willing to go that far.

"Before that hypothesis can be established, Mr Foster, you must be able to say how your unknown murderer could have left the study and, possibly, the house as well, unnoticed."

"The earliest possible time for the stabbing was while Sylvia and I were entering the front door," I said. "He could have left the study before she reached her room."

"And then?" he questioned.

"I'm stuck," I frankly admitted. "I don't know how he got out of the house. All the windows seem to be out of the picture and so is the back door."

"The front door remains," said Mr Westborough.

"Yes, but I had the front stairs under observation. And if I didn't see—well, even then I don't see how I could have helped knowing. The front door squeaks when it's opened or closed."

Mr Westborough was writing upon his scratch pad. "Perhaps a timetable of your movements will be helpful. 12:00—Mr Foster and Miss Morse in lower hall; 12:01—Miss Morse reaches her room; 12:09—Miss Morse screams. Are my figures exact so far, Mr Foster?"

I nodded. "Put down that I called the police at 12:10." He wrote an additional line on the pad.

"Can you tell me how many minutes you remained in the study?"

"Not over three or four," I estimated.

He wrote: "12:13—Mr Foster leaves study; 12:15—arrival of police"; and laid aside his pencil. "Please study this tabulation, Mr Foster. Since both exits are officially guarded after 12:15, and you yourself had the approach to the front door in view prior to 12:09, the only remaining interval in which anyone might leave the house unobserved is during the three minutes in which you were telephoning. Where was Miss Morse at that time?"

"In her own room—lying down."

"Was the door from her room to the hall open or closed?"

"Open, I believe."

"Even so, Miss Morse might yet fail to see a figure in the hall. And the time was ample to reach the front door."

"But the floors creak and so do the stairs," I burst out. "Oh, it's damning, Mr Westborough!"

He confirmed, a little reluctantly, "I fear you are right, Mr Foster. Moreover, I was given the opportunity several times during the course of the evening to observe that the opening of the front door is clearly audible from the study. But in your agitated state—"

"I'm going to be entirely honest with you. During the few minutes I spent in the study my perceptions were not dulled but heightened. I seemed to be noticing every trifling sound—even the ticking of the clock from the lower hall. But that's all I did hear. It was quiet in that house then—as still as death!"

"You are not afraid to face the truth, Mr Foster," he remarked approvingly.

"I believe in Sylvia's innocence," I answered. "There must be a rational way to explain this thing! There's got to be!"

"Suppose that Morse did not die at twelve o'clock?" he suggested.

"But Dr Hildreth's opinion?"

"It was based upon the normal time required for blood coagulation. Certain diseases—notably hemophilia—may greatly lengthen this period, I believe."

I sprang from my chair and reached for the Chicago Telephone Directory, which I had noticed lying on the phone stand. "Trowbridge," I mused, rustling rapidly through the pages. "Dr Fred Trowbridge." My eyes ran down a long column of names. "Yes, here it is."

I picked up the phone and asked the night clerk to put through the call. "Who is Dr Trowbridge?" Westborough inquired.

"Morse's physician. Attended him for years. He can tell us all about Morse's blood condition—if I can persuade him to talk."

Dr Trowbridge, his voice sleepily annoyed, answered over the wire. I endeavored to explain why I was calling at that hour, and it proved to be no easy job. If I had been previously introduced it might have been easier; as it was, I could feel that he considered himself to be the victim of a gigantic hoax. I had never thought so fast nor talked so furiously in my life; four times, at least, he was on the verge of hanging up.

Fortunately, he not only knew of my firm but had met Steelcraft personally. That helped some, particularly when I suggested he call Steelcraft at once for verification of my tale. He was willing to admit then that I might be telling the truth, but even so it was far from smooth sailing. Conforming to a rigid code of professional ethics, he was reluctant to say anything at all regarding Morse's physical condition, and it was not until I had aroused his sympathy by painting Sylvia's desperate predicament in full detail that he weakened and gave me the information I wanted.

Heartsick, I turned away from the telephone. "Morse's blood coagulation time was entirely normal," I informed Westborough. "Dr Trowbridge has the records to prove it."

PART TWO

Thursday, November 19

XII

The persistent din of the alarm clock woke me at seven-thirty, and the memory of the preceding night leaped with overpowering horror into my consciousness. I sprang from bed and ducked under the shower; then dressed and shaved as fast as I could make it. My dinner jacket was lying crumpled over the chair where I had flung it hardly more than three hours ago, and I automatically stopped to call the hotel valet.

I picked up the Chicago *Trumpet* at the lobby news-stand. The story was plastered all over the front page, and no mistake, beginning with an eight-column banner in type an inch and a quarter high: "STAB WEALTHY GOLD COASTER." I unfolded the paper and began to read:

Hezekiah Morse, retired financier, was fatally stabbed by an unknown hand no later than last midnight. The body of the 72-year-old millionaire was found in his study at 49 East Division Street a few minutes after twelve by his granddaughter, Sylvia Elaine Morse, and his attorney, Barry Foster.

Sylvia Morse, 23-year-old granddaughter of the deceased, who made her home with him, and Thomas R. Vail, age 35, formerly attached to the American consulate at Barcelona, are being held for questioning at the Water Tower district police station.

I skipped a few paragraphs, my eye caught by a subheading, "Who is Wells?"

"The police," said Lieutenant John Mack of the homicide section, "would welcome the full name and address of a Mr Wells, who is said to have called upon Morse at about eight-thirty last evening. It is believed that this mysterious visitor may possess information of importance concerning Morse's death."

The complete story occupied a full column and a half so I adjourned to the restaurant around the corner to finish my reading. However the reporter had uncovered nothing that I didn't already know. I pushed the paper aside, hastily swallowed my coffee and toast, and left the restaurant.

I was down at the office by eight-thirty, and the place was apparently deserted except for Ralph, the firm's irrepressible office boy, who was slitting the morning mail with a villainous looking paper knife. He gave me a knowing leer.

"Steelcraft's looking for you."

"Is Mr Steelcraft," I made the correction through sheer force of habit, "here so early?"

"Yep," Ralph informed. "Got in about five minutes ago. Said he wanted you to come in as soon as you got here. Say, what's the low-down on the Morse case, Mr Foster?"

They were talking about it already! Our office boy! Thousands of office boys in thousands of Loop offices! Sylvia's name bandied carelessly on everyone's lips. Sylvia

condemned without a hearing by a good portion of Chicago's three million inhabit-
ants! It was a ghastly thought.

I advised Ralph to read the newspapers and knocked upon the door of the office
occupied by the head of my firm. "Come in," Steelcraft invited. His office faced east,
overlooking the narrow canyon that was La Salle Street. It was a large room with
paneled walls and a thick carpet, a carpet that successfully muffled the footsteps of
every visitor.

Steelcraft looked up inquiringly. He was in his early sixties and, either by will
power or through consistent exercise, had retained his figure. His hair was iron gray,
his closely trimmed mustache of the same shade, and, to complete the color scheme,
he usually wore a gray suit.

"Oh, it's you, Barry?"

"They've arrested Sylvia Morse!" I exclaimed.

"Yes, I know," Steelcraft said calmly. I had never seen his habitual composure
ruffled, nor was it now.

"Sylvia isn't guilty," I blurted desperately. "I've got to get her acquitted. We're
engaged. I love her!"

The surprised glance Steelcraft gave in my direction was followed almost immediately by a frown. "Indeed? The action was, perhaps, a trifle precipitous." I waited for
a bawling out—certainly I deserved it for so jeopardizing the firm's interests. However, he delivered no further reprimand.

"You had better tell me the whole story, Barry."

I epitomized the events of the night as tersely as I could. Windy dissertations, as I
well knew, were anathema to Steelcraft, whose keen mind was always straining to
plunge directly into the heart of a problem. He shook his head dubiously as I concluded my narrative.

"It's going to be rather difficult to build a successful defense, although I noted one
or two points which tell slightly in Miss Morse's favor. The most important of them
is the statuette—obviously it had been taken from Morse's desk prior to the time
Miss Morse entered the study. Perhaps something of real value has also been stolen.
Morse had several books which were worth a tidy sum, I understand."

"Every book is going to be checked against its index cards," I told him. I had heard
Mack promise that last night.

"The wrapping paper found in Morse's wastebasket may also be of some interest,"
Steelcraft continued. "Baines's statement would apparently link it with the package
carried by Wells. And in this connection we must consider why Morse needed that
thousand in cash he procured yesterday afternoon—if he did procure it. Was any of
that money found on his person?"

"No," I answered. "At least not much of it. There were only two twenties in his
billfold. No money at all in the desk."

"A strong suggestion of blackmail," Steelcraft pondered.

"Morse wasn't the type to pay blackmail," I disagreed.

"It's impossible to lay down a hard and fast rule for such cases," Steelcraft maintained. "If the transaction with Wells had been open and aboveboard, why wasn't a receipt for the money found in the desk? Morse was far too good a businessman not to ask for one. Moreover it may be of some significance that Wells was not among the regular visitors to the Morse home."

I said excitedly, "And we don't know when he left the house. Baines couldn't even say that he did leave! Baines had never seen him before. Neither Sylvia nor Vail recognized the name. If we only had some way of tracing—"

"It will be difficult," pronounced Steelcraft, reaching for the telephone directory. "Wells isn't exactly an uncommon name, Barry." He rustled through the leaves of the directory and explained, "You can see that there are two and a quarter columns of them."

Counting the number of names in an inch, we estimated hastily that there were at least a hundred names per column. That meant two hundred and twenty-five persons to be investigated. But this particular Wells might not be in the Chicago Telephone Directory. Wells might be an assumed name. Or he might have come from New York. Or Gopher Prairie.

"It's hopeless," I said aloud.

"Very nearly so," Steelcraft agreed, replacing the directory on the phone stand. "Unless, of course, the man chooses voluntarily to step forward."

But I had little expectation of such luck. I stared helplessly at a picture on the wall, a framed enlargement of four eminent jurists who were intimate friends of Lawrence Steelcraft.

"Moreover, strict logic renders it difficult to suggest Wells as the actual murderer," Steelcraft continued. "There is slight chance that he or any other person would have been able to escape from the house unobserved, assuming, of course, that the medical examiner is right about the time of death, and it would be an impossible task to prove him wrong. Any juror, no matter how unintelligent, will see the obvious conclusion. *The murderer must be selected from among the four persons who did not leave the house.*"

"Well, I'm among the four," I said. "I had motive enough; I'm tall enough and husky enough to meet the doctor's description of the fellow who did the job."

"Naturally you will be viewed with suspicion," Steelcraft said reprovingly. "If you hadn't been so foolish as to become engaged last night—however, that's water under the bridge by now. The butler, Baines, is another legitimate suspect. Is he physically strong enough to have done the stabbing?"

"I should think so. Baines isn't any more than fifty, and he seems to be in a fair condition. But what motive could he have? Morse's bequests to the servants were ridiculously small."

"The original bequest to Baines was recently enlarged, I believe," Steelcraft remarked.

"However, that will was never signed," I reminded. "Baines benefits only to the extent of the original five hundred dollars. Not much of a motive. And Matilda Sampson gives him an airtight alibi."

"I wonder if there is such a thing as a really airtight alibi?" Steelcraft pondered. "An intensive cross-examination might reveal—"

"That she's lying to shield Baines? If that's so we ought to be able to break her story down without much trouble. She wouldn't make a particularly resourceful liar; she isn't the type who can think fast under fire. It ought to be duck soup to make her contradict herself a dozen ways." I was beginning to feel more hopeful. "And now shall I go down and sue out a writ of habeas corpus?"

"I'd advise against it," Steelcraft said. "We haven't much of a defense yet. It would be almost certain to be denied."

"You don't intend to leave her in that filthy jail!" I almost shouted.

"Calm down a bit," Steelcraft admonished. He was setting a perfect example of coolness himself, and I thought of Goldsmith's line about people generally being calm at the misfortunes of others. "Naturally you believe Miss Morse innocent. You wouldn't be worth your salt if you didn't, boy. I feel the same way about her myself. But the weight of evidence against her is appalling.

"She is tall enough and physically vigorous enough (witness her fencing) to satisfy the doctor's idea of the murderer. She had what mercenary-minded people (most people are mercenary-minded, Barry) would consider more than an adequate motive. Moreover, the murder was committed very close to twelve o'clock, and from that time until nine or ten minutes past she was in her room and blocked all possible egress from the study. These are damning facts, Barry."

No one knew that better than I. And there were other matters upon which he had not touched. Sylvia's mental condition. She had been dominated by Morse for so long! A psychiatrist might claim that she was in a fit state for a reaction. I recalled the quotation she had looked up that afternoon. Something about it being an awkward thing to play with souls. The quotation fitted Hezekiah Morse. Had Sylvia had him in mind?

But this reasoning spun round and round in a giddy circle and left me—nowhere. I turned to the only other possible suspect.

"Suppose that Mack's secret door materializes? Or that Vail had a key to the house—with or without Morse's knowledge?"

"You know we're bringing foreclosure proceedings on the Dorrion building bonds," Steelcraft said with apparent irrelevance. "Vail was one of the guarantors, and I obtained a Hill's report on him. It wasn't over two weeks or so ago. Did you know about it?"

I hadn't known, but I was very much interested. I had always considered Vail as a wealthy man. However:

"The report shows that he lost heavily all through the depression," Steelcraft continued. "A large part of his holdings are today tied up in—"

Ralph burst without apology into the room. He was carrying an envelope in his hand.

"Look what come in the mail! Letter from old Morse to Mr Fos—"

"I presume that you are referring to the deceased Hezekiah Morse," Steelcraft said sternly. I didn't hear the rest of his rebuke. I was busy tearing the envelope open.

The letter was dated yesterday afternoon. It was typed, but I recognized the signature. Unquestionably that of Hezekiah Morse, although—

"Great Scott!" I ejaculated. "Just listen to this."

Steelcraft frowned at Ralph, who left the room with obvious reluctance. I read aloud:

"DEAR FOSTER:

"Baines, who, as you probably know, has been in my employ for two decades, has been contemptibly deceiving me, I learned only today. I found it difficult to believe, but I can no longer doubt as he has made a full confession.

"Foster, will you go to an employment agency and look over suitable applicants until you find someone whom you think is qualified to take Baines' place? Frankly, I don't feel equal to doing this now: why I cannot say as I have hired and discharged many men in my life.

"Realizing full well that this is not a usual request to make of one's attorney, I am putting it to you on the basis of a personal favor. However, if you wish to send me a bill for your time, by all means do so.

"Thanking you for this and the past favors which you have been kind enough to render an old man, I am

"Yours sincerely,"

Morse's signature was wavier and more uncertain than I had ever seen it. And there was a certain defeatist attitude shown by the wording which had never been characteristic of my beetle-browed client. These, however, were minor points. The main thing was that here was a motive—and a good one—to bring Baines squarely into the picture.

I folded the letter and put it in my breast pocket. "I'm going straight to the police with this."

"Of course," Steelcraft concurred, a little absentmindedly. "But there's something else rather strange about this letter—something that isn't so apparent on the surface. Has it occurred to you that the hiring of a new servant is rather an intimate, personal service?"

"Meaning?" I asked.

"Others were closer to Hezekiah Morse than you," Steelcraft continued. "Vail, for instance, was like a son to him. Why wasn't Vail asked to select the new butler?"

Why not indeed?

XIII

As my cab purred northward on La Salle Street I remembered that I had agreed to meet Westborough that noon for lunch. ("At the Canterbury Inn where the food is delightfully English.") I was glad I would have the occasion to talk to him again; somehow I wanted to see his logic brought to bear upon this latest tangent our case had taken.

My cab pulled up before the Water Tower Station, whose dingy brick masqueraded behind the respectability of a grim stone front. I walked inside and asked for Captain O'Ryan. His office was a small cubicle of a room, and I found the Brobdingnagian occupant in a genial humor.

"Foster! All set to get her out on a writ, I bet?"

"Wrong guess," I answered, taking out my letter. "This may interest you. It's from Morse and was mailed yesterday afternoon."

"Have a chair," O'Ryan invited. He scanned the paper hurriedly and then went over it for a second and more carefully considered reading.

"Why was he going to fire Baines?" he wanted to know.

"It's beyond me," I admitted. O'Ryan reached for his telephone.

"Charley, have a couple of the boys go out to the Morse house and pick up the butler and the cook. Names are Baines and Matilda Sampson."

A bluecoat entered the cubicle.

"Dame to see you, Captain."

"Good looker?" O'Ryan inquired.

"She ain't bad!"

"Don't keep her waiting then."

I rose to my feet. "I'll wait outside."

"Stick around and see how the police work," O'Ryan invited jovially. "It isn't going to take long to find out what this dame's got on her chest."

Smartly attired in a swagger suit, a young lady with brown eyes and honey-colored hair sauntered into the office. She was a tall girl and gave the impression of being perfectly able to take care of herself.

"Captain O'Ryan?" The giant nodded. "I am Brenda Carstairs."

"Glad to meet you, miss. This is Mr Foster."

"Not Miss Morse's attorney?"

He laughed. "I see you've read the papers."

"That's why I'm here," she informed. "The *Trumpet* said you were holding Mr Vail. He was at my apartment last night until —"

"We'll take the thing in order," said O'Ryan. He reached for a pad and pencil. "Your name's Brenda Carstairs. How do you spell it?"

"C-a-r-s-t-a-i-r-s."

"Address?"

She gave him one on Delaware Place and her telephone number.

"Occupation?"

"Consolidated Appliance Distributors, Inc. I'm secretary to M. L. Itens, the supervisor of sales. He let me off work to come here."

"All right, all right," said O'Ryan. "Let's have your story."

"There isn't much to it. Mr Vail was with me all of last evening."

"When did he leave?" O'Ryan questioned.

"Not until twelve-thirty."

"What were you doing?"

"Nothing much," she confessed. "He'd taken me to dinner, and we didn't get back to the apartment until around nine o'clock. We had a few drinks and just sat around and talked."

"You sure that Vail left at twelve-thirty?" O'Ryan catechized.

"I looked at the clock."

"What kind of clock?"

"The clock in our living room. It's an electric clock and always keeps perfect time. Mr Itens gave it to me for a Christmas present—we sell them."

"I got one of 'em too," O'Ryan boasted. "Any other clocks in your place?"

"Yes, an alarm clock. It doesn't keep such good time so I always set it by the electric clock just before I go to bed. Then I'm sure I'll get to work on time."

"Were you late this morning?" O'Ryan asked casually.

"As a matter of fact I was five minutes early. Good thing because Itens raises particular Ned if I'm a min—"

O'Ryan switched the subject. "Vail with you all the time. You didn't leave him alone for a few minutes while you mixed the drinks?"

"No, he was the one who fixed them."

"What did you have?"

"Highballs. Whisky and White Rock."

"How many highballs did you have?"

"Well, more than one," she admitted, laughing.

"Was Vail drunk?" I asked.

"No," she said firmly.

"He came home plastered last night," I reminded O'Ryan.

"Well, he didn't get that way at my place," Brenda insisted.

O'Ryan asked her if she was willing to swear in court that Vail had been with her every minute of the evening until twelve-thirty.

"Certainly I'll swear it. Will I have to appear in court?"

"Maybe and maybe not," O'Ryan said evasively. "Just between you and I, you've pretty well cleared Vail. That is if you've been telling the truth."

"Well, I haven't been lying to you!" the girl flared as she went out the door. O'Ryan took a deep breath.

"I don't think she was, Foster. I've had thirty years' experience dealing with plain and fancy liars, and you get to know . . . Well, I'd better have Vail up here and see if he tells the same story."

The minute seemed propitious for my request.

"All right with you, Captain, if I see Miss Morse?"

"Why not?" he said genially. "Wait in the room across the hall, and I'll have her brought in." He nudged my ribs. "You can talk to her alone—I know how the land lays."

Thanking him with genuine fervor I stepped across the hall to a small reception room. It was not long—although it seemed so—before I heard footsteps in the corridor. A patrolman ushered in Sylvia and departed, silently as a cigar store Indian, closing the door behind him. I could hear the click of the lock, which, for the moment, made us prisoners together.

I sprang forward and caught both of her hands. "Darling!"

She smiled; that brave little movement of her mouth hurt me more than tears would have done. "It's so good to see you again, Barry." She relaxed happily for a moment; then her hand flew to her hair. "I know I must look awful! I had to wash in cold water, and they even took away my comb and compact."

"Took away your compact?" I asked stupidly.

She nodded. She was wearing a dark-blue tailored suit—smart, snappy like all of Sylvia's clothing. They had allowed her to change before leaving the house last night. No doubt the white evening dress was to figure as People's Exhibit A or B in the case which—

"They said the powder had to be analyzed," she went on. "But face powder isn't poison, is it? Even if I wanted to I couldn't—"

"And wouldn't if you could," I finished emphatically. "Sylvia, if it's the last thing I ever do, I'll get you out of this horrible—"

She laughed. "You should see where I spent the night! An iron cot without springs, and as for bed-clothing—well, far be it from me to slander this hotel, but I have a suspicion that other occupants have used it before. Only a suspicion, mind you."

Her gay courage was infectious. "Suppose you smoke a cigarette and tell me all about it," I suggested. I lit one for her and asked: "Have you any money, darling?"

"No, they took my purse."

Unfortunately, I didn't have a great deal either. There wasn't over ten dollars in my billfold. I kept a dollar bill and gave her the rest. "Can you put this away—in your stocking or somewhere they won't notice?"

She answered me by removing her slipper, putting the bills inside and fitting it to her foot again. The whole operation didn't take more than a few seconds. "Thank you, dear. It may come in handy. Now let's hear the worst!"

"There isn't any worst."

"Oh yes. If you had come to take me away you wouldn't give me money."

I had to admit her logic was correct. "Steelcraft—and I have to agree with him—thinks it would be just a waste of time to try to free you by a writ of habeas corpus. More than that; if the writ were denied, it would kick back on us when the case comes to trial."

I hadn't meant to admit that there was any possibility of things going that far, but the words had slipped out of their own accord. However, she took it like a trump.

"It doesn't matter if I do have to stay here for a few days. Or will they move me to some other place?"

"Very likely. After the inquest—"

"When will the inquest be held?" she wanted to know.

"As soon as they can make it. Perhaps today. Certainly not later than tomorrow. Sylvia, we'll have to work fast. They're not going to give us much time, and all the cards, in some grotesque fashion, seem to be stacked against us. Tell me about that knife. Have you ever handled it—to open letters or anything like that?"

"Yes, often. I opened grandfather's mail with it only yesterday morning. He—he liked to have me do it for him."

"They are looking for fingerprints," I said. "And unless the murderer was thoughtful enough to wipe the knife—"

"They'll find mine, you mean?" asked Sylvia.

"I'm afraid so," I admitted. Taking a pencil from my pocket I said to her, "Take this and show me how you hold a knife to open letters." She did so. "All right," I observed, "I think we can lick them on that point. But they're going to question you even more intensively than before. You've got to stick to your story. Don't change it by a hair's breadth at any place, or they'll be down on us like a ton of bricks."

"They did their best to trip me last night." Her courage I found remarkable. "Captain O'Ryan and six or seven detectives. There was a big glaring light; it hurt my eyes . . ."

While she talked the scene unfolded vividly before me. I could see them—grouped in a ring surrounding her—all large and burly men, modeled along O'Ryan's magnificent physique. Their questions would be tricky: leading questions, questions which begged the answer. And they would shout or yell them, endeavoring by sheer force of lung power to break down her resistance. The brutally phrased innuendoes dinned in my own ears as Sylvia continued:

" 'Were you engaged to Foster?'

" 'Didn't you know your grandfather would disinherit you?'

" 'Didn't you know about the will he was going to sign?'

" 'Didn't you kill him to keep him from signing the will?'

" 'The knife was on the desk when you took it, wasn't it?'

" 'You hated your grandfather.' (That would be O'Ryan; I could hear his deep voice tolling like a bell.)

"The light was hurting my eyes," Sylvia went on. "I tried to shield my face, and then they all began at once. It was like something out of a madhouse.

" 'How did that blood get on your dress?'

" 'Why did you wait there ten minutes?'

" 'Why did you lock the study door after you'd killed him?'

" 'You killed your grandfather. You killed Hezekiah Morse.' "

I couldn't allow her to go on.

"Don't think of it, dear. It's just everyday police routine, and it failed. It doesn't matter, because it failed. They couldn't force you to change your story."

"No," she replied in a small, tired voice. She buried her head against my coat, her entire body trembling in my arms. I stroked her hair in a futile attempt at consolation.

"You mustn't think of it. We'll talk about something else." My mind groped for a safe topic. "Your grandfather's purple parrot."

Her hands flew once more to her disarranged hair. "Grandfather's purple parrot? What can you want to know about it?"

"It didn't vanish in thin air of its own accord," I said. Associations were tumbling pell-mell through my thoughts. Westborough had insisted that this valueless object was of the utmost importance. Steelcraft, as hardheaded a lawyer as had ever prepared a brief, had been impressed by its disappearance also. And I recalled that Hezekiah Morse had referred to it in his unsigned will—and in what connection.

"Someone must have had a reason for taking it," I opined. "Sylvia, what do you know about the thing? Where did it come from? How long had your grandfather had it?"

"One question at a time!" Sylvia laughed. A faint tinge of color was returning to her cheeks, I noticed gratefully. "He'd had it—oh, at least ten years. George Smith left it with us. I couldn't have been much over thirteen."

"George Smith?" I repeated the name mechanically. "Who's George Smith?"

"The son of a man grandfather used to know when he was a boy at Dunedin. He was born in New Zealand, you know; that is, grandfather was. Mr Smith stayed with us a few days, and he gave grandfather that statuette just before he went away." She paused uncertainly. "I'm not sure but it seems to me that grandfather had helped Mr Smith to establish himself in business."

"In Chicago?" I asked.

"No, some little town in New York; I can't remember the name. I think it was a pottery, at least I seem to have that sort of association with him." She added apologetically, "It's been so long ago, and grandfather never did talk about him much."

"Your grandfather gave"—I made haste to correct myself, "lent him money?"

"I'm not sure," she faltered. "I never did know exactly."

Even through the closed door O'Ryan's bluff voice penetrated.

"Bring in Foster and take the jane back to her cell."

The unmistakable tread of a heavy policeman sounded in the corridor. We had only a few seconds left.

"How can we find this George Smith?" I asked. Our guard was now unlocking the door.

"You can't find him, Barry. He's—he's dead!"

"Dead?" I echoed fatuously.

"He died about two years ago," Sylvia said.

xiv

Back in O'Ryan's cubicle of an office, I found a preternaturally solemn Baines and an irate Matilda. O'Ryan began bluntly:

"I've got some important new dope. That's why I brought you here. I'll take you one at a time, though. Baines, you're first." Matilda, protesting volubly, was ushered outside, and O'Ryan commenced to interrogate the butler.

"Was Morse ever dissatisfied with you, Baines?"

Baines shifted uncomfortably. "I fear that he was at times, sir."

"But you were on good terms with him yesterday?" O'Ryan asked with Machiavellian duplicity.

"I—I was not, sir," Baines stammered apologetically.

"No?"

"He had announced his intention of discharging me, sir," Baines confessed.

"He had?" O'Ryan roared, as though it were fresh news to him. "Who else knew about that, Baines?"

"No one, as far as I know, sir."

"You didn't know your boss had written this letter?" O'Ryan asked.

"I did not, sir."

"Read it," O'Ryan suggested. "You can read, can't you, Baines?"

"Yes sir." Baines accepted the note and scanned it, his face puckering in an evident anxiety. "This is horrible, sir. But I cannot find it in my heart to blame Mr Morse."

"Suppose you tell us all about it," O'Ryan suggested.

"It began with the bottle of Est, Est, Est, sir. Mr Morse found out about that."

"Est, Est, Est?" O'Ryan echoed. "What the devil language are you talking? Chinese?"

"It's Latin, sir," Baines explained humbly.

"It means, 'It is, it is, it is'," I added. I don't know a great deal of Latin—the time is past when it's a necessity in law as it was in Blackstone's day—but I did happen to know that much.

"It's a wine, sir," Baines informed. "An Italian white wine."

"What's a Wop wine got to do with Morse?"

"It began because I couldn't keep away from the bookies," Baines confessed with a rueful expression. O'Ryan shook with laughter.

"My God, I didn't know you were that human. Play 'em to win, place or show?"

"Usually to win, sir. I was singularly unfortunate."

"Well, some cash in a forty-to-one shot, but most of us lose our shirts," O'Ryan philosophized. "But I still can't get through my skull what the bookies and a bottle of wine have to do with Morse firing you. Did he catch you getting drunk at the races?"

"The wine, sir, was from his own stock."

"Oh, he had a stock, did he?" O'Ryan exclaimed.

"A very fine one, sir. He purchased it from Mr Spendall at the same time he bought his house—four years ago. Mr Morse, however, was not much of a drinking man. Only rarely would he ask me to bring one of those bottles from the basement."

"Where do the bookies come in?" O'Ryan asked.

"The salary paid to me by Mr Morse was not large. In an unlucky moment I tried to augment it by wagers upon various horses." Baines sighed dolefully at the recollection. "Unfortunately, my bets were seldom well placed, sir. If I tried a long shot it fully justified the name. If I placed my money upon the favorite it was almost certain to have an unlucky day. In this manner I soon expended most of my savings, sir."

Said O'Ryan: "I know what you mean, all right, all right."

"One day," Baines continued, "I was introduced by a bookie to a very pleasant young Italian, named Giovanni or John Canzonetta. Rather early in our acquaintanceship, I happened to mention the large stock of wines in Mr Morse's cellar."

"Canzonetta!" O'Ryan exclaimed. "I know that bird. Dago John, we called him. Had some connections with the Allergi mob. Pleasant little playmate to chum around with, Baines!"

"Giovanni was a bootlegger, as you have surmised, Captain O'Ryan. He had quite an extensive clientele on the near North Side."

"And a damn good pull," O'Ryan interpolated wryly.

"I negotiated a small loan from him one day when I had lost more than usual at the races. I found him very obliging, sir."

"I'll bet!" was O'Ryan's comment.

"I borrowed two or three more sums, hoping to be able to repay him whenever. I had a lucky day at the races. Unfortunately that day never seemed to arrive, and Giovanni grew impatient. He threatened to call upon Hezekiah Morse and tell him the whole story. Naturally I did not wish my position jeopardized, and I pleaded with him for more time. Finally he said:

" 'See here, Baines, let's you and me do a deal. Then you'll be able to square up accounts and make some nice change for yourself besides.'

" 'What kind of deal?' I asked.

" 'Your boss has a whole cellarful of wines—French and Italian stuff that they'll pay any money for. Slip me a bottle of it now and then, and I'll sell it for you. We'll split fifty fifty—no, sixty forty. Forty for you and sixty for me. What do you say?' "

"What did you say?" O'Ryan asked.

"I didn't want to turn thief, sir," Baines supplicated. "But there was no alternative. Moreover, the risk of detection was small. Mr Morse touched the wines rarely, as Giovanni reminded me. I could see little chance that he would ever find out as long as I was careful to leave at least two bottles of every kind of wine in the cellar. Mr Morse had a list of the cellar's contents, and he would from time to time refresh his memory by consulting it. He took a collector's pride in his wine in spite of the fact that he so seldom drank it. However, he had never made an actual physical inspection, and—"

"Well, how did he get on to you?" O'Ryan wanted to know.

"Because, sir, I had failed to follow my original plan of reserving at least two bottles of every vintage, sir. One of Giovanni's clients evinced a particular fondness for Est, Est, Est. Just a few weeks before the repeal of prohibition I very foolishly allowed Giovanni to take away the last two bottles, sir."

"Why didn't you buy two more after repeal?" demanded O'Ryan.

"There were none on the market of that particular year, sir."

"How would Morse know that? He didn't visit the cellar, you said."

"But he had a collector's pride in it, sir—and a phenomenal memory for dates."

"Kinda on the spot, weren't you?" O'Ryan chuckled. "When did Morse ask for a bottle of the Triple E?"

"Yesterday afternoon, sir. As I explained last night he was called to the telephone from his luncheon. He returned in a very mellow mood and directed me to bring up a bottle of the Est, Est, Est.

" 'Do you believe that such a strong wine is suitable, sir?' I demurred. Mr Morse, however, was quite headstrong and he did not like to have his wishes crossed.

" 'When I want your advice about what to drink, I'll ask for it!'

" 'I'm afraid, sir,' I blurted, 'there is no more of the Est, Est, Est.'

" 'Nonsense! There are a dozen bottles of it.'

" 'You are mistaken, sir.'

" 'Baines, you scoundrel, you're lying to me! Just look at your face! You've been drinking my wines!'

" 'Not drinking, sir.'

"There was nothing to do but make a clean breast of it. He would have forced me to anyway. A very difficult man to deceive, sir. When I had finished, he said angrily:

" 'You can stay here until tomorrow—I won't be able to get anyone to take your place before then. But after tomorrow you're through, Baines.'

"I pleaded the length of time I had been in his service and the difficulties I would face in securing another situation without his recommendation, but he was deaf to all entreaties."

"Humph!" O'Ryan pondered. "His death came at a damn convenient time for you, Baines."

"It did, sir," the butler admitted anxiously. "But I had nothing to do with that. I swear it, sir."

"That remains to be seen," O'Ryan declared. He bawled for the "Sampson woman" to be brought in, and Baines was ushered away.

"I told you all I knew last night," proclaimed Matilda with a defiant glare. "I can't see why you have to keep a woman from her honest work."

O'Ryan handled this truculent witness with more tact than I had given him credit for having.

"Just answer a few questions, Miss Sampson, and we'll give you a nice ride home. I'm a good friend of yours if you'd only admit it. Didn't I make Murphy mop up your kitchen last night?"

"That's so," Matilda agreed, somewhat mollified. "What do you want to know?"

"If Baines was in the kitchen with you all of yesterday evening."

"I told you that last night."

"Yes or no?"

"Yes."

"Is Baines any relation to you?"

"Of course not!" Matilda exclaimed indignantly.

"Don't you like him?" O'Ryan asked shrewdly.

Matilda sniffed. "I'm not saying I do and I'm not saying I don't. I don't have anything against him, though."

"How long have you been with Mr Morse?"

"Four years. I came with the house, so to speak. I used to cook for the Spendalls, but they moved away to France, and—"

O'Ryan said quietly, "Baines had been stealing from your boss's private stock. Did you know that?"

"The dirty thief!" Matilda ejaculated. "Of course I didn't know that, or I would have told Mr Morse so fast it would 've made his head swim. I can't abide stealing any more than I can adultery."

"Never mind the ten commandments. Baines had been fired yesterday afternoon for it. Did he tell you that?"

"No, he didn't," Matilda returned at once.

"Well, then, did he make any threats against Morse?"

"I can't say that he did," Matilda admitted. "To tell the truth Baines never did complain much. And Mr Morse used to storm around sometimes like the devil was in him. I wouldn't stand for it either. Once I told him: 'Just because you pay me wages don't give you no right to talk to me this way. If you don't like how I do things get yourself another cook and see if I care,' I said. I told him I'd been used to working for people that was ladies and gentlemen and—"

"Let's get back to last night," O'Ryan said, interrupting the flood of reminiscences. "Are you willing to swear in court that Baines didn't go out of the kitchen even once before Miss Morse screamed?"

"He did leave to answer the doorbell."

"When?"

"A little after eight-thirty, I think it was. He came right back."

"And he didn't leave the room any other time later?"

"No. I've already told you at least half-a-doz—"

"Now wait a minute. Maybe you were out of the kitchen for a while."

"And maybe I wasn't!"

"Not even to go to the toilet?"

Matilda's face reddened. "That's none of your business!"

"Well, were you?" O'Ryan persisted.

"Yes, I did go once," Matilda admitted.

"How long 'd you stay?"

"That's a nice question to ask a lady!" Matilda exclaimed, blushing.

"Five minutes? Ten minutes?"

"It was nearer five than ten," Matilda conceded grudgingly.

"Where's the toilet?" O'Ryan demanded.

"It opens off the kitchen."

"Baines go there too?"

"Yes, once."

"When?"

"How should I know?"

"Could he get out through the toilet into the rest of the house?" O'Ryan asked.

"Not without coming back into the kitchen."

"Well, what time was it when you went there?" he questioned.

"Ten o'clock," Matilda rejoined promptly. "I can remember looking at my watch." She proudly held out a massive arm upon which was strapped an exceedingly minute wrist watch. "My married niece over at Hinsdale gave me this last Christmas."

"That's not much of a watch," O'Ryan derided.

"It's a very fine watch," proclaimed Matilda, defending her pride and joy. "My niece paid fifteen dollars for it, and I've only had to have it repaired three times since she gave it to me."

"What sort of time does it keep?"

"It keeps very good time. It only loses two or three minutes a day."

O'Ryan compared it with his own timepiece and said:

"It's only two minutes off now. Has that watch been wound or set since last night?"

"I wound it first thing this morning, but I didn't set it."

"Did you look at this pet watch of yours any other time during the evening?" the captain questioned.

"Come to think of it, I did," said Matilda, wrinkling her forehead. "It was five minutes past twelve. I'm positive of it because it seemed like hardly any time afterward when we heard Miss Morse scream."

"Five minutes past twelve!" O'Ryan ejaculated. "That didn't happen to be while Baines was out of the room?"

"No, he was right across the table from me then—he'd been sitting there at least an hour."

Dismissing her O'Ryan turned to me with a gargantuan chuckle.

"You're cagey, Foster, lawyers usually are. But if you've got the guts to admit what you're really thinking you'll say that dame was telling us the truth. You know why as well as I do. When a woman like Matilda starts out to lie she's going to invent all sorts of details to make her yarn stronger. Before long she's forgotten just what she did say and given herself away a dozen times. But Matilda didn't do that. She stuck to the straight story, and I wasn't able to trip her up on anything."

I was forced to acknowledge that had been true.

"Liars don't get far with Terry O'Ryan," boasted that gentleman, chuckling once more. "And now it looks like Baines is definitely in the clear as well as Vail. She looked at her watch at five minutes past twelve and Baines was right there in the kitchen—had been there for at least an hour she said. Vail's alibi seems to stand up, too. Too bad you can't dig up one as good for your girl friend."

I answered, more confidently than I felt, "I'll do better than that. I'll find out who really did kill Hezekiah Morse."

But, if I could have seen what lay ahead, I don't think I would have ever made such a foolish promise.

XV

As I came out of the station I noticed Vail walking on the opposite side of the street, and I hurried to catch him. He was inclined to be reserved, but melted when I outlined Sylvia's predicament. "Why it's appalling!" he exclaimed and added more in the same vein. I could detect no false notes in his consternation. Assuming complete ignorance of the visit of Brenda Carstairs, I inquired how he had managed to secure his own release.

Vail smiled—there was a likable quality to his smile. "A certain young lady of my acquaintance proved herself a real friend. I hadn't wanted to drag her into this, but O'Ryan assured me he'd keep her name from the newshounds. He isn't such a bad egg when you get to know him."

I agreed to this with all sincerity, and Vail continued:

"I tried to be tough with those fellows, and I landed in the cooler. I'm not complaining; I deserved it. However, the young lady was kind enough to explain to them where I was at midnight. Hence the release—with apologies on both sides and no hard feelings on either."

His tone was light, almost flippant, but he appeared to be speaking frankly. However, I tried to guard myself from taking him entirely at face value.

"I'd like to talk with you as soon as possible. If we get Sylvia acquitted it's necessary to clear up all loose ends. And that means"—I grasped the bull firmly by both horns—"your relations with Hezekiah Morse."

His face whitened. For a moment I could see he was on the verge of telling me to go to the devil. Then he regained control. "I can't tell you much that will do any good, Foster."

"I'd prefer to be the judge of that," I insisted, smiling in an effort to take the sting out of my words.

"Well, then, walk over to the house with me and ask as many questions as you like. I don't guarantee I'll answer them."

We started east toward Michigan Boulevard. "Vail," I began without preamble, "I received a letter from Morse this morning. He asked me to visit an employment agency and select a butler to replace Baines."

Vail whistled. "That's almost inconceivable! Baines had been with him since—good Lord, I used to borrow money from him when I was in my teens and ran through my allowance too fast."

"Didn't Morse tell you about this?" I asked. I was studying Vail's face intently.

"He did not! Why should he?"

But he knew the answer to that question. I was sure of it.

"Because you were very close to Hezekiah Morse. He always spoke of you as though you were his own son. I was comparatively a stranger to him. He wouldn't ask me to perform a favor if he could turn to you. Vail, why couldn't he?"

Vail took out his cigarette case. "He wasn't asking favors of me after yesterday afternoon."

"You quarreled with him?" I inquired. Vail puffed meditatively upon his cigarette.

"Foster, I don't see why I should tell you about it. You're not my lawyer. If you want the truth I don't even like you very much."

In his manner was the same studied insolence that he had displayed last night toward the police.

"Your opinion of me doesn't matter," I snapped. "I'm trying to find some way to help Sylvia Morse. Are you with me or against me?"

A girl, passing us on the street, nodded her recognition. It was Morse's secretary. Meeting her was such a slice of pure luck that I temporarily forgot Vail's antagonism.

"Miss Guild!" I exclaimed. "I was planning to call you this morning."

"Poor Mr Morse!" she lamented. She was a quiet little mouselike thing, and her reddened eyes told of recent tears. She was on her way to the police station now. Captain O'Ryan had asked her to come down. I noticed that the cheap fur of her brown coat had worn thin, and that a tiny hole was visible in the glove of her right hand. The girl was having a tough time of it, it was plain, and losing this job certainly wasn't going to be any help to her financially.

"As executors of Morse's estate," I began, more ponderously than I meant to express it, "my firm is empowered to liquidate all of his obligations. Under this head is included your salary, with, of course, a month's notice. How much did Morse pay you?"

"Twenty-five dollars a week," she answered. "There's about four days' pay coming to me."

"Let's say an even five weeks," I answered. "That's a hundred and twenty-five dollars. I'll see that a check is sent you as soon as I get back to the office."

"Why that's awfully nice of you, Mr Foster!" she exclaimed, her small face brightening. "I don't know just how to thank—"

Vail took out his billfold. "Our friend, Foster, is a busy man, Miss Guild, and it is just possible, although unlikely, that the matter of the check may slip his mind. Allow me, in Mr Foster's words, to 'liquidate the obligation' now."

He counted out six twenties and a five. I didn't care much for his lord-of-the-manor conduct, but there wasn't much I could do about it. Naturally she preferred cash, but I couldn't pay her myself; I had nothing but a lone dollar bill and some silver.

Vail cut her thanks short. "Foster will see I'm reimbursed." He smiled at me— mockingly. "Foster, I believe, is anxious to ask you a few questions, Miss Guild. Do you mind coming to my house while we talk it over?"

"Captain O'Ryan asked me to come to the station right away," she demurred. Vail, however, made quick work of the protest.

"That's nothing but his usual way of talking. He'll be expecting you when you get there. Here's a cab now. It won't take but a few minutes, Miss Guild. The driver will wait in front of the house, and he can take you over to the station."

The last argument won, and Miss Guild allowed Vail to assist her into the cab. What was his game? I was wondering. To make a man he admittedly disliked appear foolish? Or did he have a deeper object in view?

Nevertheless I owned, as the cab sped north, I couldn't deny that I did have a number of questions to put to Morse's secretary. There was even a possibility that her answers might open up important new lines of attack. Whatever Vail's object his forethought had put us a jump ahead of the police in the examination of this witness.

I noticed a police car drawn up before Morse's home, and a crowd of curious Chicagoans were standing around on the sidewalk. I could picture to myself what the police were doing inside at that moment: moving bookcases, sounding walls in quest of a secret doorway which connected from the Morse study to the home of Thomas Raymond Vail. If they found it—but it wasn't in the realm of common sense that they would. Anyway Miss Carstairs' positive declaration had eliminated every chance that Vail could have had anything to do with the Morse murder.

Once within the living room with its gold-framed portrait, Vail pulled up one of the vividly upholstered chairs for Miss Guild.

"What did Mr Morse do yesterday, Miss Guild?" I began.

"He dictated most of the morning. We were on a section about Burton's *Anatomy of Melancholy*, and it was rather hard going. And after lunch he spent a long time hunting for a quotation in Burton's book. He said that he wanted to use it as a sort of foreword."

"Something about 'a rhapsody of rags gathered together from several dunghills'?" I asked. She blushed, and I continued my questioning. "Did Mr Morse do any other work yesterday?"

"Yes, he dictated a letter." An odd little quirk about her mouth fought hard to keep from turning into a smile. "A letter to you, Mr Foster."

"It came to the office this morning," I told her. "When was it dictated?"

Baines had already provided the approximate answer to that question, but I wanted to test the general accuracy of this witness.

"Early in the afternoon. Just after I came back from lunch."

"Morse didn't invite you to eat with him?"

"Oh no, he seldom did that."

"What else happened yesterday?" I continued.

"Mr Vail called to see Mr Morse about three o'clock."

She glanced at Vail as though expecting that he would confirm this statement, but he remained silent.

"Did you see Mr Vail?"

"No, he didn't come upstairs. Baines brought the message that he was waiting below."

"How long did Mr Vail remain?"

She glanced once more at our host, who was smiling in a slightly amused manner.

"Until nearly four. Mr Morse didn't return to the study until ten or fifteen minutes before I left."

"You quit work at four? Wasn't that earlier than your usual time?"

"My mother isn't at all well, and I asked Mr Morse if I could leave an hour early. He was always nice to me about things like that," she added, a little shyly.

I recalled Baines mentioning that Morse had gone for a walk at four, and I made a wild stab in the dark.

"Did Mr Morse leave the house with you?"

"Yes; how did you know?"

I told her and asked: "Did he mail his letter to me then?"

"No, I mailed it. At the box on the corner of Astor Street. Afterwards he walked with me as far as Lake Shore Drive."

"Then where did he go?"

"I don't know. I caught my bus as soon as we reached the corner."

"You didn't see him at any time after that?"

"No."

That concluded my examination. Miss Guild, I reflected, had confirmed Morse's walk at four and Vail's call at three. But it was difficult to see how she could be made to fit further into this case.

Even though she had a motive for returning to the house last night and possessed a means of entering unobserved, she couldn't have stabbed Morse. She was below the doctor's height limit. Unless she stood on something . . . but that was pure fantasy. I smiled at the morbid trend my imagination was taking today.

Miss Guild turned the tables by putting a question to me.

"Are the police holding Miss Morse?"

"I'm sorry to say that they are."

"That's nonsense!" she exploded. "Miss Morse is one of the sweetest girls I've ever known, and I'll certainly tell that to Captain O'Ryan when I see him!"

I liked her for that.

Vail escorted her to the cab, and I went with them, half expecting some trick from him to get away from me. However, he made no such attempt.

We returned to the house. Vail offered cigarettes and waited, relaxed and apparently indifferent, for me to begin. As I remembered from last night, he was a hard man to handle when the conversation turned upon personal issues. And there was no way on earth to keep it from turning that way.

"Why did you and Morse quarrel?" I asked, resuming my inquiry at the point we had reached prior to the advent of Miss Guild.

Vail coolly flicked his ashes into a large brass receptacle standing upon a tripod. "I don't know that it's any of your business, Foster."

My own temper was beginning to rise, and I answered tartly, "Anything that bears on the welfare of Sylvia Morse is my business. Are you refusing to help clear her of this charge?"

Vail, studying my face as I had studied his own not half an hour before, suddenly extended his hand.

"Accept my apologies, Foster. You're right, but this story involves a woman. There are some things—"

"I'm not a gossiping old maid," I said. "A lawyer is used to confidences—the same as a doctor or a priest."

"I'll trust you," Vail decided abruptly. He smiled in a pleasant manner. "If I begin at the beginning, as I should, this will be a long story, and you may find it a dry one. Let's start with a scotch and soda."

He rang for Hudson, who brought a tray containing glasses, a pinch bottle and a siphon. Vail poured a good stiff potion into each glass.

"Perhaps you've wondered why Morse should will such a large portion of his property to me? Or why he brought so much pressure to bear to induce Sylvia to become my wife?"

I answered, sipping at my drink, that I had never understood why Morse had resorted to such coercive tactics.

Vail pointed to the portrait.

"It's her story—Dolores, lady of sorrows, but always known by the affectionate diminutive, Lolita. And it begins with her father—my grandfather—Don Ramon Rusiñol y Milá."

It is impossible to describe the manner in which the long sonorous name rolled from his tongue. The scotch had the peculiar smoky taste that good scotch ought to have, and I took a deep swallow as Vail continued.

"Don Ramon, as a true Catalan gentleman, was active in politics. Also he possessed the Catalan genius for allying himself with the losing side. An ardent supporter of Don Carlos during the furious days of the early seventies, he was exiled from Spain with ten thousand others when Carlism was finally quelled in 1876. My mother was born that year, the very year he came to Chicago.

"Like most Catalans, Don Ramon was energetic, progressive, commercial. This city appealed to him. He became a success, and in so doing he had business dealings with Hezekiah Morse. This portrait was painted in 1894 when Dolores was just eighteen. That was the year in which Uncle Hezekiah first visited my grandfather's house."

I calculated mentally. Morse would have been thirty then. Since he had come to Chicago from New Zealand in his early twenties, I recalled his mentioning, he must have been almost a stranger in the city himself.

"Yes, his foot was still on the bottom rung of the ladder," Vail confirmed. "My grandfather was one of those who helped him to rise. Morse never forgot an obligation, and this partially explains his feelings for me. Lolita, however, explains by far the greater part of them."

"But why didn't they mar—"

"Because Hezekiah Morse was already married and had a five-year-old son to boot at the time they met. Lolita was a Catholic; divorce was out of the question. Any other alternative was unthinkable to them. Catalan women are rigorously virtuous, and Morse, a descendant of the Scotch Presbyterian founders of Dunedin, was something of a moralist himself."

Vail drained his glass. "It wasn't much of a love affair by today's standards. Stolen glances at meetings at which Lolita's parents were always present. Several clandestine letters, daring in their utter hopelessness. The inevitable renunciation. Another drink, Foster?"

I declined, and Vail refilled his own glass. "She married four years later. Am I boring you, Foster?"

"No, go on."

"Morse's frustrated love affair had unfortunate repercussions upon his son Philip. Morse disliked him intently from that date. It was rottenly unfair, of course, but I doubt if Uncle Hezekiah ever paused to analyze his feelings. When he was twenty-one Philip ran away from home and married a ballet dancer. The marriage turned out surprisingly well, I believe, although Uncle Hezekiah would have nothing to do with either of them. After nine years Philip and his wife were killed together—in a train wreck. Sylvia was only six. Uncle Hezekiah took the child; there was no one else to do it."

Vail deposited his glass upon the tray. "My own mother died twenty years ago; my father soon after. Morse was guardian and father rolled into one. I was eighteen when little Sylvia came to live with him. Twelve years older, I never thought of her except as the merest baby. She was just a long-legged, lanky kid of thirteen when I left for Barcelona. Through the influence of my grandfather's family I had secured the appointment."

He talked of Barcelona, and his words sketched the city before my eyes. The flower market—*Rambla de las Flores!* In the cool freshness of early morning an entire street assails the nostrils with perfumed fragrance, and the eyes are stabbed with the flamboyant brilliance of scarlets and yellows and crimsons. A great cathedral—relic of Spain's proud grandeur—with darkened nave and dim aisles and glowing stained-glass windows of the fifteenth century. Towering over all, Mount Tibidabo, from whose top the city is spread out like a fantastic checkerboard, and the blue shimmer of the Mediterranean merges imperceptibly with the horizon.

Barcelona! Factories and clanging tramcars, sidewalk cafes, broad plane tree-lined boulevards. A bustling modern city above whose teeming harbor the outstretched arm of a gigantic Columbus points forever west. In whose heart Roman columns crumble—forgotten, unnoticed.

"A city can be like a mistress, Foster, loved like a mistress. And yet," Vail paused self-consciously, "I left Barcelona."

"Because of Sylvia?" I hazarded.

He reached for the bottle and poured himself another drink. "Yes, Sylvia. Five years ago I came to Chicago intending to close out my affairs and return for good to Barcelona. But I never did go back. I couldn't leave her—even though she wouldn't have me I couldn't leave her." He drained his glass, his voice thickening. "She was only eighteen then; I thought at first that it was because she wasn't yet ready for marriage. Later I wasn't so sure. It was plain, unvarnished hell, Foster, and I'm only human. Jonas Spendall lived next door then. He was a cold-blooded icicle of a man, and his wife Dorothy, a pretty brunette in her twenties, was about as sexually unsatisfied a woman as I've ever met. Jonas played bridge with three old cronies regularly two evenings a week. It didn't take long to learn those evenings."

Lighting a cigarette Vail blew a series of debonair smoke rings.

"I didn't compromise her by calling openly; the servants were given no opportunities to suspect that anything was amiss. Dorothy had the front room—yes, the same room in which Uncle Hezekiah was killed. An ornamental iron balcony ran from under her window to the window of my own bedroom. It was entirely practicable, particularly on a dark night when one couldn't be seen from the street, and the romantic side of it appealed to Dorothy's nature. Our affair lasted several months until old Jonas happened to come home unexpectedly and found me there."

Flicking the ashes from his cigarette Vail laughed sardonically. "It was like something from the *Commedia dell' Arte*. Harlequin scurries around for his trousers while Pantaloon storms and Columbine dissolves in tears! Some men would have shot me outright. Jonas wasn't one of them. He didn't even ask for a divorce; couldn't stand the scandal. Uncle Hezekiah made him an offer for the house soon afterwards, and they sailed for Southern France. He was tickled to death to sell, because it gave him an excuse to take Dorothy permanently out of Chicago."

"You haven't explained why you quarreled with Morse," I reminded.

"No?" said Vail. "Well, I asked Sylvia to marry me for the umpteenth time. She refused—uncertainly—but still refused. That was according to precedent, but Morse happened to overhear the proposal and from then on made the child's life miserable. I believe I could have persuaded her if he hadn't interfered; as it was I didn't have a chance. However, I didn't really take a definite stand against him until he gave you instructions to draw up that will disinheriting Sylvia. I spoke to him about it several times, but I couldn't make him change his mind. Yesterday afternoon I determined to have one more try."

"So that's it!" I exclaimed.

"Yes," Vail confirmed grimly. "As his secretary told you I dropped in about three o'clock. I began by pointing out that he was being very unfair to Sylvia. He retorted by referring to her as 'a silly chit who doesn't know her own mind' and to me as a 'chivalrous fool.'

"I lost my own temper—and I have a good one as you've probably noticed. 'If you weren't a blind, obstinate old fool,' I said, 'you'd know what sort of man you were forcing your granddaughter to marry.'

"I gave him the whole Dot Spendall story and threw in one or two others for good measure. Foster, the old boy went purple! He was so mad he couldn't talk; just pointed at the door and said in a squeaky sort of whisper that wasn't at all like his usual roar, 'Get out!'

"I went, feeling—well, you can imagine how. Foster, you'll have to take my word for it, but that's the last time I ever saw him alive."

XVI

After leaving Vail I stopped for a paper before catching a southbound streetcar. The news I had expected and feared was spread all over the front page:

FIND SYLVIA'S FINGERPRINTS
ON DEATH KNIFE

Fingerprints on the knife used to stab the retired financier, Hezekiah Morse, who was killed last night in his home at 49 East Division Street, were today identified as those of Sylvia Morse, granddaughter of the deceased, by O. A. Schmidt, assistant chief identification inspector.

"The prints were blurred, although readily identifiable," stated Inspector Schmidt. "This might mean that an unsuccessful attempt had been made to wipe them off prior to the arrival of the police."

Questioned at police headquarters, where she was taken this morning from the Water Tower district station, Sylvia Morse admitted that the prints might be hers. She said that she had frequently used the knife to open letters, but denied that she had ever tried to remove the prints from the knife handle. . . .

There were a few more details concerning the identification of the fingerprints, and then came the news that the inquest was slated for 2 P.M. tomorrow and that Lewis M. Teagan was handling the case for the state's attorney's office. The paper slipped to my lap while I stared dully from the car window.

Assistant State's Attorney Lew Teagan had a deadly record of convictions. He would be all set to make a killing in this case, particularly if public sentiment turned against Sylvia Morse, as it seemed likely to do. And the fact that Sylvia had over a million dollar stake in her grandfather's death was going to look ugly to a jury.

Juries, generally speaking, feel an unconscious resentment toward anyone with money. It's the psychology of the old adage—the one about it being the high hat that gets the snowballs.

Of course, if your client happens to be hard up, the thing works just the other way. Maybe the washer-woman who is suing the tramway company on account of a broken leg had been so drunk that she had lain down to take a nap right across the car tracks. Prove that fact, and six juries out of ten will allow her damages just the same. It's easy to be generous with someone else's money, and it gives you a nice feeling of satisfaction.

In this case, however, ordinary human sympathies were alienated from the start. Greed is the most likely motive for murder. It is the motive that people can best understand, and it is the one that they are the least apt to condone. Of course, if Morse had been able to sign that will before his death, if Sylvia actually were to be disinherited, the situation would have been vastly different. Then all these imponderable psychological factors would be in our favor instead of working against us. However, there wasn't much use in dwelling upon *that*.

Our financial disadvantages were counterbalanced somewhat by other resources. Sylvia's youth, looks, voice, her obvious sincerity—but it was out of my line to weigh the probable influence of such qualities upon the "twelve good men and true." I wasn't going to attempt to plead the case in court. A very clever criminal lawyer would be required for that, and Sylvia was going to have the benefit of the cleverest that could be obtained.

Nevertheless, the surest and only really satisfactory way to secure an acquittal was to prove that someone else had killed Hezekiah Morse. And, if that were humanly possible, it was going to be done, I resolved grimly.

My thoughts turned to Westborough, whom I was meeting for lunch. He had made some excellent points in our favor last night. Who was he? What had he done to give him the respect of such men as Lieutenant Mack and Captain O'Ryan? Steelcraft had promised to make some inquiries for me upon these points, and as soon as I had left the streetcar I hurried into a drugstore to call the office.

Steelcraft was out, but he had left a rather lengthy message, which Miss Birch, his secretary, read to me over the phone. Westborough, I discovered, had been the prime over in the solution of two murder cases, one of them a very baffling affair upon a large Wisconsin estate.* And the little fellow was halfway on our side already! Altogether I was considerably heartened.

I stopped at my bank to cash a check, which made me a minute or two late for my appointment with Westborough. As I was walking west along Randolph Street I noticed him standing on the sidewalk, wearing his black Homburg of last night and a huge black Chesterfield which almost totally engulfed him. He was peering anxiously down the street, but did not recognize me until I was within about fifteen feet.

"Mr Foster! I was hoping that you had not forgotten our appointment."

I apologized for keeping him waiting, and we went into the restaurant, where we were shown to a table well toward the center and directly beneath a colossal oval mirror, one of the largest I had ever seen.

"The Canterbury Pilgrims make their way to the Canterbury Inn's luncheon—food with a story behind it." Westborough was quoting from the menu. "Shall these pilgrims start with blue points? And then may I suggest the grilled mutton chops with kidneys? I can recommend this dish with a good conscience."

I assented without much enthusiasm. Food held little interest for me that day. While we waited for the oysters I began by telling him of Morse's letter, which, like a voice from the dead, had reached me that morning. The blue points arrived, large and succulent and served with an excellent sauce. I continued with the statements of Miss Carstairs, Baines and Matilda at the police station and ended with a full account of Vail's rather fantastic tale.

Swallowing the last of his oysters Westborough observed:

"Mr Vail is undeniably obstinate, headstrong and proud, as only a Spaniard can be. But, rather curiously, he does not appear to possess a modicum of the characteristic Catalan practicality. His finances are at a low ebb, yet he ventured to provoke a quarrel which might easily have resulted in his removal as a beneficiary of the Morse will—had Morse lived long enough to make the necessary revision." He shook his head distressingly, "Dear, dear, I believe that the scent of the too familiar Ethiopian may be discerned behind the firewood. Or, as Lieutenant Mack puts it so picturesquely, 'There's something screwy about it.' "

"I see," I cogitated. "Then you think Vail's lying?"

The arrival of the waitress prevented his immediate answer. Our mutton chops were sizzling hot and done to a perfect brown, and Mr Westborough smiled as his knife and fork began the attack.

"Our present knowledge, Mr Foster, may be likened to a tangle of underbrush under which a tiny white flower is hidden. We must find that flower, Mr Foster."

"Are you with me?" I fired at him point-blank.

"The problem interests me strongly."

"Show me Morse's murderer, and you can name your fee!" I cried.

He swallowed another morsel of chop. "I am not a businessman, Mr Foster. I should not have the slightest idea how to appraise the merits of my services. Moreover, my financial resources are ample for my simple wants."

It was no use arguing; he simply refused to listen. Money as such had no interest for this curious little man. It was the baffling nature of the puzzle which had caught his fancy—and held it until the end.

Of his own accord Mr Westborough changed the subject.

"You will be surprised, Mr Foster, to learn where I have spent the forenoon. In the public library, improving my knowledge of New Zealand."

I was surprised—and showed it.

"Entirely because of Mr Morse's purple parrot," he explained, and that did take me aback. However, his eyes were beaming so earnestly behind his gold-rimmed bifocals that I held my peace.

"The parrot is, like Joseph's celebrated coat, of many colors," said Mr Westborough, his knife and fork delivering a fresh assault on the mutton chop. "There is the common American green parrot, its plumage often variegated with blue, red and yellow. There is the gray parrot of Africa. There is the giant black ara of New Guinea—largest of all the order *Psittaci*—and there is a certain Australian parrot which is a vivid blood-red. There are cockatoos: a snowy white or tinged with rose or saffron or orange. There are macaws: blue-and-yellow, blue-and-red, even with all-blue plumage. Nature, however, appears to have entirely neglected the color purple in her decorative schemes for this interesting hook-billed bird. I think that I may safely venture the predication that a purple parrot is, to say the least, something of a rara avis."

I smiled; it appeared to me a matter of small importance.

"The kakapo," he continued, "is a species hitherto unknown to me, and I wondered if its plumage actually was purple. You will think me extremely foolish, Mr Foster, but I assure you that I was unable to set my mind at rest until I had answered this question."

I inquired (rather impatiently) what he had found out.

"A great many interesting facts," he replied. "I was amazed to discover how little I knew concerning the Dominion of New Zealand. In an area no larger than the state of Colorado one may have one's choice of Switzerland's peaks and glaciers, Japan's volcanic cones, Norway's fiords, Italy's lakes, the waterfalls of a Yosemite, the geysers of a Yellowstone—but I fear that I am digressing. Even more impressive than the scenic wonders is the incredible remoteness of these islands. Find them upon a globe, and you will see how they lie under the very rim of the world—alone in the vast stretches of the South Pacific."

My knowledge of geography was a trifle hazy, but I ventured to argue the point. "New Zealand's right next door to Australia, isn't it?"

"It takes nearly as long to sail from Sidney to Wellington as to cross the Atlantic," he informed. "Keeping this amazing isolation in view one might naturally assume that New Zealand flora and fauna would possess unique characteristics, and I assure you that such is indeed the case. Giant ferns flourish in great abundance; fuchsias grow to a height of forty feet, and there is a white buttercup with blooms four inches across. But the fauna are even more singular than the flora. Oddly enough, it is the omissions which strike one the most."

"All this is very interesting but—"

He was not to be hurried. "There are no indigenous mammals with a few unimportant exceptions. There are no indigenous snakes. There are birds which can not fly."

"Including a purple parrot?" I asked, grinning.

"That would scarcely appear startling among the avian marvels I did discover upon this voyage in print," he returned soberly. "The extinct moa, for example, which must have stood at least fourteen feet high. The odd-looking kiwi, which violates physical and natural laws by laying eggs a quarter of its own weight. And the kea, whose sharp beak incises the side of a living sheep and tears out the kidneys. But I digress again. The kakapo is the only New Zealand bird in which you could possibly be interested, and yet I fear that you will now find it something of an anticlimax. It is a bird about the size of a raven, and it has radiating wreaths of feathers about its eyes which give it a slight facial resemblance to an owl. The name, kakapo, is derived from a Maori word meaning 'night.' "

"A night parrot!" I interjected.

"Yes, it is often referred to by that very name and with some reason, for, like the owl it resembles, the kakapo is nocturnal and predatory. It has wings, but is unable to fly. And it is said to make an affectionate and amusing household pet."

"What about its color?" I reminded. "Is it purple?"

"Dear me, no. It is green varied with brown above and a yellowish-green varied with brown and yellowish-white below. Not in the least like Mr Morse's missing statuette. And the eyes are not red but black."

"Maybe Morse's parrot was a futuristic conception of a kakapo," I chuckled. "Artists don't always stick to hardboiled facts."

"Are you familiar with the four Laws of Thought?" he inquired.

"I haven't paid much attention to them since my logic course in college," I confessed.

"Nevertheless, you will be able to recognize the particular truism known as the Law of Sufficient Reason. The purple color is a discrepancy; there must be some adequate explanation for—"

My attention had wandered to the giant oval mirror hanging on the wall above our heads. There was a man at an adjoining table leaning toward us a trifle too anxiously. He had a stubby mustache, small gray eyes and a grim, square jaw.

"Look in the mirror!" I said in a low voice. "We're being watched."

He nodded calmly. "Naturally, Mr Foster, you are on the list of official suspects. Doubtless you have been under police surveillance the entire morning."

PART THREE

Friday, November 20

XVII

I was dreaming of detectives. They commenced to follow me as I left the Water Tower Station, lay patiently in wait before Vail's home, took up the trail to the Canterbury Inn. Then the city suddenly melted away in the disconcerting topsy-turviness of dreams, and Sylvia and I were running for our very lives through a shadowy forest with unknown foes in hot pursuit. We sought refuge in a round tower—a sort of Norman keep. I have an extraordinarily vivid impression of the massive, nail-studded door which, in the nick of time, we providentially succeeded in shutting and bolting. Then "they"—their faces always appeared as a blur although the terror they inspired was very real—commenced a hammering like all the demons of Sheol upon the entrance . . .

Sleepily I struggled to the conscious realization that someone was actually rapping on the door of my own hotel bedroom. Wondering if an important message had come concerning Sylvia I sprang from the bed and hastily donned my dressing gown. But it was only Charles, the hotel valet, returning my dinner jacket.

"Why wake me up to bring that here!" I exclaimed irritably. Glancing at the alarm clock I discovered I had overslept half an hour and added in a more amiable mood, "You should have left it in my room yesterday."

Charles, a small, swarthy Latin with the suavity of a diplomat, regretted beyond measure that he had disturbed my repose. He had, however, discovered a certain letter in a pocket which he thought advisable to return to me in person.

"What letter?" I asked in genuine puzzlement. Charles handed it to me and I discovered it was the advertising letter I had found on the floor of Morse's study and completely forgotten.

I gave Charles the tip for which he had been angling, and he went his way. Closing the door I read the missive again, secretly hoping that there might be some clue between its lines. But I didn't see how it could have had any more to do with the case than Mack's Aunt Harriet up at Niles, Michigan. It was so patently and obviously exactly what it seemed.

ROY N. PICKENS
Advertising
333 North Michigan Ave.
CHICAGO, ILL.

DEAR SIR:

"A good cigar's a smoke," as Kipling so aptly observed. You know from your own experience what a smoke Sir Andrew is—we don't have to tell you about its prime Havana filler and its costly wrapper from distant Sumatra.

You know also that Sir Andrew has hitherto been available only to the discriminating smoker who has found it worth the extra trouble to order a box at a time by mail.

The makers of Sir Andrew are considering a change in policy. They feel that the mellow goodness of Sir Andrew should no longer be limited to a favored few. They would like to give all cigar smokers a chance to select a Sir Andrew—even if it does cost a little more than an ordinary cigar.

This can only be done through advertising. Will you help us to plan the advertising for Sir Andrew?

We don't want a testimonial—we don't even ask for your name if you prefer to remain unknown. All we ask is that you list the three biggest reasons why you like Sir Andrew on the three lines below and mail this letter back to us in the enclosed stamped envelope.

Will you do it?

....

....

....

Thank you.

Idly I flopped the sheet over. On the back a small number, "56", had been written with pen and ink in the upper right-hand corner. Evidently, it appeared, Mr Pickens didn't intend that the endorsers of Sir Andrew should remain as unknown to him as he had pretended. I smiled as I thought how incensed Morse, who had been a devoted cigar smoker, would have been had he discovered this little trick of the advertising profession.

However, there was no time to be wasted in trivial speculations that morning. I dressed and shaved hurriedly, bought a paper and rushed across the street to read it while I swallowed a cup of coffee. There was another story on the Morse case on the front page:

MORSE CASHES CHECK
AFTER BANKS CLOSE

Milton R. Penrose, manager of the large and opulent Hotel Duke on the near North Side, appeared at the Water Tower District station yesterday afternoon to inform Captain Terence O'Ryan that he had cashed a $1,000 check for Hezekiah Morse on the afternoon preceding the financier's death. He declared that he had been acquainted with Morse for several years, but that the latter had not informed him for what purpose the money was wanted.

Morse, Penrose asserted, had visited the hotel shortly after four o'clock. This statement corroborates the accounts of Morse's butler, Judson Baines, and his secretary, Evelyn Guild, both of whom mentioned that the deceased had gone out at four.

Well, that was interesting, but it left unanswered the important question of what had become of the thousand. I turned the page and found something else of interest:

SEEK SECRET DOOR;
REMOVE RARE BOOKS WORTH THOUSANDS

In frantic search of the Morse residence, with the object of finding a secret passageway or other concealed means of egress, Patrolmen Daniel Riley, Stanislaus Maniskowski and Lawrence Callahan shoved contemptuously aside rare first editions and other volumes valued at many thousands of dollars.

Up to late last evening they had discovered no such exit, although they had re-

moved practically all of the 2,000 volumes from their shelves and had sounded carefully the walls of the study behind the bookcases.

Lying upon the desk top, just as it had been found on the night of Morse's murder,
was a first edition of Robert Burton's *Anatomy of Melancholy* dating from 1621.
This book, which the financier had evidently consulted a short while before his death,
is worth about $750.

A more expensive member of the Morse collection is a first-edition copy of John
Milton's *Paradise Lost*, published in 1667 and conservatively valued at $1,250.

Stacked in a heap in one corner were three volumes of *Sketches by Boz* with
Cruikshank etchings. This set, a first edition published in 1836, is easily worth $450.
Another Dickens' work, the familiar *Christmas Carol*, was represented by a first-
edition copy published by Chapman & Hall in 1843. Any book collector might be
willing to part with $200 to secure this treasure.

A first edition of another book in the Morse library, although equally familiar to
children, would bring no more than $40. This volume, published in 1872, is *Through
the Looking Glass and What Alice Found There.*

A volume with a rather ponderous title topped a pile of books in another corner of
the library. This treatise is credited with having done more than any other work to
revolutionize the thinking of humanity. Its full title is "On the Origin of Species by
Means of Natural Selection, or the Preservation of Favored Races in the Struggle for
Life," and the author is Charles Darwin. The copy which belonged to Morse is valued in the neighborhood of $150.

Mack's concealed doorway, as I expected, had been a total flop! I gulped down the
last of the coffee and made for the door. At the cigar counter I stopped abruptly.
Something I should remember was buzzing around like a wasp inside my brain. It
was connected with cigars. Did Morse order his cigars by mail? And what brand of
cigar did he favor?

There was a telephone booth in the restaurant, and I was dialing in two seconds.
Baines answered the call.

"Mr Foster, Baines. Do you know what kind of cigars Mr Morse smoked?"

"Corona Coronas, sir."

"Anything else? A cigar called Sir Andrew for instance?"

Baines's voice sounded positive. "He was very particular not to smoke anything
but Corona Coronas, Mr Foster."

And that was that! I phoned Westborough's hotel at once. "This is Foster. I'm on
the track of something which may turn out to be important. If I learn anything I want
to talk it over with you as soon as I can."

He answered that he was entirely at my disposal during the whole day, and we
agreed to meet at the northwest corner of State and Lake in an hour, which would
give me ample time for a call upon Roy N. Pickens.

I dashed out of the restaurant and flagged a cab. Pickens' office was on the twelfth
floor of the building, and I entered it through a cubbyhole of a reception room, which
was furnished in the ornate style that advertising agencies often affect. A blasé plati-

num blonde with a movie accent scrutinized my card and looked unimpressed.

"Mr Pickens is very busy just now. Do you have an appointment?"

I answered that I didn't, but that I was calling on an urgent legal matter. Finally I succeeded in persuading her to send my card into the holy of holies. She returned a few minutes later with word that Pickens would see me.

Pickens, who was sandy-haired and blue-eyed, was just banging down the receiver of his telephone as I entered the door. His face mirrored an ill-concealed annoyance.

"A legal matter, eh? Well, we haven't run any pictures without a release. If you knew how I checked you—"

"It's nothing like that. There's no lawsuit in the offing."

"A lawyer who doesn't want to sue!" Pickens smiled, extending his hand. "What can I do for you, Foster?"

"I'm after information. You sent out a certain form letter, which—"

The desk telephone set up an insistent ringing. "Sorry, Foster, you'll have to wait," Pickens said, picking up the receiver. "Hello, Paul, have you still got the form standing on the Beatty Furniture spread? Well, they want the head changed to 'Thousands of satisfied owners acclaim the Beatty trademark dash the hallmark of excellence.' Yeh, hallmark, h-a-l-l-m-a-r-k. Yeh, I know it's long for Ultra Bodoni—put it in eighteen point if it won't go in twenty-four. And listen here—it's got to go off on the two o'clock plane—*The Home Courier* goes to press tonight. Sure you can make it. Just rush the corrections through as fast as God Almighty 'll let you, bundle up the original form and shoot it in a taxi over to the municipal airport. Yeh, I did say the original form. Sure, I know type costs money—we're not asking you to stand the expense!"

Jerking down the hook he barked into the telephone, "Get me Morgan of *The Home Courier* in New York." He slammed down the receiver. "Sorry to keep you waiting, Foster. You said something about a letter?"

"A letter about Sir Andrew—the cigar."

"Damn fine cigar!" Pickens observed. "Lot of rich old buzzards smoke them. We're planning a new campaign if you're interested."

"Yes, I know. You sent out a form letter—"

But the New York connection had been completed in a surprisingly rapid time.

"Well, Morgan, I saved your two-page spread for you! Yeh, Turco are putting the original type with all corrections on the two o'clock plane, which gets in at seven-fifteen at the Newark airport. If you make arrangements to hash out some sort of electro tonight you can go to press as per schedule."

Breathing a deep sigh of relief he replaced the receiver. "This is the world's craziest business, Foster. What is it you were saying about Sir Andrew?"

"You sent out a form letter asking for recommendations," I reminded. "Those letters were numbered to correspond with your mailing list, weren't they?"

Pickens said, with noticeable exasperation, "If they were that's our business. Why the cross-examination?"

"Because one of your letters with the number '56' on it was found on the floor of

Hezekiah Morse's study the night he was killed. And Morse didn't smoke anything but Corona Coronas. Do you see?"

"You bet I see!" Pickens ejaculated. He picked up the telephone again. "Miss Gillis, look up the file of those letters we sent out for Fortunatus Tobacco and bring me the name and address of number '56'."

"What was the idea of the numbers?" I asked.

"New advertising campaign as I said before. Play up the slogan, 'Sir Andrew, the cigar smoked by the successful.' No harm to know who our friends are. Later I can make a few personal calls on the biggest shots and get their okay on testimonials."

"But when they see that number on your letter they ought to be good and mad," I objected. "Especially after you tell them you aren't looking for their names."

"Ninety per cent of them are never going to see that number," Pickens told me. He handed me a blank sheet of copy paper. "Try it yourself, Foster. I'll make a cross right here to represent the number in the upper right-hand corner. These letters were mailed in a number 10 envelope with a 6¾ return envelope. The letter has to be folded in sixths to fit the return envelope. Now turn the sheet over so that the number's on the back and fold it in half. Now fold it in thirds. See what you do? You turn it ninety degrees clockwise and fold it twice. Now you'll put it in the return envelope; if you don't turn over your folded sheet—and why should you?—you'll never know the number was there."

"Ingenious," I agreed. He waved his hand deprecatingly.

"Nothing at all. Say, leave your card, Foster, and I'll give you a ring the next time some chiseler starts to sue—"

The blasé blonde with the bored voice marched into the room with a slip of paper. "Here's the name and address you wanted, Mr Pickens."

Pickens handed the slip to me, and I read:

"J. Worthington Wells, 1924 Russell Avenue, Chicago."

I thanked him and left the office. J. Worthington Wells! The name had an aristocratic ring to it, I mused, while I waited for an elevator. And Pickens had implied that his letters had gone to men of wealth. Still, plenty of men who could have qualified in that category only a few years ago were now wondering where the next plate of beans would come from. I stepped into the elevator, reflecting that possibly the address might give a clue to Wells's present status. But it didn't help. Russell Avenue, I remembered vaguely, was in the far northern section of the city, somewhere in the Rogers Park district, but I didn't have the least idea in what kind of neighborhood Number 1924 would be.

As I stepped out of the elevator I received a big surprise. There was my stubby-mustached friend again. No, I couldn't be mistaken. He was standing by the cigar counter, apparently engrossed in conversation with the clerk. Considerably nettled I strolled toward him and asked for a match. Without saying anything he handed me a packet.

"Thanks," I said, returning the matches. "Your face is familiar to me. Haven't we met somewhere?"

Stubby Mustache grunted. "Don't remember it if we have. My name's Jones. Ted Jones."

"Well, I can't place any Joneses, but I'm glad to know you anyhow. I'm Barry Foster." I handed him one of my business cards, which he accepted uncomfortably. "I'm a lawyer," I added. "What's your line?"

"Broker," he returned, a little sullenly.

"Good!" I exclaimed. "I'd like some reliable advice on the market. What would you do with American Motors today?"

He hesitated perceptibly. "I'd stay out of it."

"Thanks, I will." (American Motors had been moving upward steadily for about three weeks, and was generally known as one of the blue chips of the market—only slightly more of a risk than government securities.) "We must have lunch together some day, Jones. I usually eat at the Canterbury Inn."

That was pure idiocy; there was nothing at all to be gained by letting this fellow know I recognized him. He'd only be called in and a new tail sicked on to me. However, I got a simple, human satisfaction out of telling him.

"Yeh, good idea," he grunted and turned back to the cigar clerk. As I left the building I stifled a Little Audreyish impulse to "laugh and laugh." If Jones continued to follow me during the next half hour he was due for a shock.

Westborough was standing on the corner even though the hour I had given him wasn't quite up. I told him of my discovery, and he agreed that our best move was to go straight to police headquarters. While we were riding south on a State Street car he produced a newspaper clipping from his billfold.

"I ran across this in the *Bugle* this morning. It will undoubtedly interest you, Mr Foster."

"There were a couple of stories in the *Trumpet*," I told him in return. "Some new developments—"

"Yes, I recall the items quite well. Particularly the description of Mr Morse's library. But tell me your opinion of this bit of pertinent information, Mr Foster."

I took the clipping from him. It was, I noticed, the picture of a young lady, whose attractiveness, despite the necessary coarseness of newspaper reproduction, was distinctly discernible. "The Merry Widow" was the facetious tag inserted above the picture, and the caption underneath it read:

"Vivacious Dorothy Spendall has left the Riviera to enliven Chicago society. Mrs Spendall, a former Chicago resident and well known here, has been at Nice during the past four years with her husband, the late Jonas Spendall."

"Vail didn't say a word about Spendall's death," I mused aloud. "I wonder if he's going to be glad or sorry to learn that his former inamorata is back—minus her elderly husband."

"The data are too meager to hazard a prediction," was Westborough's answer.

At police headquarters, a curt desk sergeant directed us to Mack's office.

"There's no use your trying any hocus pocus to get your girl friend out," was the detective lieutenant's greeting. "All we need to hold her is reasonable grounds of suspicion—you know that as well as I do. And we've sure got that."

"Have you located Wells?" I inquired.

"No," Mack returned shortly. He directed a long shot accurately into a cuspidor. "There's over two hundred fellows with that moniker in the phone book. Some of 'em are well-known citizens, too. We can't drag two hundred people like that down to the station on the off chance that Baines may be able to identify one of 'em. It 'd stir up a hornet's nest. What's the answer, wise guy?"

Westborough, his eyes twinkling, replied for me.

"Mr Foster has the full name and address of our Mr Wells."

"What?" Mack shouted.

I presented the slip of paper Pickens had given me, and he sniffed suspiciously.

"How'd you get hold of this, Foster?"

I explained about the Pickens letter—and how it had happened to be in my dinner jacket.

"That's concealing evidence," Mack growled.

"I suppose so."

Mack continued the bawling out as he thumbed the pages of the telephone directory. "You're a lawyer. You ought to have known better."

"If you weren't deaf, dumb and blind," I cut in hotly, "you'd know I didn't walk away with it on purpose. And, while we're on the subject, I'm tired of being tailed. There's no need for it. I've played square with you fellows; I've given you every bit of information I had."

Mack, intent on the pages of the directory, didn't appear to be listening. "Yeah, there's a J. Worthington Wells—address checks, too . . . Say, what were you saying, Foster?"

"I'm tired of being tailed," I snapped.

"What's eating you?" Mack demanded in wonderment. "There hasn't been any tail on you, Foster."

XVIII

I was utterly nonplussed. "You didn't have a man following me?"

"We did not," Mack said. "You can take my word for it."

Even if he were lying I didn't see anything to be gained by telling him so. As it was our relations hadn't been any too amiable.

"Dear me," Mr Westborough sighed. "I, too, had a distinct impression—"

"You saw him, too!" Mack yelled. "What kind of guy was he?"

"He had a fair, stubby mustache, light-brown hair, and pale-blue eyes," I was able to recall. "Square face—big jaw. And he was wearing a pepper-and-salt suit."

"Yesterday it was a brown suit," Westborough contributed. "And the gentleman had a very thick neck and somewhat large feet. That is no doubt why Mr Foster and I mistakenly assumed—"

Mack roared with laughter, then suddenly sobered. "You weren't being tailed by us, Foster. That's the straight dope. If you see him again get to the nearest phone booth and call headquarters. Then stall around with him until we get a chance to pick him up. If that bird really was tailing you I'd give a lot to know his game."

"So would I," I confessed wholeheartedly.

Mack glanced at his watch. "Quarter to eleven! There's plenty of time to make a call on Wells before the inquest. You fellows like to come along?"

I agreed, and Westborough murmured politely, "Indeed yes."

"Well let's make it snappy," Mack gruffly advised.

There was plenty of room for three in the front seat of Mack's car, particularly with Westborough, who didn't take up much room, in the middle. Mack drove fast— somewhat recklessly, but with consummate skill. We discussed the case as we sped northward.

"The Morse girl's a damn nice kid!" Mack conceded. "I don't like to see her take the rap for this, but who else is there?"

Unfortunately, I wasn't able to answer nor was Westborough. The little man, however, had a question of his own.

"Were any volumes missing from the Morse library?"

"Just got the final report this morning." Mack shot through a light that was shifting from orange to red, dexterously avoiding a car coming at right angles. "We had three men on that job—two to check the index cards and one at the books. Every book checked with both sets of cards."

"What about your hidden door?" I reminded maliciously.

"Ouch!" Mack exclaimed and made a wry face. "That's out for good! Those walls are solid everywhere."

"It was an excellent idea—by no means improbable," Westborough said consolingly. He paused hesitantly. "Had any article other than the purple parrot been removed from the house?"

"Baines said no; nothing so far as he knew. We looked into Morse's deposit vault— nothing to be learned there. Morse hadn't visited it for a week anyhow."

"What's your theory about the thousand dollars in cash?" I asked as we sailed through Lincoln Park at a forty-mile clip.

"What's yours?" Mack retorted, his eyes focused on the road.

"The one-thirty call might easily have been from Wells," I speculated. "Suppose he made an appointment for the evening—and wanted money! Wouldn't that explain why Morse cashed the check?"

"Then why was there not a receipt for the sum in Mr Morse's desk?" Westborough inquired. "A businessman as shrewd as the late Hezekiah Morse would surely not neglect this elementary precaution."

Steelcraft, I recalled, had taken much the same position.

"Not if the deal was on the level," Mack stressed the last three words. "But Morse might 've been paying blackmail."

"How reconcile that hypothesis with the package which Mr Wells was known to have brought with him?" Westborough objected.

"That's easy! Wells delivered a document to him and collected the grand."

"You've been through all the stuff in Morse's desk," I put in excitedly. "Was there anything there that would fit the bill?"

"Hum," Mack pondered, skillfully weaving in and out of the Sheridan Road traffic. "I'm not so sure there wasn't. A locked steel box in the bottom drawer had some old letters in it. They were signed by a dame named Lolita, and some of 'em were pretty hot!"

Lolita! The name evoked Vail's words: "Dolores, lady of sorrows, but always known by the affectionate diminutive, Lolita." And again: "Several clandestine letters, daring in their utter hopelessness."

Yes, Morse, hardened as he had become, might still have possessed that core of sentiment. He might have paid well to get back such letters.

"Suppose that Wells did deliver those letters," I interjected. "Suppose that Morse paid him his thousand and locked the letters in his steel box. What would happen then?"

"You tell me," Mack drawled, his eyes busy on the road.

"Morse would tell Wells what he thought of him. He would make threats. They wouldn't be idle threats, either, I can testify. Wells got panicky and—"

"Yeah!" Mack scoffed. "Morse wasn't stabbed until midnight; Wells came at eight-thirty. How long do you think it takes to deliver a pack of letters? Morse would get rid of the fellow as soon as he could. He'd just as soon have a snake in the house as a blackmailer."

He had me there, all right, and I acknowledged my defeat. However, it wouldn't do any harm to thresh out other problems—particularly since Mack was in a position where he had to listen to me.

"The hall-door key is a weak point in your case against Miss Morse." (I had done no little thinking on this subject.) "There weren't any fingerprints so whoever turned it must have been wearing a glove. But the key was bloodstained so the glove must have been that way too. Your men searched the house carefully and searched Miss Morse's room completely. They didn't find any bloodstained glove."

"She had plenty of time to wash it," Mack growled.

"Strongly open to question. But if she had washed it your men would have still found a damp glove."

"There was a bottle of cleaning stuff in her room," Mack pointed out. "She could 've cleaned the glove with that, and it wouldn't be damp by the time we got there."

"An excellent theory, but not in accord with physical facts," Mr Westborough commented. "Only yesterday I consulted a work upon the removal of stains. Organic solvents, such as benzol or carbon tetrachloride, which are the basis of most cleaning fluids, do not seem to be particularly effective upon bloodstains. Why I do not know. Cold water or hydrogen peroxide is recommended if the stain is on silk, wool or rayon; ammonia, hydrogen peroxide or javelle water if it is on cotton or linen."

"There you are!" I exclaimed. "Your cleaning fluid wouldn't have worked. And you didn't happen to find a bottle of ammonia or javelle water in Miss Morse's room, did you? Such things are kept in the kitchen, and you know that she didn't go down there."

"Well, there was a bottle of peroxide in the bathroom cabinet," Mack said. "I can remember seeing it there."

"Miss Morse is not a practicing chemist!" I objected heatedly. "You can hardly expect her to know that peroxide will take out bloodstains."

"Moreover, hydrogen peroxide is no more volatile than water," Mr Westborough added. "In the event of its use, the glove would have still been damp."

"You see!" I grinned. "You're right back where you started from."

"Oh, to hell with it!" Mack snapped. "It's going to take more than ammonia and hydrogen peroxide to get your girl out of this jam, Foster." He turned left from Clark Street and drove under the elevated tracks of the Chicago and Northwestern Railway. "Here's the street now."

The dwellings in this part of Russell Avenue were staid two-story houses, set comfortably back from the sidewalk. Tall elms ornamented the parkways; the neighborhood, in startling contrast to the uniform rows of apartment buildings only a block or so away, had the leisurely charm of a small town. Mack drove by a yellow frame house with a high-gabled roof and a spacious porch.

"That's the place. Can you spot it from the alley, Foster?"

I nodded. "With that color it would be hard to miss."

Mack pulled up to the curb — at least half a block away from the yellow house.

"All right, run down the alley and watch the back door. If anybody tries to make a getaway stop him and yell for me. Get it?"

The thrill of the chase stole upon me as I sneaked up the alley in accordance with Mack's tersely expressed commands. Leaning against a telephone pole I waited expectantly. There were no signs of movement from within the house. The shades had been tightly drawn, and the place wore a bleak air. Deciding it could do no harm to reconnoiter I lifted the latch of the back gate. Just as I stepped inside the yard Mr Westborough came walking briskly from around the side of the house.

"Come at once, Mr Foster," he said. "Mr Wells is at home."

Mack was standing by the front door, talking to the most unprepossessing female I have ever seen. She was all angles, her hair was strained back in an uncompromising knot at the back of her head, and she had a face beside which a glass of vinegar would have been as palatable as fruit punch.

"Why don't you let them come up, Hannah?" a man's voice called from above. With a loud and reluctant sniff the woman stepped aside.

The house had evidently been furnished at least twenty years ago, and nothing had been done in the way of interior decoration since. There was even an ancient carved umbrella stand in the front hall. The light from the leaded glass window on the landing, allowed me to discern that the stair carpeting was badly worn, almost threadbare in places.

"Good morning. Will you be kind enough to come this way?" said the man who greeted us at the top of the stairs.

He was slight—no taller than Westborough—but it was too dark in the upper hall to make out his face. His voice, however, had sounded tired and a little uncertain. He opened the door to a front room. It had a large bay window facing south, through which the sun was cheerfully streaming.

"Will you be seated, gentlemen?" His manner was courteous, his tones gentle.

"Is your name Wells?" Mack demanded.

Our host bowed. He was in his late sixties, I judged. His features were refined, delicate. They were the features of a scholar, an impression augmented by his nose glasses and his neatly trimmed, gray Vandyke beard. His blue suit was freshly pressed, but the serge was shiny, and his shirt, although spotlessly white, was slightly frayed at the cuffs. He was stoop-shouldered, and his eyes were reddened and squinting.

The room was in obvious keeping with this hermit of a man. Like Morse's study it was lined with books. They stretched to the ceiling, and there was a stepladder sort of thing on casters to be shoved around to reach the upper shelves. A massive Elizabethan refectory table with melon-bulb legs took up most of the center of the room, and there were two large black chairs with markedly worn leather upholstery. In one corner was an old-fashioned iron safe.

"Yes, I am J. Worthington Wells," our host replied. "And you, gentlemen?"

"Lieutenant Mack of the homicide squad. This is Mr Foster and this is Mr Westborough."

"Westborough?" Wells repeated. "Are you the author of that splendid work: *Trajan: His Life and Times?*"

"I have enjoyed that slight distinction," Westborough answered, his manner noticeably self-conscious. Mack broke impatiently into the conversation.

"We didn't come here to talk about books. Wells, you called at Morse's home on Wednesday night." Seating himself in one of the leather-upholstered chairs he crossed his legs aggressively. "That was the night Morse was killed. You called on him that night, and it won't get you anywhere to lie about it."

"But I do not intend to lie about it," Wells said, with the hurt surprise of a child. "I did call upon Mr Morse, but I left him at nine."

"You sure of that?"

"It was certainly no later."

"Morse's butler didn't know when you left," Mack objected.

"No, I did not see him then. Mr Morse himself went to the door with me."

"Where did you go after nine o'clock?"

"To Kimball Hall on South Wabash. I took a taxi and was there by nine-fifteen."

"Hum! Anybody see you there?"

"Several friends. I was making a talk before a small group of bibliophiles. The subject was—"

Mack waved this aside as of slight importance. "Why did you go to see Morse?"

"To sell him a book."

"A book!" Mack ejaculated.

"Dear me," exclaimed Westborough. "I had already conjectured that such was the case."

"One of those antiques that Morse collected?"

"Yes, an English translation of Boccaccio's *The Fall of Prynces*."

Mack asked incredulously: "Did Morse pay you an even grand for one book?"

"A grand?" Wells inquired. "I do not believe I know—"

"Hell, where have you been all your life?"

"Lieutenant Mack wishes to know if you accepted a thousand dollars for the book," Westborough interpreted.

Wells smiled, a shade wistfully. "Necessity, gentlemen, is frequently a sad task-master. I was compelled to part with it at that price."

"An even grand for just one book?" Mack repeated.

"But this is the edition printed by Richard Pynson in 1494! There are only ten known copies."

"You may be assured, Lieutenant Mack, that the volume *is* a collector's rarity," Westborough confirmed. "In more propitious times than these it would have fetched an even larger sum."

"Well maybe." Mack sounded as though he didn't in the least believe it. "Did Morse give you cash or a check?"

Wells replied, "He was good enough to pay in cash. I had made that request of him."

"You asked him for cash? Why? His signature was as good as gold on any check he cared to write."

Once again Wells smiled his wistful smile. "I am no longer fortunate enough to have a bank account. It is an open secret that I have been living from hand to mouth for some time now, parting one by one with these old friends whom I have spent the better part of a lifetime in amassing."

"Dear, dear!" Westborough sighed. "That is really too bad."

Mack's attitude was more realistic. "You're living anyhow. And when you can collect an even grand for just one book, I'd say you didn't have much to worry about. Did Morse ask for a receipt?"

"Yes, I gave him a receipted invoice."

"What became of it?"

"Is it missing? It was lying on the top of his desk when I left the room."

Mack leaned forward in his chair. "What do you know about Morse's purple parrot?"

"Purple parrot?"

"Yeah! Little statue of a parrot about six inches high. Did you ever see it?"

"Yes." Wells's eyes were fixed on the oaken top of the refectory table.

"When?"

"That evening."

"You saw it lying on top of the desk?"

"Why, no. Mr Morse brought it from a lower drawer to show me."

"What made him do that?"

Wells's face appeared rather strained, I fancied. "Why does anyone show his curios to anyone else? I can't recall the circumstances clearly—it seemed of such trivial importance. But I believe that Mr Morse asked me if I could tell him what a kakapo was. I answered that I believed it was a New Zealand bird, and he brought out the statuette from the drawer."

"Did he put it back in the drawer before you left the room?"

"I—I can't remember."

"You didn't take the thing?" Mack demanded bluntly.

Wells's glance shifted uneasily to his bookcases. Then he turned and said in a surprisingly peppery tone, "I did not. That question is an insult, sir."

Mack's fist banged down on the table.

"Maybe you're lying and maybe you're not! But I'll have the truth if I—"

"May I ask Mr Wells a few questions?" Westborough interrupted.

Mack grudgingly yielded the floor.

"I should like to know the subject upon which you addressed the association of bibliophiles."

"It was reviewed in the paper," Wells answered. "Merely a few paragraphs, but I was surprised to learn that my subject had even that much interest for the general public. I believe that I preserved the notice." He opened the table drawer. "Yes, here it is."

He handed a newspaper clipping to Westborough who read aloud:

PRINTED IN 1462, BIBLE
IS WORTH $30,000 TODAY

The first dated Bible was printed in Mainz, Germany, in 1462, and a copy is worth about $30,000, J. Worthington Wells of 1924 Russell Avenue told members of the Bibliophile Club last evening.

This is probably the fourth printed Bible to be produced, Mr Wells explained, and it was preceded in time by only the "Gutenberg" or "42 Line Bible", the Bamberg Bible, and the Mentelin Bible. Incidentally, Mr Wells reminded his listeners, there is no conclusive evidence to show that the so-called "Gutenberg" Bible, printed in Mainz before August, 1456, was actually the work of Gutenberg.

About as few copies are known of the "1462" as of the "Gutenberg", Mr Wells said. Only four have been placed on the market during recent years, and these have been sold at prices ranging from $19,000 to $35,000.

Mack chuckled. "My Aunt Harriet's got an old Bible I could have for nothing. Who'd pay thirty-five grand for such a thing?"

"I have refused an offer of thirty thousand dollars for my own copy," Wells answered. Mack shook his head in baffled astonishment.

"Nuts! Clear nuts! Anyway, if I had something worth thirty grand, I wouldn't leave it laying around loose here."

"I take the obvious precautions," Wells replied, pointing to the safe.

"That cheesebox!" Mack explained derisively. "Any good cracksman could split it wide open in ten minutes."

"Would it be too great a favor to see this rarity?" Westborough ventured.

With the air of a high priest about to unveil the holy of holies, Wells opened the safe. He lifted the book out tenderly and laid it reverentially upon the table. A tinge of awe was in his voice as he pointed out that this was the first Bible to carry the name and address of its printer.

Well, I took his word for it. The book was in Latin, printed in Gothic characters, and was about as intelligible to me as one of the Rig-Vedas in the original Sanskrit. Westborough, however, was tremendously impressed.

"Remarkable!" he breathed. "An amazing sight which I shall long treasure in my memory. I do not wonder that Hezekiah Morse offered you the thirty thousand dollars."

"Morse made that offer!" Mack exclaimed blankly. "Wells didn't say that. How did you find it out, Westborough?"

"A mere surmise," the little man disclaimed with his habitual modesty. "I noticed that Morse's collection contained few incunabula. It seemed inevitable that he should attempt to purchase such a gem as this."

"Yes, it was Morse who offered me that sum," Wells confirmed. "Naturally I did not accept."

"Naturally not," Westborough agreed.

Mack, however, did not think the procedure to be so natural. "Both of you are clean screwy, if you ask me. Say, how long ago was it that Morse wanted to buy this thing?"

"He had never withdrawn his original offer," Wells explained.

"Did he say anything to you about it Wednesday night?"

"Ye-es," said Wells, hesitating once more. "He did."

A vivid picture of the two men talking in Morse's study flashed before my mind. Morse, who didn't take defeat easily, would have been very insistent in his demands.

"There must have been a quarrel," I said aloud. "You refused him and he got nasty. Wasn't that it?"

"The quarrel was solely on his side," Wells answered. He returned the 1462 Bible carefully to the safe, slammed the door and spun the dial. "I merely reiterated that I did not wish to sell. Eventually he accepted my position, and we parted on excellent terms."

Mack's loud snort was singularly expressive. "How long were you down at Kimball Hall?"

"Until nearly eleven. At that hour a friend drove me home in his car."

"What friend?"

"His name is Peter Whealon."

"Pete Whealon!" Mack ejaculated. "Not the paving contractor, Pete Whealon!"

Wells nodded. "He also is a book collector. We have many common ties."

"You sure get around with the big shots!" Mack observed admiringly. "Did he drive you straight home without making any stops?"

"Yes."

"If you didn't leave the Loop until eleven you couldn't have made it out here until at least eleven-thirty."

"I didn't notice."

"Did he come inside with you and stay for a while?"

"No, he drove on at once. Mr Whealon, I am sure, will confirm this story."

"Well," Mack deliberated, "I don't see how you could have got back to Division Street by twelve o'clock. If Whealon confirms that story you're cleared, Wells."

The relief in the man's face was very nearly ludicrous. Mack noticed it, also, for he added sternly: "But take a tip from me—tell the police all about it the next time you happen to be calling on a guy who gets murdered."

Wells said humbly, "I'm sorry. I was confused, upset. I didn't know just what I ought to do."

"You should 've come straight to headquarters," Mack told him severely. "That would have saved us a lot of bother and yourself some embarrassment. Remember it next time."

"I will, indeed," Wells promised with fervor.

Wells had contributed one important bit of new information. The purple parrot had not been taken earlier than Wednesday evening; it was now known definitely to have been in Morse's possession up to as late as nine o'clock on the night of his death.

But, as we left the house, I was not so certain that Wells had told us everything he had known concerning Hezekiah Morse. Walking down the stairs I reviewed the entire scene, and by the time we had reached Mack's car I had reached a definite conclusion.

Wells had been patently anxious several times during the course of the interview. But his uneasiness had reached its peak at the time Morse's purple parrot was under discussion!

XIX

Public interest in the dramatic Morse case was at white heat. The inquest room at the county morgue would seat about a hundred people, but at least three times that number were pushing and crowding for places.

Sylvia sat beside me in the front of the room. Her black crepe dress accentuated the whiteness of her throat, the pallor of her face. Although she was undoubtedly fighting hard to retain her poise her lips quivered slightly.

Coroner Gerald E. Hunt, the white-haired veteran of several thousand inquests, fidgeted with the black ribbon of his pince nez and frowned on the male and female sensation seekers who were fighting their way into the room. He reminded me of Shakespeare's description of the justice—"in fair round belly with good capon lin'd." And the "good and lawful" men prescribed by Illinois statute, looked as though the worthy coroner had picked up the first six fellows he had happened to meet on the street.

One of them, a fussy little man with glasses, obviously wore a toupée—at least there were two shades of hair on his head which didn't quite match.

The coroner's deep bass droned the oath administered to the jury foreman—no other than my friend of the toupée.

"You, as foreman of this inquest, do solemnly swear that you will diligently inquire and true presentment make how and in what manner and by whom or what the body which here lies dead came to its death, and that you will deliver to me, the coroner of this county, a true inquest thereof, according to such evidence as shall be given you, and according to the best of your knowledge and belief, so help you God?"

The foreman answered resolutely, "I do," and the coroner turned to the other jurors.

"The same oath which John J. Piersons, your foreman, has just now taken on his part, you and each of you do solemnly swear to keep on your respective parts, so help you God?"

"I do," the jurors chorused.

I glanced over at Assistant State's Attorney Lew Teagan, who was a Napoleonic sort of man with a prominent aquiline nose. He was swaying nervously in his chair—like a race horse pawing the ground before the starting gun.

O'Ryan, big and blustering in his blue uniform, was the first witness called. The coroner, after putting the conventional routine inquiries, directed:

"You may tell the jury what you found at the Morse residence on the night of November 18."

"I got a call from headquarters at twelve-thirteen and went immediately to the home of Hezekiah Morse at 49 East Division Street, arriving there at twelve-twenty." O'Ryan stressed each sentence as though cognizant that it would become a matter of public record. He was conscientiously thorough in his inclusion of details, and I realized what an ordeal this inquest would be for Sylvia.

"The deceased," O'Ryan concluded, "was slumped forward and resting against the edge of the desk. A knife was sticking in his chest, and he had his hand around the handle of it. The door from the hall into the library was locked from the inside, and the key was in the lock. A second door to the library was standing wide open. It opened through Miss Morse's room."

"There are only two doors to the room in which you found Morse?" Teagan inquired.

"Yes."

Mack confirmed O'Ryan's account and also mentioned the bloodstained door key. Teagan began to question him.

"Were the windows of the study closed and locked?"

"They were both closed, but only one was locked."

"Do you think it possible for a person to have left the house by the unlocked window?"

"No."

A juror, rubbing his hand across an unshaven chin, leaned forward.

"Why couldn't they? Anybody can go out an unlocked window."

"Anybody leaving by that window would 've had to drop a good fifteen feet to a plot of turf," Mack explained. "He couldn't do it without leaving his footprints, and there weren't any footprints."

"What about a ladder?" persisted the inquiring juror. Mack looked at him witheringly.

"A ladder would 've left a couple of dents to show where it rested. The turf was perfectly smooth."

I rose to my feet. "The ground is partially frozen. Are you sure that footprints or the marks of a ladder would necessarily appear?"

"I don't care how hard the ground is," Mack maintained. "A fifteen foot drop or the weight of a man on a ladder would be bound to leave some marks."

"Would it be necessary to rest the ladder on the grass in order to enter the house?" I persevered. "Might it not have been placed on the concrete sidewalk?"

"If it was I'd hate to go up on it."

Two or three jurors snickered, and the diminutive foreman, who took his new dignity seriously, glared at them. The coroner, after a number of questions, most of which had to do with the position of the deceased when found, dismissed Mack and called Baines. The butler was allowed to tell his story uninterrupted until he mentioned Sylvia's scream.

The coroner fingered his black ribbon. "What did you do then?"

"I went upstairs, sir."

"You may tell the jury what you saw."

"The first thing was Mr Foster running up the front stairs. We met in the hall, sir."

"Where was Miss Morse?" Teagan put in.

"Also in the hall, sir."

"Did you see her come out of her room?"

"No sir."

"Did you see her before or after you noticed Mr Foster?"

"I hardly know, sir. We all three met in the hall."

"What did you do then?"

"We entered the study."

"Through which door?"

"The door from Miss Morse's room, sir."

"Why not the door from the hall?"

"That door was locked, sir."

"How did you know that?"

"I tried to open it, sir, and so did Mr Foster."

"Was the door to the study from Miss Morse's room open or closed?"

"Open, sir. Mr Morse's body was plainly visible."

Teagan took up the questioning. "Had you left the kitchen at any time prior to the scream?"

"Once," Baines admitted. "To go to the toilet, sir."

A juror guffawed and was given a reproving look by the foreman.

"At what time?" Teagan interrogated.

"I don't recall. I was not away more than two or three minutes, sir."

Matilda was the next witness. She admitted that her name was Matilda Sampson and her occupation that of cook for the deceased. She added a number of other statements that were not particularly relevant. Finally:

"Could Mr Baines, while out of the room, go upstairs without your knowledge?" the coroner inquired.

Matilda shook her head with positive assurance. "No, he would 've had to come back through the kitchen. He didn't go upstairs unless he went there while I was out of the room."

"When was that?"

"About ten o'clock."

"Was Mr Baines with you when you heard the scream?"

"Yes."

"Had he been with you for some time prior to that?"

"Yes, at least an hour or so."

Matilda swept to her seat with the air of a good woman who has done her lawful duty, and I heard my own name called. I tried to keep my statement as noncommittal as possible.

"... I remained downstairs while Miss Morse went up to speak to her grandfather. I heard her scream and rushed upstairs. She had just gone into her grandfather's room—"

Teagan darted at me with the swift swoop of a hornet.

"How do you know she had just gone into her grandfather's room?"

"It's obvious—or she would have screamed before," I snapped.

"Oh, is it? Not if she killed him herself, she wouldn't."

I applied to the coroner. "The assistant state's attorney has no right to make such an assumption."

"You know that this is not a judicial proceeding, and that we are not bound by the formal rules of evidence," Coroner Hunt replied. Teagan returned to the attack.

"Are you engaged to Miss Morse?"

I hesitated. "Are you or aren't you?" Teagan snarled.

"Yes."

"Didn't you wait in the Morse living room because Miss Morse was going to ask her grandfather's consent to your marriage that night?"

"Yes." (The fellow had a fiendish knack of picking out his adversary's weak spots.)

"Wasn't it extremely unlikely that such consent would have been granted?"

This question, however, wasn't up to his usual shrewdness.

"I can't say whether it would have been or not."

Teagan sallied from another direction. "Is it not a fact that you drew up several wills for Hezekiah Morse?"

"Yes."

"Will you tell us the provisions of the latest will—the will which had not been signed prior to Morse's death?"

"Is this relevant?" The coroner ruled that it was. "The will divided the great bulk of Morse's property between his granddaughter and his friend, Thomas Vail. There were bequests for the two servants and for several charitable organizations."

"There was also a provision disinheriting Miss Morse if she married anyone but Mr Vail, wasn't there?"

I was forced to admit that there had been such a provision. Teagan was satisfied, but my ordeal was by no means finished.

"You may describe your first view of the body of the decedent," the coroner directed. I could see Sylvia shuddering as I complied with the request.

"Did you notice that a pool of blood had formed on the surface of the desk?"

"Yes."

"Will you tell the jury what the blood looked like?"

"Like blood."

Several people laughed, and the coroner rapped for order. If I could play the imbecile long enough—

"Had the blood you saw commenced to coagulate?" the coroner inquired.

"Coagulate?" I echoed, striving to keep my face an uncomprehending blank.

Very patiently, as though dealing with a subnormal intelligence, the coroner elucidated. "Had it commenced to thicken, or was it still a thin liquid?"

There was no escape from it. I was forced to give that devastating testimony against Sylvia. "A thin liquid."

I was dismissed after a few more minor questions, and the coroner called a new witness: O. A. Schmidt, assistant chief identification inspector.

Schmidt was a jovial, bearded German, who spoke with a faintly discernible accent. The coroner exhibited the cloisonné-handled letter opener.

"Did the Identification Bureau discover fingerprints on this knife?"

"Yes."

"Were you able to identify those fingerprints?"

"Yes."

"Whose fingerprints were they?"

"They were made by the fingers of Miss Morse's right hand."

I asked permission to question the witness.

"I understand that the prints found on the knife were blurred?"

"That is correct."

"How then are you able to identify them with such assurance?"

A broad smile swept across the face of the German. "We used the fingerprint projector."

"Fingerprint projector?"

"Yes, an instrument which throws together on a lighted screen the enlarged images—magnified to about the size of a man's head—of two separate fingerprints. If the two fingerprints are identical, the convolutions will flow into each other."

I switched to another line of inquiry.

"What prints were on the knife?"

"The four fingers."

"Were they on the blade or the handle?"

"Upon the handle and perpendicular to it."

My next question, I considered parenthetically, might save Sylvia, or it might utterly damn her. Nevertheless, I felt justified in going on.

"Was the little finger or the index finger toward the blade?"

"The index finger was toward the blade, the little finger toward the end of the handle."

"Miss Morse frequently used this knife to open her grandfather's letters. From the position of the fingerprints does it seem probable to you that the knife had been held for this purpose?"

"No," Schmidt maintained after a few minutes' thought. "The normal way to open a letter is to hold the knife between the index and second fingers and to extend the index finger along the blade in a direction nearly parallel to it. This knife was held for stabbing."

"It's the way you would hold a sword," I declared. "Or even a knife if you were going to stab somebody facing you. But Morse was stabbed from behind."

Picking up the knife from the coroner's desk, I handed it to Schmidt.

"I am seated in a chair, my back toward you. Grasp the knife, reach around and stab at my chest."

Teagan rose to his feet. "This is an inquest and not a third-rate melodrama."

The coroner repeated what he had earlier told me. "We are not bound by the formal rules of evidence."

"There are some things not admissible," Teagan grumbled.

"In my opinion Mr Foster's demonstration is relevant," the coroner ruled.

I grasped Schmidt's wrist and raised it toward the jury. "Do you see how he holds this knife? The little finger is toward the blade, the index finger toward the handle. If a knife is held the other way with the index finger toward the blade—and the fingerprints show that this knife was held that way—then it's necessary to turn the wrist in a very awkward manner in order to stab downward from behind."

Taking the knife from Schmidt I held it with my index finger toward the blade.

"When Miss Morse made the prints Mr Schmidt identified she held the knife in this manner. If any of you gentlemen of the jury care to experiment you will find it quite easy and natural to open an envelope with this grip."

I extended the knife to the jury foreman, who grasped it in the manner I had described, and, an air of grim determination on his face, opened several imaginary envelopes. Two or three jurors nodded their heads.

Teagan took the floor hastily.

"Didn't you state, Inspector Schmidt, that the fingerprints you found on the knife were blurred?"

"Yes. Such is the case."

"Might not such blurring result from a gloved hand grasping the knife and thus smearing the prints already on it?"

"Yes, that might cause the blurring," Schmidt admitted. Teagan addressed the coroner.

"You can see that it makes little difference whether or not Miss Morse was responsible for the fingerprints discovered by the Identification Bureau." The coroner nodded his agreement and called for Dr Basil Hildreth, who, after the regular routine had been concluded, was asked to state the cause of death.

"Shock and hemorrhage resulting from a knife thrust," the doctor said briskly. "The knife entered the body in an obliquely downward direction, penetrating the chest wall at the fourth interspace and puncturing the aorta a short distance from the point where that artery joins the left ventricle."

"Could such a wound be self-inflicted?" the coroner asked.

"In my opinion—decidedly not. The knife traversed the deceased's coat, vest, a heavy shirt of Oxford cloth and his underclothing, and, in spite of the considerable resistance opposed to its passage, entered the body with sufficient force to drive a small fragment of the underwear into the wound. Only a person standing behind the deceased and striking downward with the full momentum afforded by this position could deliver such a blow."

The coroner requested him to identify the knife, and he did so after a brief examination of it. Then he was asked to tell the jury the time at which Morse's death had occurred.

"In my opinion between midnight Wednesday and five minutes past that hour."

"How does he know so exactly?" murmured a juror in an extremely audible stage whisper. The coroner suppressed an incipient laugh from the audience.

"You may tell the jury your reasons for believing that the decedent was killed at the time you have named."

"Blood begins to coagulate in from five to ten minutes. When Mr Morse's body was discovered at ten minutes past twelve the blood had not yet coagulated."

"Who told you, Dr Hildreth, that the blood had not coagulated?"

"Mr Foster."

"Just what were his words to you?"

"I don't recall his exact words. The substance was that the blood appeared to him to be a thin, red liquid."

Hearsay evidence, provided it was relevant, might be introduced at the inquest, I knew. However, the coroner left no doubt in the minds of the jurors.

"You remember, gentlemen, that Mr Foster stated that the blood was a 'thin liquid' when he first saw it."

Teagan hurried to make the doctor affirm the point. "You are positive that Morse's death did not occur before twelve o'clock?"

"As positive as one can ever be in these cases."

I rose to my feet, grasping at the one tiny loophole. "Would you say, Dr Hildreth, that Morse could not have been killed as early as five minutes to twelve?"

"There might be a small variation from the time I have stated. I do not believe it would be as long as five minutes before twelve, but I'd be willing to allow you that much time after twelve."

"In your opinion," asked the coroner, "is Miss Morse able to deliver the blow which caused her grandfather's death?"

"Will you ask Miss Morse to stand, please?"

His searching glance of Sylvia seemed interminable.

"Yes," he declared at length.

The coroner called for the next witness.

Sylvia Elaine Morse!

"It is my duty to inform you that any testimony you might give in this hearing may be used against you," his heavy bass boomed. "Knowing this, do you still wish to testify?"

She nodded, and the coroner administered the oath.

With gratification I noted that she had been able to control all traces of the anxiety I had remarked at the beginning of the inquest. Her voice was clear and resonant, and she kept her eyes fixed squarely on the faces of the jurors. Teagan interrupted her account after half-a-dozen sentences.

"Why didn't you go into your grandfather's room immediately?"

"I was—hesitant about approaching him."

"Because you had just become engaged to Foster?"

"Yes."

Striding toward her Teagan extended his finger threateningly. "Did you or did you not go near the body of your grandfather?" he demanded curtly.

"I can't remember."

Teagan spoke to the coroner in a low voice; the next instant he was holding out a white evening dress for Sylvia to examine.

"Is this the gown you wore on the evening of November 18?"

"Yes."

He turned the dress so that the jury could see the red smudge across its hem.

"When did this dress become stained?"

Sylvia nervously clenched and unflexed the fingers of her right hand. Her eyes sought mine imploringly—but I could do nothing.

"I don't know."

"You don't remember going near the deceased?"

"No! I tell you I don't!"

"Did Mr Foster remain downstairs the entire ten minutes prior to your scream?"

"Yes," she affirmed steadfastly.

"He didn't come through your room while you were waiting at the dressing table?"

"No."

"Miss Morse, you may be charged with the murder of your grandfather," the coroner admonished imposingly. "Knowing this, do you wish to persist in your statement that Mr Foster didn't enter your room at any time prior to your scream?"

"Yes."

Her eyes were fixed straight ahead with a confidence nothing on earth could break down, and I felt a lump rise in my throat. I would have given anything to have been able to save her from this.

The testimony concluded at last, the coroner instructed the jury:

"Remember, gentlemen, that it is not your function to decide whether or not any certain person is guilty of the death of Hezekiah Morse but to decide whether or not the evidence you have heard is sufficient to justify that any person or persons be held for trial."

They filed from the room. Minutes dragged like great black hours across the face of time until Foreman John J. Piersons, fussily important, delivered the verdict:

"We find that the deceased, Hezekiah Morse, was murdered, and we recommend that Sylvia Elaine Morse be held to the grand jury."

XX

The verdict of the coroner's jury had been no more than I had expected. Yet it made me realize, as nothing else could have done, the appalling weight of the evidence against Sylvia. Still, there must be another solution to the problem—a solution which would also provide the answer to:

(a). The disappearance of Hezekiah Morse's purple parrot.

(b). The reason why I had been shadowed.

My thoughts turned to Stubby Mustache as Westborough and I continued our walk along Division Street. For the hundredth time I gave a quick glance backward over my shoulder with futile results. I had not seen him since our encounter that morning. Apparently my bit of bravado had frightened him into abandoning the trail for good. What an idiot I had been! I had deliberately severed the one thread which might have led to the heart of the labyrinth.

"Come, come, Mr Foster!" Westborough entreated sympathetically. "Surely it cannot be as bad as that?"

I returned no answer. My eyes were mechanically picking out the glowing reds and blues of Neon tube signs. My mind, however, was completely obsessed with Sylvia. She needed me — needed every gram of mental fibre my brain possessed. Sylvia in the County Jail! Sylvia surrounded by its hardened and calloused inmates! And I was doing nothing — nothing at all!

We neared State Street, and a tall hotel loomed from the shadows. There was a florist shop across the street; I had once stopped there to buy flowers for her. How long ago had that been? A week? Or a hundred years?

My mood, however, did not affect Westborough's invariant cheerfulness. "Who knows?" he continued genially. "Perhaps tonight we may be fortunate enough to clear away a little more of the underbrush which conceals our white flower."

We reached the Morse house. I was going there for a confidential talk with the servants, and Westborough, for some reason of his own, had been eager to accompany me. Baines opened the door for us, and we went upstairs at once to the study. Something had been bothering Westborough ever since the inquest. I wasn't sure just what it was, but it was something connected with that room.

The study, however, was much the same as it had always been prior to Morse's death. The stain had been washed from the desk and rug, I noticed the first thing. With the tall desk lamp lighted, the room bore a pleasant, cheery air that was not at all in keeping with its recent history.

Westborough deserted me without compunction for the bookcases. He was examining titles, his eyes, like those of a true bibliophile, dwelling upon each volume with a caressing tenderness.

"What are you looking for?" I asked.

"The missing receipt which Mr Wells gave Mr Morse."

"But the police —"

"The police," he interrupted, "did not then possess the knowledge that we have now. I have a deep-rooted conviction that they failed solely because they did not know where to look. Perhaps my theory is entirely wrong, but I should like to put it to the test. Can you tell me if that exceedingly rare volume, *The Fall of Prynces*, is still in Mr Morse's library?"

I consulted the olive-green cabinet on the desk. The index cards were there all

right—made out in Hezekiah Morse's own handwriting. After some search we found
the volume among the folio editions; it was a book with a handsomely ornamented
black calf cover.

Mr Westborough held it reverentially in his hands.

"The binding, if I am not mistaken, is early sixteenth century." He pointed to the
ornaments. "Note the four royal badges of the period: the Tudor rose, the royal ini-
tials H.R., the Tudor portcullis, and the fleur-de-lys. Dear me, what a treasure for a
collector to acquire."

He opened the cover, and Wells's receipted invoice stared us full in the face. A
brief notation upon the back of the receipt explained why Morse had elected to keep
it with the book: "There are about ninety missing pages. Of the nine other copies of
this work known to exist, not one is entirely perfect and most of them, like this, are
large fragments—J.W.W."

But something else had also been placed within *The Fall of Prynces*, a white card
which fell to the floor. I stooped to pick it up. It was a card of the size and shape
Morse had used for his indexing, and there were a few lines on it in Morse's bold
handwriting:

BIBLE, "1462"

Fust and Schoeffer, Mainz, 1462. Printed on vellum; Latin in Gothic characters. First
dated Bible. First Bible to bear name and device of its printer—Johann Fust and
Peter Schoeffer.

"Dear, dear!" Westborough exclaimed. "This is most interesting. I must remember
to see that it is brought to Lieutenant Mack's attention." He laid the card, together
with the receipted invoice, upon the desk while I restored *The Fall of Prynces* to its
shelf. "And now," he continued, "shall we press our luck with regard to another
matter?"

"What matter?" I inquired.

"That concerning the somewhat enigmatic George Smith—the erstwhile owner of
the purple parrot. Surely you have not forgotten him?"

I had not.

"You think we may be able to trace his family?"

He shrugged his slight shoulders. "Dear, dear, I would not care to be that optimis-
tic. But Miss Morse, I recall your saying, mentioned that her grandfather had ren-
dered financial assistance to this emigrant from his boyhood home. Doubtless there
is a record of the transaction."

Morse had kept books, we soon discovered upon rummaging through the desk
drawers. Every item of income and expenditure had been meticulously entered in a
small ledger, which, however, did not contain any entries further back than the beginning of the current year. While Westborough, making no effort to disguise his curiosity, was poring over the ledger, I leafed through a bundle of canceled checks. They

were carefully arranged by months, a rubber band securing the checks for each monthly period, but, like the ledger, they did not extend back any further than the current year. Westborough continued his intent study of the ledger. Hoping that there might be a letter from George Smith or his family, I went through the entire desk. The only letters I found were those in the steel box which Mack had mentioned—the ones from Lolita. These I did not disturb; I could not bring myself to trespass upon their very personal contents.

I slammed the last drawer shut. "There's no reference to George Smith in this desk. I'll swear to that."

Westborough closed his ledger. "No doubt the older records are stored in some other place. Let us go downstairs and consult Baines."

The single lamp bulb in the center of the long hall afforded so little illumination that it was almost necessary for us to grope our way toward the back stairs. But if the hall was dim the stairs were worse. I wondered how Baines had escaped breaking his neck a dozen times a day in traversing this passage.

We paused on a small landing, half-a-dozen steps from the kitchen, which, despite the gleaming electric refrigerator in one corner, appeared definitely dingy and out-moded. Matilda—our lady of the skillets—was nowhere in evidence, but I could see Baines. Evidently he had not heard us approach, for we caught him very much off guard. He was in his shirtsleeves; his chair was tipped back at a comfortable angle, and he puffed clouds of smoke from a villainous smelling briar as he perused the pages of *The Saturday Evening Post*.

"Baines!" I called from the landing.

Down banged the chair, the pipe clattered to the table, and the magazine dropped to the floor while Baines hastily donned his coat.

"I am sorry, sir. I did not hear you."

"Reading a good yarn?" I smiled.

His coat on, Baines had regained his professional dignity.

"Quite amusing, sir."

"Where's Matilda?" I asked. "This her night off?"

"That day falls on a Thursday, sir. Miss Sampson has retired to her room with a slight headache."

"That's too bad. I wanted to talk to both of you. But if she's sick—"

"I do not believe it is at all serious, sir. I will inform her at once."

I stopped him on his way to the stairs. "Not just yet, Baines. Mr Westborough and I wish to examine Mr Morse's old records."

"Is Mr Westborough a detective, sir?"

"An amazingly clever one," I informed.

Westborough's face flushed. "You are far too kind, Mr Foster."

"If I may be allowed the liberty of speaking out of place—" Baines began.

"You may," I told him.

"Then I sincerely hope his efforts may be crowned with complete success, sir. It is unthinkable that Miss Morse could be concerned with Mr Morse's death. I have known her since she was six years old, and there never was a more lovable child nor a sweeter young lady, if I may be allowed to say so, sir."

I clapped him on the shoulder. "Bully for you, Baines. You can count upon Mr Westborough getting to the bottom of it."

"I fear that you paint my abilities in far too glowing colors," Westborough returned. "One can only do one's best. And now, Baines, will you tell us where Mr Morse's old ledgers and canceled checks have been stored?"

"In a trunk in the storeroom, sir."

"Where's the storeroom?" I queried.

"In the basement, sir. I will show you the way."

The door to the basement stairs opened from the kitchen. After pressing a switch at the head of the stairs to turn on the lights below Baines reached upward for a ring of keys, which were hanging on a nail behind the door. Westborough was examining a small shelf protruding from the wall, upon which was reposing a pair of white cotton gloves.

"Do your duties, Baines, include the firing of the furnace?"

Baines affirmed apologetically that they did. He seemed to feel that he was losing caste by the admission. "The house is so small, sir."

The furnace was of the old-fashioned hot-air type. The pipes, which radiated in all directions from above, gave it a marked resemblance to a gigantic octopus. "The ashes have been emptied recently?" Westborough inquired.

"Daily, sir. The storeroom is here."

The door was locked, but the key was one of those on the ring which Baines had brought with him from the head of the stairs. He flung the door inward to disclose a dusty, cobwebby sort of room, which contained four or five trunks and innumerable truck of all kinds. Strangely enough, the only items I can specifically recall are an empty bird cage suspended from the ceiling and an ironing board stacked behind the door, neither of which has the slightest thing to do with this account. Selecting another key from those on the ring Baines unlocked the largest of the trunks.

"All the old records are here, sir. I have myself conveyed many armloads of them to this place."

I could well believe it. The top of the trunk was crammed with papers, and it looked as though we were letting ourselves in for a man-size job. Baines withdrew from the room, and we settled down to tackle it as methodically as possible. Presently Westborough called that he had found several bundles of canceled checks. He carried them over to the light for a better examination.

"They appear to be arranged by years, Mr Foster. Dear me, our search will be considerably facilitated."

"Sylvia said he was here ten years ago," I reminded. "Find 1926 if you can."

I had caught sight of some ledgers like the one upstairs and I began to hunt for the one covering the same year. I soon found it and commenced an impatient search

among the entries. Since Sylvia had not told me what month it had been when George
Smith had visited them, I was forced to start with January. I had gone clear up to June
before I found what we were after. I read the amount and whistled.

"Great Scott! Morse gave the fellow ten thousand!"

Mr Westborough found the canceled check. It was endorsed "George Smith," and
it had been cashed at Morse's own bank.

"Probably Morse himself took him there," I mused. "He had to be identified, and
a stranger from New Zealand couldn't have known many people. It's a slim chance,
but somebody may have remembered him."

"Perhaps we may be able to discover a letter concerning Mr Smith," Westborough
suggested.

But Morse appeared to have been in the habit of destroying his personal correspondence. An hour's exhaustive search yielded no further results. Only the canceled
check and the single ledger entry testified that George Smith had actually been a
reality.

Shamelessly leaving the entire search to me, Westborough had retired to a far
corner of the room with the old ledgers. He seemed to have developed an inordinate
curiosity regarding the details of Hezekiah Morse's personal finances. Finally I gave
up the quest.

"It's no use. The bank is our only lead."

We carried the ledgers back to the trunk, shut the lid and locked it with the key
Baines had left. Our discoveries had apparently terminated in a blind alley. Still it
was something to know that Hezekiah Morse had paid ten thousand dollars to the
fellow who had given him the purple parrot. Although that fact probably had about as
much to do with Morse's death as Mack's Aunt Harriet.

Baines was waiting for us at the top of the stairs. Eyeing his hands ruefully Westborough asked to be directed to the nearest lavatory, and Baines showed him the one
adjoining the kitchen. My own hands being in an equally grimy state, I employed the
same facilities. As I stepped inside the door, I made a close examination of the diminutive room. There was only the one door and a single small window, which was
high in the wall and too tiny to admit anything much larger than a monkey. Matilda
had been right; Baines would certainly have had to return to the kitchen. Besides, I
remembered, the time was all wrong. He hadn't been here at midnight or even at all
close to it.

"Miss Sampson will be down in a few minutes, sir," Baines informed as I returned
to the kitchen.

I directed him to bring her into the living room where Westborough was now
waiting. It was true that I didn't have anything to tell her that Baines couldn't have
relayed, but Westborough wanted to question her. I didn't see what earthly good it
would do, however; O'Ryan's thorough catechism and the examination at the inquest
had undoubtedly exhausted Matilda's meager portion of information. Nevertheless, I
agreed wholly with Westborough that even such unpromising straws must not be

slighted, so bizarre, so inexplicable was this puzzle from every ordinary standpoint.

Walking into the living room I found Westborough standing by the fireplace, his hands locked behind his back in a manner that made me think of Felix the Cat. He was regarding the cold grate with a thoughtful preoccupation, but glanced up as I approached.

"That was a very odd loan, Mr Foster. Not only did Smith apparently give no security, but, even more remarkable, he did not pay any interest. Or, if he did, Mr Morse had not recorded its receipt, an equally unusual circumstance."

"Maybe Morse gave him the money," I suggested. "After all, ten thousand to him was no more than ten dollars to me. And if Smith was the son of a boyhood friend—"

But I couldn't visualize Hezekiah Morse as such a sentimental philanthropist. Nor could Westborough.

"A purchase appears to be more probable than a gift."

"But what could Smith sell him that was worth that much?"

"So far we know of only one object."

"But that's absurd," I objected. "Anyone willing to pay ten thousand dollars for a bit of purple crockery is stark, raving loony."

"I am well aware that the theory verges upon the fantastic," Westborough smilingly conceded. "On the other hand—"

"I hear you wanted to talk to me," said Matilda, sweeping belligerently into the room with Baines in tow.

I invited them to be seated. Baines expressed a preference for standing, but Matilda seated herself stiffly on the edge of a large wing chair. She was wearing a black dress as stiff as her manner, a dress a bit too tight for her voluminous form. I explained that as Morse's will had named my firm the executors of the estate, we were empowered to pay all legitimate expenses in connection with it and that their salaries would go on as usual. Venting a sigh of relief Matilda sank deeply back in her chair.

"Now that's real nice of you, Mr Foster! I'll admit I didn't know where my next two weeks' pay was coming from, what with Mr Morse in his grave and Miss Morse in—"

A chill look from Baines silenced her. I turned to the butler.

"You understand, Baines, that this arrangement holds only until Miss Morse is once more able to assume the supervision of the household? I have not yet spoken to her about the matter of the wine cellar, but it is my belief that she would wish to give you another chance. Is she able to count upon your future honesty?"

His eyes met mine without flinching. "She is, sir."

Fumbling through his pockets, Mr Westborough exclaimed, "Dear me! I do not have Mr Wells' receipted invoice, which I wished to show Lieutenant Mack. Did you return it to me, Mr Foster?"

"We left it on Morse's desk," I recalled.

"Perhaps Baines," Westborough suggested, "will be good enough to fetch it. There is also a white card with it, I believe."

The butler bowed low. "Certainly, sir. I shall bring them at once."

As he left the room, Matilda pushed her hand across her temple.

"Lordy, I have another of my headaches. They're the bane of my life and make no mistake about it, Mr Foster."

In the special voice which one reserves for the suffering I said that I was very sorry to hear she was troubled by such an affliction. Then I asked if she felt up to answering a few questions, which Mr Westborough desired to put to her.

"I guess so," Matilda groaned faintly.

"Do you like Miss Morse?" Westborough interrogated with surprising abruptness.

"The pretty thing—I should say I do!" Sincerity showed in every line of the cook's middle-aged countenance. "She was always so bright and gay; it was like a tonic every time she came into my kitchen."

"Do you believe that Miss Morse killed her grandfather?"

"Of course not!" Matilda snorted indignantly. "She was too tenderhearted to kill a fly! And she thought the world and all of him—who should know that if not me. Many a time I've seen him so grumpy there was no livin' with him, and her a-coaxin' him out of it with her pretty ways. Lord, Lord, this headache's a-comin' on sure!"

"A most distressing affliction!" sympathized Mr Westborough. "Perhaps a wet towel on your head while you lie down in a darkened room might be of some assistance?"

"It don't do no good! Nothing does much good when one of 'em gets really started. But go on with your questions," she added, with the air of a martyr determined to do her duty although death snatched her bodily the next instant. "What else do you want to know?"

"I should like you to think back to Wednesday evening." He held up his hand to stifle her unvoiced protest. "Dear me, I know that you have already done that, but if you are able to recall anything else, no matter how trivial it may seem, you may be of great assistance to us in securing Miss Morse's acquittal."

"I'll try, Mr Westborough," she promised. "I'll try to do the best thinking I can." Her labored breathing informed us that she was indeed indulging in a very unusual concentration. Her recollections, however, soon terminated in a disgusted sniff.

" 'Tain't a particle of use. I told that Captain O'Ryan everything that happened— him and his impudence." Her hand fluttered again to her temple. "My head's a-achin' to split! These sick headaches is awful things, Mr Foster."

It was plain that there was nothing to be obtained from Matilda. Probably her discussion of her symptoms would be interminable. Nevertheless, I felt constrained to manifest a show of interest for politeness' sake.

"Do you have them often?"

"Off and on, I have 'em." Matilda, evidently delighted to have found fresh listeners, launched into a long account. "Sometimes I won't have 'em for months, and then again they come every few weeks." (The jeremiad was even worse than I had anticipated, and it appeared to be interminable) "I've had 'em so bad I had to lay down for a whole day, and sometimes they make me deathly sick to my stomach. Once I vomited five times . . ."

"Migraine, perhaps," Mr Westborough conjectured. "Have you secured competent medical counsel?"

"You mean have I been to a doctor? Bless you, Mr Westborough, I can't say that any doctor's been able to help me much. Lately, Mr Baines has been givin' me Christian Science treatments. That seems to do about as much good as anything. I ain't no Scientist, don't hold with 'em at all. I'm a Methodist, I am, and always have been. But that don't stop me from saying—Oh my Gawd, what can that be!"

The crash had sounded from upstairs—a noise like that of a heavy body falling to the floor. I ran to the foot of the stairs and called for Baines, but there wasn't any answer.

"He's been killed!" screamed Matilda.

"Be quiet," I ordered. "I'll soon find out."

"I shall not allow you to go alone," Mr Westborough declared firmly. Considering his size and his age, he was certainly dead game.

"You're not going to leave me here!" Matilda shrieked. I had already reached the top of the stairs and didn't stop to answer her.

The door to the study was open, and there was a light burning within. Except for Baines the room was empty.

We found the butler along the west wall, lying face down at the foot of the bookcases. On the floor, not far from his unconscious head, was one of Hezekiah Morse's cherished iron candlesticks.

XXI

"Sakes alive! Is he dead?" shrieked Matilda from the doorway.

Half raising the prostrate butler I laid my hand over his heart and was relieved to feel its steady beating. "Not dead, but it looks like it had been a close shave for him," I said.

"I shall notify the police at once," announced Mr Westborough, who was already at the telephone. While he inquired for Mack I made a quick survey of the study.

Three books were scattered on the floor. A yawning gap in one of the upper shelves of the bookcase showed where they had originally rested. The glass door was still open. I turned my attention to the desk. One lower drawer had been partially pulled out—just as one had been on the other night. Yet I was positive that Westborough and I had closed all the drawers before we left the room.

"Lieutenant Mack is coming at once," Westborough informed as he replaced the receiver.

I took my turn at the telephone in order to dial Dr Trowbridge's number. He was at home, fortunately, and promised to come at once. Returning to the unconscious butler I started to lift him from the floor.

"Just a minute, please, Mr Foster," Westborough requested. While I telephoned he had gone into Sylvia's room, and the familiar scent of her perfume hovered about the large, round box of bath powder which he carried. Opening the box, he took out the mammoth powder puff and, by holding it on its edge, managed to trace the outlines of Baines' body in broad powdery strokes. Not until he had completed this task did we carry the butler to the bedroom across the ball. Being no doctor, I made no attempt to diagnose Baines's condition. I couldn't help observing, however, that there was a large swelling at the back of his skull. It was obvious that he had been struck from behind.

Belatedly, it occurred to me to search the house. I ran down the back stairs. The kitchen was empty, of course, and the back door was closed. I had started to take hold of the doorknob when I thought of fingerprints and used my handkerchief. To my surprise I found that the door wasn't locked.

I stepped out into a tiny yard, paved with flagstones and surrounded by a high stone fence which melted imperceptibly into the house. The back gate was also unlocked, but its lock was rusty, I discovered upon striking a match to make a closer inspection. It probably hadn't been used for years. The alley was completely deserted, and no wonder! If Baines's assailant had fled that way he would have had time to get at least as far as the Loop.

I returned to the kitchen, where I found Westborough. He was examining the kitchen floor, which was immaculately scrubbed and bore no signs of outside dirt. But then, I told him, the alley as well as the yard was paved.

We searched the whole house, beginning with the basement and finishing with the servants' quarters on the third floor. There wasn't a sign of any intruder. Somehow I hadn't expected that we would find anything. If I had dashed down the back stairs right away instead of— However, it was too late to worry over that now.

The doorbell rang, and I went down to admit Dr Trowbridge, the same person whom I had talked with over the telephone the other night. There was something about his broad, square jaw and lean figure that told me Baines would be in safe hands. We found the butler moaning deliriously, and Matilda was wringing her hands in dismay.

"The poor man's been groanin' somethin' terrible!"

Dr Trowbridge stooped over the recumbent figure, his long, bony fingers skillfully exploring the lump on Baines's head.

"A severe contusion! Doesn't seem to be any fracture, though."

The doorbell rang once more, and Westborough and I left him issuing terse instructions to Matilda. Mack greeted us with a curt:

"What the hell's it all about?"

Westborough explained briefly on our way upstairs. Mack took a quick look around the study.

"Where is he?"

"In the bedroom across the hall. A doctor is now with him," Westborough replied. "You can readily see how he fell from these powder markings. We found him lying parallel to the bookcase, his head in the direction of Miss Morse's room."

"What 're the books doing on the floor?" Mack wanted to know.

The question was something of a poser. For the first time I examined them closely. They were large folio editions, too tall to fit in an ordinary bookcase. I picked up the nearest volume: *The Workes* of Benjamin Jonson. The other two books were volumes one and two of Samuel Johnson's *Dictionary of the English Language*.

"If just one book was worth a grand three of them ought to be worth some real dough," Mack conjectured.

Westborough was of the opinion that the identity of the books made some slight difference in this matter. "The set of Jonson's *Workes*—I notice that the second of the two volumes is still upon the shelf—I have seen quoted at $250. And an original edition of Johnson's dictionary probably could not be sold for more than $150."

"Well, that makes four hundred," Mack declared as he picked up the first volume of the dictionary. He turned to the title page and the spell of the old book asserted itself over even his matter-of-fact mind. "Say, this was printed way back in 1755—long time ago. 'In which,' " he read aloud, " 'the words are deduced from their originals and illustrated in their different significations by examples from the beft—' Must be a misprint here! They've used an 'f' for an 's'."

Westborough refrained from even a suggestion of a smile.

"If you care to look further inside the volume you will find some very quaint definitions. Samuel Johnson was a gentleman of forthright opinions, and he saw no reason why, even in a dictionary, he should not maintain them. Pension he defined as generally meaning in England the pay given to a state hireling for treason to his country and excise as 'a hateful tax levied upon commodities and adjudged by wretches.' " The little man chuckled softly. "My own favorite bit of Johnsoniana, however, concerns itself with the good doctor's reply to the woman who queried why he had defined 'postern' as he did. 'Because, madam, I knew no better,' the lexicographer is reputed to have thundered."

Mack, however, had now lost interest in Samuel Johnson. "Somebody might 've been trying to cart these books out when Baines butted in and got himself slugged. There was a newspaper yarn about how much dough these books are worth. How does that idea strike you, Westborough?"

"But the newspaper did not mention Jonson's *Workes* nor Samuel Johnson's dictionary," demurred the little man. "Six other volumes were described, none of which are to be found on this particular shelf of the bookcase. Would not such an intruder choose to pick out those volumes of whose market value he had been informed rather than others which, for aught he knew, might well have been worthless?"

Mack thought this over. "Maybe this yegg had been to college. He might 've known these books would bring him four hundred berries."

"But, in the event he possessed such knowledge, he would surely know also that these volumes are by no means the most valuable in the library. *The Anatomy of Melancholy* and *Paradise Lost*, both of which were mentioned in the newspaper article I may remind you, could be sold for a total of two thousand dollars. And a single volume, *The Most Noble and Famous Travels of Marcus Paulus*, would bring the same amount."

"One book worth two grand!" Mack ejaculated.

"An exceedingly rare work," Westborough pointed out.

"Humph! Morse should 've put up bars on these windows," was Mack's spoken thought. He crossed the room to make an inspection of them. "Say, here's something else funny. The window's unlocked again. The same window that was unlocked on Wednesday night."

An odd coincidence certainly, but it was hard to see how it could be anything else than coincidence. Probably Baines had overlooked locking the window since Wednesday night; yes, that might easily prove the true explanation. Moreover, there was the matter of the unlocked kitchen door. I explained this to Mack, and he declared with conviction:

"Somebody sneaked in that way while you had Baines and Matilda in the living room—beat it the same way after he'd slugged Baines. But, if he didn't come here to swipe the books, what did he come for?"

"I cannot say," Westborough returned, "but Mr Morse's desk has also been searched. That lower drawer was not pulled out in that fashion when Mr Foster and I left the room. And here is further contributory evidence." He pointed down to the floor, and I noticed a broken rubber band about three inches long. It was the first time I had seen it. "I am almost certain that came from the desk," Westborough added. "Mr Foster and I found several such rubbers around various rolls of papers."

"And left them there," I affirmed. "At least I'll swear I put every one of them back."

"All right, the desk was rifled," Mack agreed. "So what?" He picked up the receipted invoice, which was still lying with the card we had found on top of the desk. "Where the devil did this thing come from?"

Westborough explained.

"Well, that proves Old Whiskers' yarn was the real McCoy," Mack declared cocksurely. "Pete Whealon checks his alibi, too. That puts Wells definitely in the clear on this thing, I'd say."

Westborough, however, was not of the same opinion. "If I may be permitted a suggestion I should deem it advisable to procure a warrant to search Wells' house."

"For the love of a constipated cat, why?" Mack demanded.

"Because I believe that Mr Wells is withholding certain essential information. I am almost certain that he knows the whereabouts of—"

"Morse's purple parrot!" I exploded.

"Yes," Westborough confirmed. "I received the distinct impression that Wells was acutely uncomfortable while that topic was under discussion."

"Can't say I didn't get the same idea," Mack grunted. "But Whealon is a good friend of the fellow, and Pete Whealon has a hell of a pull in this man's town. We can't search Wells' house without more to go on than the chance we might find a dinky little two-bit statue. Whealon would raise one hell of a stink!"

Westborough's answer was to exhibit the canceled check.

"Well? What difference does it make if Morse paid a guy named Smith ten grand back in 1926?" Mack wanted to know.

"Smith gave Morse the parrot statuette at just that time," I informed.

"Well, why didn't you say so? Who is this George Smith? Where can we find him?"

"He died two years ago."

"Then where's his family?"

"We do not even know that he had one."

"Well, where did the fellow come from?"

"New Zealand. All we know about him," I concluded, "is that he was the son of one of Morse's old buddies."

"New Zealand is a long ways off," Mack observed. "It's going to take quite a while to make inquiries." He folded the check into his wallet. "I'll ask about this at the bank, but it 'll be a miracle if I learn anything. Ten years is a long time to expect a fellow's memory to hold out."

"What 're you going to do about Wells?" I demanded angrily.

"That's my business," Mack returned curtly.

"You're not going to keep an innocent girl in jail just because you can make out a case against her on slim circumstantial evidence?"

"Our case is a damn good one, and don't you forget it, Foster."

"I'm not likely to." There was a good deal more I was going to add to this, but Mr Westborough intervened.

"Wells is not a man who can readily screen his emotions. Do you recall how anxiously he glanced towards his bookshelves when you questioned him concerning the missing statuette? Possibly he has removed the article since our visit, but I am very nearly certain that at that time it was concealed behind the books in the third shelf from the top in the northeast corner of the room."

"That's definite enough, anyhow," Mack laughed. "Why didn't you tell me this before?"

"Because you had no authority to search the house. Nor was I sure until we found the canceled check that the article had an intrinsic value."

"You think it's valuable?" Mack asked.

The little man nodded. "I am almost certain."

"Why?"

"Candidly, I haven't the least idea," Westborough replied.

"Can't say I ever found you very far wrong before," Mack admitted, staring thoughtfully at the floor. "All right. Pete Whealon or no Pete Whealon, I'll do it."

"I do hope that you will have no cause to regret the step," Westborough murmured.

"I'll take the risk," Mack answered shortly. "Now what about this desk? Foster, have you any idea what the fellow could be looking for?"

I shook my head. I couldn't name a single item with market value among the papers I had so recently perused. Westborough had a suggestion to offer.

"Doubtless Mr Foster and I will be able to ascertain if anything has been taken."

Mack gave an approving grunt, but Dr Trowbridge came into the room before we were able to begin our search. The doctor had already donned his overcoat.

"The patient is conscious," he said laconically. "A nasty crack, but no particular harm done. He ought to be quiet the rest of the night, but he'll probably be all right tomorrow."

"Can I ask him a few questions?" Mack inquired.

"Shouldn't do any particular harm—if you don't keep him talking too long. Good night, Mr Foster, Mr Westborough."

"Hey, wait a minute!" Mack called. "Take a look at this iron candlestick, will you? No, don't touch it—we have to go over it for prints. Take the one on the stand—it's just like this one. Heft it and tell me if it was the thing used to slug Baines."

Dr Trowbridge "hefted" as directed and made a few tentative swings through the air. Then he studied carefully the round iron base.

"In my opinion this could do it. Nor do I believe that a very hard blow would be necessary."

Mack produced pencil and memorandum book. "Give me your name and address, Doc. You may he hauled into court to testify."

"Testify to what?" Dr Trowbridge snapped. "All I know about this affair is that a man was hit on the back of the skull with an object which may or may not have been this iron candlestick. You can get my name and address from Foster. I'm in a hurry."

He strode angrily out the door and down the stairs.

"Doc seemed sore," Mack grinned.

"So many doctors are overworked," Westborough observed.

"Well, see if you can find anything missing from the desk," Mack directed. "I'm going to talk to Baines."

I did not share Westborough's optimism that we would be able to tell if anything had been taken from among that mass of receipts, leases, bank statements, canceled checks, correspondence and catalogues from English booksellers to be found in Morse's desk. However, Westborough had scarcely opened the wide top drawer before we made a discovery.

"Are you sure you saw it when we were looking through this before?" I questioned. The question, however, was a purely rhetorical one. Westborough's reply made no difference. I was sure that *I* had seen it.

"But why was it taken?" I asked. "By a chance prowler?" I paused, a little uncertainly. "Or is there some definite object?"

I had never seen Westborough's face so grave.

"I fear that there is a certain pattern not yet apparent from the surface—like the submerged seven tenths of an iceberg! Mr Foster, we are confronted by certain forces which might almost be termed hyperphysical. Sinister forces which—"

"Baines was able to talk all right," Mack informed, stepping genially into the room. "Doesn't know much, though. Saw the light in the study on when he came upstairs, he says. The door was open and the first thing he noticed was that one of the book-cases was open and some books were lying on the floor. He stooped to pick 'em up, and zowie! That's all Baines knows. I tried to check about the back door, but Baines didn't remember. Matilda first said it was locked and then she switched around and claimed it wasn't. What a face that hen's got! It 'd stop more than a—"

He broke off abruptly. "Say, what the devil's eating you fellows?"

Westborough answered for us.

"Something *has* been stolen from the desk. Mr Morse's revolver!"

PART FOUR

Saturday, November 21

XXII

I was trying to catch up on some work I had allowed to slide during the past two days. There was nothing particularly urgent except the Lingley matter, a dispute in the title of certain South Side real estate which threatened to necessitate a thoroughly trouble-some search of old records before we were ready to go to court. I was wondering whether or not it would be advisable to ask for a continuance when Steelcraft came into the office and sat down on the other side of the desk.

I hadn't seen him since Thursday's conversation, and I had some hopes that he might be able to shed some light on the George Smith incident. Steelcraft had handled Morse's legal affairs personally before he had turned them over to me, and he had known the financier for a long time. However, it turned out that he had never heard Morse mention the name, George Smith.

I informed him that Mack had promised to get a warrant to search Wells's house for the purple parrot.

"But, even if he finds the thing there, I don't see how it will be any help to us," I opined. "Wells has a first-rate alibi. He was driven home and left on his own doorstep at eleven-thirty. He couldn't get from Rogers Park back to Division Street in time to kill Morse, and that lets him out."

Admitting the truth of this Steelcraft inquired how many witnesses Wells could produce to testify to the hour at which he had arrived home.

"Only one," I answered. "But he's as good as twenty. It's the political big gun, Pete Whealon."

"Not the paving contractor?" Steelcraft exclaimed.

"Do you know him?"

Steelcraft returned surprisingly, "Hezekiah Morse did. It very nearly came to an action for slander."

"Whealon was going to sue Morse?"

"The other way around. However, the matter was settled out of court."

He gave me details: Whealon had traded in certain stocks upon Morse's recom-mendation. There was no reason to suppose that Morse had not acted in good faith; it was during the postwar depression of 1921 when the market was in a hectic state. But Whealon, after losing a considerable sum, had lost his head as well, and he had called Hezekiah Morse a swindler and some other things before two witnesses.

Morse had threatened suit. He had excellent proofs of malicious slander, and there appeared to have been little doubt but that he would have won in court. However, after Whealon had retracted his former statements publicly before the same two wit-nesses, Morse had allowed the matter to drop.

"Whealon was forced to apologize," I ruminated. "That wouldn't sit so well with him."

"I don't believe it did," Steelcraft agreed drily.

"Still fifteen years is an unreasonably long time for a man to hold a grudge. Did their paths ever cross again?"

"Not that I ever heard of."

Vail, Wells and now Whealon! The number of suspects was certainly broadening. But, assuming that alibis could be smashed (which I doubted), how had any of these three been able to enter the house? Or, a still bigger problem, to leave the place unobserved? At this juncture my phone rang, and I asked Steelcraft to excuse me.

Scarcely had the voice at the other end of the wire spoken two words before I realized that this call was going to be decidedly out of my ordinary routine. The tones were rough, low, obviously disguised, yet the voice had a tantalizingly familiar quality. But, search my memory as I would, I could not recall where or in what connection I had heard it.

The very first thing the Voice said was:

"Will you pay ten grand for the name of the guy who bumped off old Morse?"

Fortunately there was a scratch pad and pencil conveniently near at hand. I wrote: "See if this call can be traced," and handed the note to Steelcraft, who at once left the room.

I stalled for as much time as I could possibly gain. If the telephone company could get into action while we were still talking the call could be traced. I had heard Mack say something to that effect the other night. But I didn't have any idea how long it would take to persuade the company to act, nor how long the operation would require after they started.

"Ten grand is a lot of money. Have you evidence that will stand up in court?"

There was a derisive snort from the other end of the wire. "Offer a lawyer the moon, and he'll ask you to put a red fence around it. No, I haven't any evidence, but I can give you the name of the guy who bumped off Morse. The rest is up to you—and the cops, goddamn 'em."

"Do you know how it was done?" I asked. "How he left the house without being seen?"

"Hell, yes! I can give you the works!"

"How do I know this isn't a practical joke?" I inquired.

"Because I'm telling you."

"Well, if you're acting in good faith, give me a test of it. Tell me how Morse's murderer left the house."

The Voice instructed ribaldly, "You go slit a fat pig. I'll talk when you give me ten grand and not before."

"I haven't got that much money."

"Hell, you're Morse's executor, ain't you? That's chicken feed to the pile he left."

"But I'm not empowered to draw on the account."

"You pay his bills, don't you?"

"Only the legitimate debts of the estate. I would be criminally liable if I employed the funds for other purposes."

"You make me sick," the Voice informed wearily. "You're engaged to the Morse girl, ain't you? Is it or isn't it worth ten grand to get her out of the mess she's in?"

"It's worth a good deal more," I assented. "It's worth everything. But how am I to get the money?"

"Cash a check on old Morse's account."

"Even if they gave me the money I'd be arrested before I could leave the bank. I'd have to get a court order and you're crazier than you sound if you think the probate court will allow such a claim."

The excuse passed muster.

"Borrow it then!"

"Who from?" I returned. "You can't go around borrowing ten thousand dollars at a minute's notice."

"The hell you can't!"

"Maybe you can," I qualified. "I certainly can't."

"Then to hell with you, Foster."

"Wait a minute," I cut in hurriedly. "I've got a thousand of my own. I'll give that to you."

"Make it five."

I hesitated as long as I dared. "All right, maybe I *can* borrow four thousand. I'll have a check for you."

"You know what you can do with a check," the Voice returned in annoyance. "I want it in cash—one thousand five-dollar bills."

I agreed that this sounded reasonable.

"And I don't want new bills either," the Voice went on mandatorily. "One thousand old bills—the dirtier the better."

"But what if the bank doesn't have that many old bills?"

"It better have, or we don't do business."

"All right," I assented. "I'll do the best I can. When shall I meet you?"

"Tomorrow night."

"Where?"

"By the Buckingham fountain. Walk over and keep staring at it. Don't look around. I'll come up behind you and give you an envelope with all the dope in it. Then I'll take the satchel."

It was my turn to be derisive. "I wasn't born yesterday, my friend. At this time of year the Buckingham fountain will be as deserted as the beach. All you have to do is to stick a gun in my ribs and collar the money. If you do leave an envelope there will be nothing in it but torn-up newspapers."

"No, this is on the level. You pay me the five grand, and I'll give you the straight dope."

"Then make a more reasonable proposal."

"All right, you go to the Sherman tomorrow night. Register under the name of John Jacob. I'll come up to your room some time before eleven, tell you what I know about the guy who bumped off Morse, and you give me the sugar afterwards. I can't make any fairer proposition than that, can I?"

I affected to consider this carefully, wondering if Steelcraft had had time as yet to induce the telephone company officials to start tracing the call.

"When I open the door to let you in you'll flash a gun and take the money," I objected.

"Suspicious as hell, ain't you?"

"I believe in going halfway to meet trouble."

"Well, get a rod yourself. Pull it on me as soon as I come in if that 'll make you feel safer."

"Now you're talking sense," I said. "But if I have you covered with a gun, how will you know I won't turn you over to the police?"

The Voice swore profusely. "Try it, you bastard, and they'll carry you out in a wooden overcoat."

"Don't worry," I said apologetically. "I don't intend to do anything of the kind. What time will you be at the Sherman?"

"When I get there! I'll try to make it before eleven."

"What time should I be there?"

"God almighty, do you want a wet nurse? Any time after eight. And one more thing, Foster."

"Yes?"

"The deal's off if you tell the bulls."

"I don't intend—"

"And don't think I won't know it if you do. You've been watched since Thursday, and my men know everything you do. If you're as much as seen talking to a dick this deal's off."

I assumed as much alarm as I could conveniently throw into my voice.

"I won't even say hello to a traffic cop. But you haven't told me your—"

A click from the other end of the wire was the only answer. Steelcraft returned to the office. "They promised to trace the call, but they didn't start until a moment or so ago. It took some time for me to get to the proper parties and explain what I wanted and why. I doubt if there's been—"

The phone rang again. A feminine voice from the telephone company reported that they were sorry but they had been unable to trace the call.

"Too bad you couldn't stall a while longer," Steelcraft remarked. "Although you did a first-rate job as it was."

"You listened?" I asked.

He nodded. "I asked Miss Fisher to plug me in on an extension while Coleman talked to the telephone company."

"Did you think it was anything more than a stage setting for a first-class holdup?"

"It's hard to say," Steelcraft returned cautiously.

"Well, I'll see if I can borrow a revolver somewhere," I said. "It's pretty hard to hold up a man who has you covered when he opens the door."

Steelcraft shook his head dubiously. "That was his suggestion, Barry. It may be a trick."

"Anyway, I'm going through with it," I answered grimly. Rather to my surprise Steelcraft did not attempt to talk me out of the decision.

"I'll see you through on the money end."

"That's decent of you," I said fervently.

"No, it's merely business. It's a legitimate expense of the Morse estate. But even if it wasn't it would be worth all that and a good deal more to help Sylvia Morse. I like that girl, Barry."

There was a whole lot I could have said to that but I wasn't given the opportunity. The phone was ringing again, and I picked up the receiver, wondering if the Voice had changed his mind and was going to insist upon "ten grand" after all. But this time it was Mr Westborough.

"Good morning, Mr Foster. I have a rather peculiar request to make. However, I believe that my reasons are good and sufficient. Are you able to obtain a key to the Morse home?"

"I guess so. Why?"

"I should like to have one. But please do not tell anyone for whom it is wanted."

I was taken aback. He could get into the house at any time—day or night. If Baines did happen to be out, which rarely occurred, Matilda would surely be there.

"Why on earth do you want a key?" I asked.

"Dear me, I should prefer not to say at the present time. There are so many conflicting threads—one must exercise unusual caution in making his way through the tangled maze of the labyrinth."

"All right, when do you want it?"

"If possible, today."

"You'll get it today," I promised.

"One thing more, Mr Foster," he added as I started to hang up the receiver. "Will you come to police headquarters at once? Lieutenant Mack has just discovered Mr Morse's purple parrot."

XXIII

I was impaled upon a dilemma with two exceptionally sharp horns. I had the sworn word of the Voice that if I went to police headquarters negotiations would be broken off completely. But if the purple parrot had been found it was certainly my duty to be on the spot as quickly as possible. Moreover, not to comply with Westborough's natural request would undoubtedly arouse Mack's suspicions and might lead to definitely unpleasant consequences. A plan leaped into mind, and I made a quick decision.

"I'll be there, but I'm tied up for a while. Will it be all right if I'm down there in an hour?"

"I will ask Lieutenant Mack if that suits his convenience," Westborough replied with old-fashioned punctilio. A minute later: "Yes, that will be entirely satisfactory."

"Did Wells have the purple parrot?" I questioned, but Westborough wasn't inclined to give details over the telephone. Replacing the receiver I asked of Steelcraft: "Doesn't Coleman commute on the Northwestern?"

"Yes, why?"

"Just a wild idea of mine."

I found Coleman at his desk and borrowed a timetable. There was a train which left at eleven-sixteen—I had just time to make it. I rushed downstairs and caught a cab.

Maybe the Voice had been doing a bit of tall bluffing about the diligence with which I was kept under observation. On the other hand there had been the evidence of Stubby Mustache, and there was certainly no sense in taking any foolish chances.

I left the cab at the Northwestern Station, walked through to the ticket window and asked in a loud voice for a ticket to Evanston. Then I bought a paper and climbed on the train. Taking a seat near the end of the coach, I unfolded the newspaper. While pretending to read it I managed to keep one eye on the door. Two men came into the car before the train pulled out, and I noticed that one of them took a seat just across the aisle from me. Although he didn't seem to be paying me much attention I knew that a really clever operator could easily give that impression. He was not Stubby Mustache, but then, I reflected, the Voice would hardly employ him again.

Climbing down from the train at Wilson Avenue I waited for a while on the platform. Nobody else got off but a middle-aged woman, who walked briskly down the stairs. I followed her to the street and watched her disappear along Wilson Avenue. She hadn't even once glanced back at me; I was sure of it. I waited a few more minutes at the foot of the stairs, but I might as well have been at the bottom of the Grand Canyon for all the attention I was attracting. I flagged a cab and ordered the driver to take me to headquarters.

The tall gray building towered like a monolith from amidst the squatty edifices surrounding it. Before stepping out of my cab I remembered that it would be very easy for the Voice to have a watcher posted nearby. If so all my efforts at confusing the trail were utterly useless. I glanced cautiously up and down the street before leaving the taxi, but, seeing no suspicious looking loiterers, I decided to take the chance.

The purple parrot was in Mack's office, sitting on the detective lieutenant's desk. I inspected it closely. A funny-looking bird, shaped with feathers around its red glass eyes and perched upon a purple rock. As a work of art it wasn't so hot. If, as Westborough seemed to think, Morse had really paid ten thousand dollars for this thing he certainly should have had his head examined.

"Did you find this in Wells' house?" I asked.

"Right behind the books in that room upstairs where Westborough said it 'd be," Mack informed.

"Where I said it *might* be," the little man corrected.

"What did Wells have to say for himself?"

"His explanation is a very curious one," Westborough stated. Mack guffawed.

"It's all right, if you believe in fairy stories. Wells claims—in fact, he insists—that he didn't know he had the thing until he found it in his overcoat pocket the next morning. He didn't know what to make of it; he had no idea at all he'd carted it out with him. He didn't find it, he says, until after he read about Morse's death, and then he was scared stiff. Especially so when he read we were looking for him."

"If he was so scared why didn't he get rid of it?"

"He was afraid to, afraid he might be seen."

Westborough nodded gravely. "That is psychologically understandable, I believe, as Mr Wells is a shy and retiring recluse, almost wholly absorbed by his scholarly pursuits. Such a sharp contact with an exceedingly unpleasant reality might well paralyze his powers of decision."

"Hell, he was so scared that he didn't even think of asking his friend, Pete Whealon!" Mack chuckled. "But Pete knows all about it now, you bet. We allowed Wells one phone call and he got Pete on the wire the first thing."

"Wells' story might be true," I suggested. "He might be a kleptomaniac—I've heard they can take things and not know they're doing it."

"An act of impulsion committed in a transitory dream state," Westborough corroborated. "Bright-colored objects of little monetary value are frequently pilfered, if I am not mistaken."

Mack jerked a large broad thumb toward his desk. "Well, that doohinkus is bright enough and worthless enough to satisfy any of them. But kleptomania's not likely as far as Wells is concerned. I talked to Doc Zeiss, who's over at the Criminal Court Behavior Clinic, and he told me that most kleptomaniacs are middle-aged women. Said it was a manifestation of a repressed sexual something or other. Lord, the lingo those psychiatrists—"

The ringing of his telephone interrupted the sentence. Mack said, "Oh yeah" several times to the transmitter and then hung up.

"Well, I told you there 'd be a stink," he said to Westborough. "Guess who's coming up here with blood in his eye?"

"Mr Whealon?" the little man conjectured.

"Right the first time," Mack returned cheerfully. "He's all set to get my scalp, they say."

"I've got some dope on Whealon," I was beginning, when a large, angry man strode indignantly through the door.

When I say large, I mean large—along the O'Ryan dimensions—six feet three or four and correspondingly broad across the shoulders. But where O'Ryan's bulk gave you the feeling it was mostly muscle, you realized that there was a lot of fat on Pete

Whealon. He was still husky enough; he could probably have licked the tar out of me in a rough and tumble, but I was willing to put up ten bucks, if there had been any takers, that his wind was bad. His face was a brick red. He wasn't blushing either; that seemed to be its natural color. And he had a thick and heavy neck that made you think of something like a steel girder. A tough customer and no mistake.

And he was mad clear through. So mad he didn't even notice Westborough and I were in the room.

"I'm here to tell you you've made a damn fool mistake!" he shouted.

"What's all the fuss about?" Mack asked, glancing up from his desk as though the matter were of minor importance.

"You know damn well what it's about. Wells is a friend of mine." His tone implied that the recipient of his friendship received a license forever after to commit murder, rape and mayhem without interference from the police department. "Only a prize damn fool would think he had anything to do with the Morse killing."

"Wells called on Morse the night of his murder," Mack retorted. "He should have come clean and he didn't."

"He's a man of no practical experience," Whealon answered, his voice softening slightly. "As I told you before I can answer for him personally from nine o'clock until eleven-thirty."

"Do you also collect rare books, Mr Whealon?" Westborough inquired gently.

For the first time Whealon noticed our presence. "Who are these fellows?"

"Friends of mine," Mack said laconically. "That's a good question, Whealon. Why not answer it?"

Whealon's face was a study. "It's none of your business, but as a matter of fact, I do."

Well, all sorts of people collect postage stamps, so why not first editions? And I couldn't think of any other tie in or out of Christendom that would hold together such an ill-assorted pair as Wells and Whealon.

"Why don't you let Wells go?" Whealon asked truculently. "You haven't got anything on him."

Mack pointed to the purple parrot. "That belonged to Morse, and it was stolen on the night Morse was killed. We found it hidden in your friend's house."

"How do you know it belonged to Morse?" Whealon countered instantly.

"There couldn't be two of the things," Mack asserted. "And, besides, it's been identified."

"Who identified it?"

Mack jerked his broad thumb in my direction. "Foster."

Whealon glared threateningly. "Foster! Morse's attorney makes the identification! What kind of dirty frame-up is this?"

"Frame-up is a hell of an ugly word," was Mack's comment.

"It's a frame-up as plain as your nose," Whealon retorted. "You know damn good and well who killed Morse; you got her down in the jail now. Foster hasn't a ghost of a chance to clear that girl. She's guilty as hell, and he knows it. And here's a fellow who was known to have called on Morse the night of the killing—it doesn't matter if he's a harmless little cuss who wouldn't hurt a beetle, and has an ironclad alibi for the time of the murder in the bargain. Since there's not any real evidence Foster decided to manufacture some. So he bribes you with some of Morse's dirty millions—"

Which was about as much as I could stand.

"See here, Whealon, let me tell you a thing or two. Once you called Morse a swindler before witnesses, and had to back down and eat humble pie or you'd have paid plenty for it in court. If you're not careful history is going to repeat itself."

"You goddam shyster," Whealon roared.

He swung for me but somehow Mack got between us. Mack isn't nearly as big as Whealon; as a matter of fact, he's a couple of inches shorter than I am. But he caught Whealon's arm, and, in spite of his bulk, Whealon couldn't seem to shake himself loose from the detective's grip.

"Sit down," Mack ordered. "You've raised enough hell for one morning, Whealon. Now I've got a few questions for you to answer. What about this story of Foster's?"

"It's true," Whealon admitted. He was still trying vainly to shake loose from Mack's fingers. "What difference does it make?"

"May make a lot," Mack informed. "You didn't have much use for Morse, I take it?"

"I did *not*," Whealon confirmed. "He was a dirty skunk if there ever was one!"

PART FIVE

Monday, November 23

XXIV

The jangling of the telephone aroused me from a sound slumber. Drowsily I opened one eye and wondered where I was. Certainly not in my own room. Then it came to me in a single illuminating flash.

The Sherman!

I sprang out of bed and grabbed the phone.

"Eight o'clock, Mr Jacob," informed a pleasantly cheerful voice.

"Any message for me?" I asked, hoping still against all reason. However, there was nothing. The Voice had definitely let me down!

Had it been just a ghastly practical joke? There were, I knew, people who were capable of such jesting. Or had the Voice's unknown agents seen me enter the police station and reported the fact to their employer?

That would be supremely ironical, because if ever instructions were faithfully executed to the letter, these had been. I had not told the police. I had not even told Westborough, much as I disliked breaking faith with the little man.

But Westborough was too close to Mack to take the risk. Moreover, I told myself consolingly as I shaved, his flawless logic couldn't be employed upon this matter, which was merely the sordid business of paying a stool pigeon his thirty pieces of silver. Or rather (my legal training compelling the correction for the sake of accuracy) his thousand five-dollar bills. Wrinkled bills, dirty bills—exactly as the Voice had ordered. They were still in the suitcase under the bed. Or were they? My face covered with a mask of lather, I hurried across the room to see.

However, the suitcase was there—locked. I hastily opened it. Inside was my own brief case and in it a great sheaf of bills—seemingly as many as I had put there on Saturday afternoon. If the object of the Voice's plan had been robbery he had not succeeded in carrying it through.

I thought it over as I finished shaving. The locked hotel door undoubtedly did make robbery difficult, but the hotel room had been his own idea. I had acquiesced in every detail, taking no precautions beyond the obvious one of borrowing Coleman's revolver. And even that had been the Voice's suggestion; not mine.

What was the answer, then? I tried to reason it out while I finished dressing, but my brain refused to click. Maybe some of Westborough's logic was needed after all. My own mind couldn't produce anything better than the old idea of a practical joke. Perhaps that would explain why the Voice had been so hauntingly familiar. Perhaps one of my so-called friends—"

I ran the list over in my mind, but I couldn't conceive of one of them capable of such macabre humor. I packed my soiled shirt, socks and toilet articles into the suitcase and started out of the room. As I reached the door I remembered Coleman's revolver—I had put it in the drawer of the writing desk, where it would be handy to the door and yet out of sight.

It was still there, looking coldly menacing as I opened the drawer. I dropped it into my overcoat pocket, but it bulged conspicuously and made me recall there was a stiff law against carrying concealed weapons. Opening the suitcase again I stowed it in there.

I walked toward the elevator, reflecting that if the police should see fit to arrest me at that moment, I'd have some difficulty in explaining why I was registered at a hotel under an assumed name and why I carried a suitcase containing five thousand dollars in bills and a revolver.

However, there were no detectives in the lobby, at least none who were looking for me. While paying my bill I asked once more if there had been any message for Fos—Just in time I caught myself and substituted Jacob.

There had been no message; I hadn't really expected that there would be. On my way to the coffee shop I noticed a pile of morning newspapers stacked on the counter of the cigar stand.

There had been another murder in Chicago said the black headlines which were smeared all over the front page of the *Bugle*. But I didn't buy a paper. This, obviously, had nothing to do with the Morse case, and I was in no mood to read the gory and gruesome details of another killing. After breakfasting I took a cab to the office and was deep in the intricacies of the Lingley case by the time Steelcraft arrived.

"A complete washout," I answered in response to his inquiring look.

"Your man didn't show up?"

"No."

"Strange," he meditated.

"Probably nothing but a practical joke."

"I doubt that," he took issue. "Not many people think in that manner. Practical jokesters run in well-set grooves as a general rule. They will give you the number of the city zoo and tell you to ask for Mr Fox or the number of the city incinerator and tell you to call Mr Berner. This seemed to me to have all the earmarks of the real thing." His forehead knitted meditatively. "Perhaps something happened to your informant."

This was an aspect I had never considered, and the implications left me momentarily speechless.

"It's rather a dangerous game to peach on a murderer," Steelcraft continued. "Perhaps—"

Perhaps I *had* been a bit hasty in refusing to read about the details of last night's killing. If this theory of Steelcraft's should be right—

The telephone shrilled in my ear, and I answered it hurriedly, hoping that it would be the Voice after all to set another appointment.

It was only Westborough—but a very excited Westborough.

"Mr Foster, good morning! I have another ridiculous favor to ask of you. Doubtless you are thinking I am completely unbalanced, but I assure you that such is not the case. I have indeed a very good reason for this strange request, but, unfortunately, it would take too long to explain over the wire."

After all this prologue I thought I was ready for almost anything. But I was not prepared for the "strange request" when it finally did come.

"Mr Foster, am I correct in my belief that the stone in Miss Morse's ring is one of those curious gems which are named after the Czar Alexander II because found in the Ural mountains on his birthday—an alexandrite?"

"Yes," I returned, a little impatiently. "What on earth—"

"Very good indeed!" he exclaimed. "Miss Morse did not remove the ring prior to her incarceration?"

"I don't think so. Whatever—"

"Mr Foster, will you be kind enough to procure it from her at once and meet me at Lieutenant Mack's office?"

"Why in the name of—"

"Dear me, there really isn't time to explain, Mr Foster. I may count upon seeing you within an hour and a half? At the most? And another matter: will you inquire of Miss Morse if her grandfather had ever belonged to any organization of book collectors? I allude in particular to the Bibliophile Club."

He hung up before I was able to ask any questions.

"Sylvia's alexandrite ring!" I exploded to Steelcraft. "He wants me to go out to the County Jail and borrow Sylvia's alexandrite ring."

Steelcraft's look said plainly that either I had suddenly gone insane or Westborough was demented. Or both.

"And on top of that key business Saturday," he fumed. "What's the matter with the man? I'm beginning to think—"

I cut in quickly. "I promised to get it at once. But I forgot that visiting hours aren't until—"

Steelcraft waved that difficulty lightly away. "I know the sheriff slightly. If you really believe this man knows what he's doing—"

"I'm sure of it," I said confidently. Steelcraft did some hectic telephoning.

Several minutes later I settled myself in a green plush seat on the Douglas Park "L" and unfolded the latest edition of the *Bugle:*

MURDERED IN LINCOLN PARK

Lying face down on a Lincoln Park bridle path, a bullet through his brain, the body of Carl ("The Skate") Gronstein, notorious underworld character, was found last night by Lincoln Park police.

A thirty-two calibre revolver containing an exploded shell was discovered behind a clump of bushes a block or so southward. Its powder-blackened barrel revealed that it had been fired recently. This weapon "might have done the job", police officials say . . .

Coleman's revolver was also a thirty-two, I remembered. But it was still in my suitcase at the office. And it hadn't been fired.

I returned to my reading, searching vainly through the paper to find in what branch of underworld activity Carl ("The Skate") Gronstein had distinguished himself. The reporter was annoyingly reticent upon that topic. Nor could I find a picture of the murdered man, but that, doubtless, would appear in a later edition.

Although on a chilly November evening Lincoln Park was not likely to be over-populated it appeared rather odd that only one witness had been found who had heard the shot. This witness (he preferred to remain anonymous) had given the alarm to the police around ten o'clock, but the assassin had succeeded in making a complete escape.

The *Bugle* article concluded with the enigmatic reference that the police had several clues in their possession, but did not care to divulge them at the present time.

Was Gronstein's the voice that had spoken to me over the telephone? Had he been killed because he was going to squeal on the Morse murderer? The idea seemed a bit farfetched. The killing of a "notorious underworld character" is, after all, by no means a rarity in Chicago.

The conductor called my station, and I folded up the paper. It was an odd commission that Westborough had given me, I reflected as I walked to the front end of the car. The little fellow's methods might be effective, but there was no denying that they were — to say the least — eccentric. The request about the key had been equally peculiar, too. I had given it to Westborough on Saturday afternoon, but why he expected to need it was a mystery entirely beyond my ken.

Leaving the "L" at California I walked the five blocks to Twenty-sixth Street. The Criminal Courts building could be seen some distance away: a grim square fortress in one corner of which, ironically enough, was carved the word "Libertas." The County Jail, like a poor and undesirable relation, was shunted to the rear and across a small yard from its more architecturally prominent companion.

Stepping inside the smaller building I gave my name to a deputy. Steelcraft's call to the sheriff had worked miracles. I had expected to wrangle for some time before being permitted to see Sylvia, but not even a minor altercation was necessary.

A guard escorted me to a small reception room and locked a sliding steel door behind me. A row of booths, ranged on both sides of a barred partition, permitted a prisoner to talk to her counsel in comparative privacy. Presently Sylvia was led in from the other side of the partition.

For the moment we forgot everything except that by some miracle we were together again. But as soon as I was able to talk coherently I remembered Westborough's instructions.

"Mr Westborough wants to borrow your ring. Don't ask me why. I don't know. There are things about Westborough one has to take on faith."

Smilingly she passed the ring through the wire mesh separating us. "Take it to him with my compliments. He's a dear, and I like him."

"I believe that he also likes you," I conjectured. "Which reminds me that he told me to ask you something else. Did your grandfather ever belong to an association of rare book collectors?"

Her eyes were frankly puzzled. "The Bibliophile Club? I believe that's the only such organization."

"That's the one Westborough specifically mentioned."

"Grandfather refused to have anything to do with it, because he didn't like one of the members," she continued.

"Mr Whealon?" I hazarded.

Her eyes widened. "Are you reading my mind?"

"Not in the least," I assured her. "It isn't even moderately brilliant deduction. I knew Whealon was a member of the club, and Steelcraft told me about the rumpus your grandfather had with him."

A morose deputy entered to inquire if I expected to linger in that particular spot the rest of the day. "I'm going now," I told him. Sylvia's look was so sorrowful that, without regard for the deputy's sour visage, I stepped back to the partition.

"My poor darling!"

"Don't, Barry." She smiled bravely, but there was a telltale trace of moisture in her eyes. "Don't make me feel sorry for myself. It really hasn't been so bad."

The deputy made some sarcastic observation to the effect that if I didn't go soon it would be necessary to build a fire under me. Regretfully I left her to go to headquarters.

I found Westborough gazing blankly from a window, while Mack fiddled with some papers on his desk.

"I've got it," I proclaimed as soon as I came into the room. "Now tell me what—"

Mack's shout prevented me from getting out another word.

"Foster! Look at these pix!"

I inspected the pix—numbered photographs from the police file—a front view and a profile. They were both of the same fellow—no other than Stubby Mustache.

"Recognize the guy?" Mack asked, his eyes studying my face shrewdly.

"It's the fellow who was shadowing me. Where is he now?"

"Morgue," Mack returned tersely. "Bullet through his left temple. A thirty-two cartridge that was fired from Morse's revolver."

"Morse's revolver!" I echoed incredulously. "How did you identify it?"

"If it wasn't Morse's gun it was a Smith and Wesson thirty-two that was its twin brother! And here's a question for you to answer, Foster, and answer damn quick. What the hell was your card doing in Gronstein's pocket?"

xxv

I goggled idiotically. For the moment I wasn't able to answer. Then I remembered that I had given him the card myself in the lobby of 333 North Michigan. I explained, but it didn't take me long to see that my story wasn't going over at all with Mack.

"Humph!" he grunted. "You thought he was from headquarters and so you handed him your card. Sounds pretty thin, Foster."

"I wanted to let him know I was on to him," I elucidated.

Mack remained accusingly silent, but Westborough came to my assistance.

"However, we do know that this man *was* shadowing Mr Foster," he said. "I recognized him myself as the individual who was watching us at the Canterbury Inn."

Mack's voice was ominously calm. "Just the same, Foster, you can tell me where you were last night."

The request was only reasonable, but it put me in a predicament. If I didn't tell him I'd probably be arrested on suspicion, and if I did—

I thanked my lucky stars that Steelcraft had listened in and could corroborate my goofy story.

"I was staying at the Sherman under the name of John Jacob."

"What!" Mack roared. "*What!*"

I told about the Voice. Westborough looked at me reproachfully, but said nothing beyond a brief, "Dear, dear."

I concluded my account with the statement that Steelcraft, whose reputation for respectability was on par with that of an ordinary bishop, had listened in on the extension and could corroborate what I was saying.

Mack thundered belligerently, "Why didn't you tell me about it?"

I explained that the Voice had expressed himself with undisguised clarity that any such action would lead to the breaking of all negotiations. Mack groaned in disgust.

"Same old stall! How do you expect us to get anywhere on a case when the public won't cooperate?"

He read me a lecture on the subject, and in all fairness I had to admit that he was entirely right about it. In my own defense, however, I stated that I had acted as I had believed to be in the best interests of my client, and since the police had already fixed upon a solution presumably they didn't need my help. Our discussion was rapidly becoming heated when Mr Westborough interrupted with a pertinent question:

"Was it Gronstein's voice you heard over the telephone, Mr Foster?"

I answered that it had been an obviously disguised voice, and I hadn't been able to identify it, although I did have the feeling that I had heard it before.

"It must have been Gronstein," he answered with unwonted assurance. "Everything fits, even his occupation."

"What was that?" I asked.

"Jewel fence," Mack returned laconically.

"Which reminds me of Miss Morse's ring," Westborough said cheerfully. "You have it, have you not, Mr Foster?"

I answered by taking it from my pocket and handing it to him. He carried it over to the window for inspection: the stone, I could see, was now a bright green.

" 'An emerald by day and an amethyst by night,' " Mr Westborough quoted softly.

"The stone absorbs the red part of the spectrum, which is strongest in artificial light."

"Is *that* why you wanted the ring?" I asked.

"Oh dear, no. I wanted it for quite a different reason, which will be at once apparent to you. Lieutenant Mack, do you still have Mr Morse's purple parrot in your possession?"

Mack brought it from a drawer of his desk. He was as much mystified as I was, I could tell.

"Before beginning my little experiment," said Westborough, "I should like to ask what Mr Foster has learned concerning Mr Morse's membership in the Bibliophile Club."

"He didn't belong—couldn't stick our friend Whealon," I answered.

"I surmised that Mr Morse was not a member," Westborough stated quietly. "Otherwise it would have been quite impossible."

"What would?" Mack wanted to know.

Westborough did not reply. He had taken the statuette from the detective and was scrutinizing it closely.

"I think I mentioned to Mr Foster," he recalled, "that the kakapo is not purple, which is indeed an uncommon color among the order *Psittaci*, but green varied with brown. If I am not mistaken I hazarded at the time that the purple shade might be of some significance. Now I feel fairly certain that the purple glaze was selected solely for camouflage."

"Camouflage!" Mack and I exclaimed together.

"Yes," Westborough explained. "The bird was tinted purple because a true verisimilitude in color was impossible without one incongruous detail. The eyes of the kakapo are black—not red."

Mack shook his head doubtfully. "Have you gone screwy, Westborough?"

"I hope not," smiled the little man. Holding the parrot in his left hand, he pressed Sylvia's ring against the thing. The stone was brilliant cut—like a diamond—and he drew the edge of one of its facets lightly over the round, protruding eyes. Then he returned the statuette to Mack.

"Examine the eyes carefully, please."

Mack did so. "They're just the same as they were before," he said disgustedly.

"Exactly the same as they were before," Westborough beamed. "But ordinary glass would not be so unmarred. Jewelers, defining hardness as the ability to resist abrasion, have established an arbitrary scale with which to make comparisons. Upon Mohs's scale of hardness, the diamond is given the top rating of 10. Alexandrite, as a form of chrysoberyl, is well up on Mohs's scale, ranking 8½. Glass, on the other hand, usually averages between 5 and 6."

I broke in excitedly. "The stone would make scratches if those eyes were glass! But they weren't scratched, so—"

"Quite right," Westborough finished. "Your syllogism can lead to but one conclusion. The parrot's eyes are not glass."

"Then what are they?" Mack demanded imperatively.

Westborough smiled. The little man appeared to be enjoying himself hugely. "Upon Mohs's scale chrysoberyl is exceeded only by the diamond, with rank 10, and the sapphire, the ruby and other corundum gems with a rating of 9."

Mack yelled, "Those eyes are rubies?"

Westborough nodded. "I would not have taken the risk of damaging the stones by this experiment had I not been reasonably certain of their identity. The red is that characteristically true-red shade, known to the jewelry trade as 'pigeon blood', and it is a color seldom found in stones other than the ruby. The red of garnets is much darker; zircons are inclined to a slight brownish cast; spinels are either more yellow or more purple, and tourmalines verge upon pinkness. However, even experts may be deceived in their identification of a stone solely through color. The hardness test, on the other hand, is conclusive evidence, since all of the red stones I have named rank below chrysoberyl upon Mohs's scale and hence could not fail to be scratched by it."

Mack was not yet entirely convinced.

"All the rubies I ever saw were cut with a lot of facets to reflect the light and make 'em glow. These are rounded—as though you sliced 'em off a ball."

"Yes," Westborough confirmed. "They are cut *en cabochon*, and hence make very satisfactory eyes. It is undeniably true that rubies are best in color when in full step cut—with parallel and horizontal facets—but the cabochon cut, older and more economical, is often preferred by purchasers of quiet taste. Moreover, it is the only proper cut for star rubies."

"Are these star rubies?" I asked.

Westborough shook his head. "Apparently not, and yet their value is by no means to be sneezed at. I do not see how they can weigh less than three carats each, and a three carat ruby of the desirable color and fire these stones have is something of a rarity. I am the veriest layman in matters concerning jewels (here, as always, Westborough underrated himself), but I believe that prices for fine natural rubies of as high as twenty-five hundred dollars per carat are by no means uncommon."

Mack began to calculate. "Two rubies, three carats each. Six times—say, that makes these things worth fifteen thousand bucks. But how do you know they're not synthetic?"

"I am not enough of an expert to tell," Westborough admitted. "However, I should think it unlikely that Hezekiah Morse would pay ten thousand dollars for them without having an appraisal by a competent jeweler."

"I'm going to take this thing down and get a jeweler's report myself," Mack declared. "But if you're right and they are rubies, how the devil did they ever get sunk in a lousy little purple parrot?"

"George Smith must have put them there," I speculated. "I remember Sylvia saying that the money her grandfather gave him went to establish a pottery. He probably owned one, or at least worked in one, in New Zealand. That's how he could make the thing himself, and that's just what he did. He put the rubies in while the clay was moist and then fired it."

"Nuts!" Mack exclaimed. "The heat 'd melt 'em."

Westborough shook his head. "I have already considered that question. The average clay is fired at a temperature of 1,800 degrees Fahrenheit. Rubies do not melt under a temperature of 6,000 degrees."

"Well, the oven 'd break the stones up or spoil their color or something," Mack persisted.

"Not in the least," Westborough demurred. "A graduated increase of heat will not fracture the stone. And while it is true that the ruby does change color upon being heated, the color is not altered permanently. The pristine tint is restored as soon as the stone has cooled again."

Mack yielded. "The thing could have been done then. But why in blazes did this fellow Smith do it?"

"Smith emigrated from New Zealand," Westborough reminded. "I can see a very simple and very obvious reason to justify his trouble."

"To smuggle the rubies through the customs?" Mack asked.

Westborough nodded. "Yes. Under the tariff act then effective a tax of twenty per cent was imposed upon such stones. If these rubies are worth, as we have conjectured, fifteen thousand dollars the tariff would amount to three thousand dollars, a not inconsiderable sum. Dear me, I can only paint the picture with extremely broad strokes. Many of the details must remain forever obfuscated. But it is not too improbable that Mr Smith was unable to pay such an amount, nor that he should be pessimistic concerning his ability to procure the required ransom during the three years allotted him to release the rubies from a government warehouse."

"If he wanted to fool the fellows at the customs he took a hell of a big chance," Mack grumbled. "Leaving these rubies right out in the open where anybody could spot 'em! If he must bring 'em over in a purple parrot why not bury 'em inside?"

"But," objected Westborough, "in that event Mr Smith could not know how his rubies had survived their ordeal by fire. Nor could he exhibit them to a prospective purchaser without destroying the statuette, which might not have suited his purpose. There was indeed the risk that the stones might be detected as such, but if the statuette had been obviously purchased for a small price from a New Zealand pottery (and I do not doubt but that Smith secured a bill of sale to testify to this fact) then its examination by customs officials might easily be perfunctory. It is the Purloined Letter psychology once more, and that it succeeded is sufficiently well evidenced by the fact that the rubies are now here."

Mack grudgingly admitted the explanation might not be too unreasonable. "But," he objected, "why did Morse keep 'em in the statue like this, instead of locking 'em away in a safety deposit vault, like anyone with any sense ought to do?"

"I fear that is one of the details which must remain in obscurity," Westborough confessed. "However, I believe it suited Morse's caprice to see such valuable jewels taken without question for worthless glass by all to whom he showed them." He sighed. "Dear, dear, it is pitifully ironical that such a harmless whimsy as his purple parrot should have sealed Hezekiah Morse's death warrant."

"Morse was killed for that thing?" Mack shouted.

"I am nearly sure of it."

"Who knew it was worth real money?"

"Obviously its secret could not have been known to many people," Westborough opined. "George Smith is dead, and—"

"The jeweler!" Mack interrupted. "If Morse did take it to one for appraisal."

"I think that we may except the jeweler," Westborough averred. "Jewelers, like lawyers and doctors, retain the confidence of their clients."

I had an idea of my own at this point. If Westborough was right in his belief that Morse had been killed to obtain the purple parrot then the financier's death could not be laid to Sylvia. For, by terms of the unsigned will, it was the one object which would conclusively and undeniably be hers. I voiced these thoughts aloud and, to my delight, Westborough confirmed them.

"Yes, in my own mind at least, that unfortunate child is entirely exonerated."

"Humph," Mack grunted skeptically.

Well, it was a long way from Westborough's mind to Mack's, and probably a still longer journey from Mack's mind to Lew Teagan's, but Westborough's words comforted me, nevertheless. He had never said before, in so many words, that he believed Sylvia to be innocent.

Mack grumbled, "I can't check with you that Morse was killed for the rubies. Too simple, by far. There might be a hundred other reasons. But if that was the answer, then the guy that did it was the guy who stole 'em. Wells. And Pete Whealon gives him—"

"Mr Wells could not possibly be Mr Morse's murderer," Westborough interrupted. (I was willing to concur in that belief, because Wells was the least likely person to commit murder that I had ever encountered.) "There is still the Gronstein affair to explain. After the killer—shall we depart from tradition and designate him by the Greek letter Xi?—after the killer had delivered his blow, he found the purple parrot gone; it had already been taken from the drawer in which it was habitually kept. Suspecting Mr Foster, who had been deeply in Mr Morse's confidence, of knowing its location, Xi immediately communicated to his accomplice Gronstein that Mr Foster should be watched. Mr Wells cannot be cast in the role of Xi because, setting aside all psychological considerations, he is needed in another part. The purple parrot left Morse's study in his overcoat."

"He stole it," Mack exclaimed emphatically. "Well, that's grand lar—"

"But Mr Wells is entirely innocent of the theft," Westborough demurred.

"You mean he's a kleptomaniac?" Mack demanded. "How about Doc Zeiss—"

"If Mr Wells were a kleptomaniac he would not be entirely innocent of the theft. The law recognizes no such escape from responsibility. Neither knowingly nor unknowingly did Wells stow away the purple parrot in his overcoat pocket."

"Then how did it get there?" Mack demanded in baffled bewilderment.

"It was," Westborough answered slowly, "to use your own picturesque phrase, 'a plant'."

Mack was speechless for at least three seconds. "It couldn't be," he asserted finally. "There was no one there to plant it."

"I am sorry, but I must differ," Westborough returned. "There was Hezekiah Morse."

"Have you gone clean screwy?" Mack wanted to know when he was finally able to say anything at all.

I found the implication equally difficult to accept. "Do you mean to say that Hezekiah Morse, a millionaire and a man of some position, deliberately framed this poor little bookseller?"

"That is exactly what I do mean," Westborough insisted. "You cannot deny, Mr Foster, that Mr Morse had at times been a trifle unscrupulous in his methods? In other words, that he was a believer in the dictum concerning the justification of the means by the end?"

"Hell and high water wouldn't stop him when he wanted something," I admitted. "But to frame this poor little scholar for no reason at all! And to use for the frame-up the one thing he was planning to leave to Sylvia without any strings attached to it!" I shook my head doubtfully. "You're asking us to believe a great deal, Westborough."

"Let me answer your last objection first, Mr Foster. I fancy that the purple parrot was to enjoy no longer the distinction of being the only object left unrestrictedly to Miss Morse. From Mr Vail's account we can guess that Mr Morse, had he lived, would undoubtedly have made still another alteration in his will. And the purple parrot was the only object of adequate value and sufficiently small size to serve his purpose."

"What purpose?" Mack asked.

"Dear me, it appears so obvious. What was Morse's greatest interest in life?"

"His books," I answered without hesitation.

"And what did Wells have that Morse wanted?" Westborough continued to catechize.

"An old Bible," said Mack. "The one he offered thirty grand for. Good Lord! Would he pull such a lowdown trick just to get that?"

Westborough was sure of it. And, I conceded, if Hezekiah Morse had wanted Wells's 1462 Bible badly enough, he wouldn't care much about the shabbiness of the trick employed. As Westborough had mentioned some of the steps in Morse's career had not been overly scrupulous.

"I do not believe the plan to have been at all premeditated," Westborough resumed. "I think that Morse acted impulsively and upon the spur of the moment, after his scanty store of patience had been exhausted by Wells's persistent refusal to sell. Morse accompanied Wells to the front door. While traversing the darkened stairway the statuette might easily be slipped into Wells's pocket. Its bulk is not large enough to attract undue attention; it is entirely within the realm of probability that Wells is speaking the exact truth when he says that he did not notice it until the following morning."

"Then the next day Morse was going to call up and raise the devil," Mack speculated. "He meant to claim Wells had swiped rubies worth fifteen thousand bucks, and there was going to be hell to pay about it."

"Something of the kind was no doubt his intention," Westborough concurred. "Mr Wells, for all his knowledge of rare books, is an amazingly unsophisticated person. After he had found the parrot statuette in his own possession he would be helpless against such an attack from Morse."

"And Morse, after putting on the screws for all they were worth, would finally calm down and agree to let the matter drop if Wells would return the purple parrot and give him the Bible," Mack continued to theorize.

Westborough had a slight correction. "I feel sure that Mr Morse had fully intended to purchase the book at his original offer of thirty thousand dollars. His object, I believe, was merely to break down Wells's obstinacy, not to benefit financially."

"Wait a minute!" Mack exclaimed. "Wells was a good friend of Pete Whealon, and Morse would've had sense enough not to monkey with him. Whealon can pull ropes and plenty of 'em in this man's town, and Whealon hated Morse. Boy, oh boy, how he hated him! Morse'd know if he tried a stunt like that on Wells, he'd land behind bars so fast it wouldn't even be funny."

"That would undoubtedly have been the outcome had Morse survived," Westborough admitted. "But it was not the outcome that Morse had foreseen. Morse did not know that Wells was a friend of Whealon's."

"He didn't? What makes you think that?"

"Baines had never seen Wells before, and the name conveyed nothing to Vail nor to Miss Morse. Moreover, Morse was not a member of the Bibliophile Club to which Wells and Whealon belonged. The conclusion is inescapable that Wells and Morse were not intimately acquainted, and hence it is reasonable to assume that the close association between Wells and Whealon was unknown to Hezekiah Morse."

"Well, it's a sweet theory," Mack admitted. "Trouble is you haven't a speck of proof."

"On the contrary the proof is in Morse's own handwriting," Westborough smiled. "*What!*"

"On the card which we found with Wells's receipted invoice."

"Oh, *that* card! I remember now. There was some dope on it about the Bible."

"The card, Lieutenant Mack, was identical in form to the other cards in Mr Morse's card index file. The conclusion is almost inescapable. Mr Morse had been so sure of acquiring the 1462 Bible for his library that he had actually gone to the trouble of indexing it."

"Well, I'll be a son of a gun!" Mack ejaculated. "Now how does Gronstein fit into this?"

"Gronstein was the accomplice of Morse's murderer, our unknown Mr Xi. Doubtless he had agreed to dispose of the two rubies when Xi succeeded in obtaining them. But in the place of the rubies Xi was able to offer only the excuse that, after killing Morse, he had found them missing. In an attempt to divert Gronstein's suspicions, Xi suggested that Mr Foster knew where the rubies were secreted. Gronstein's clumsy shadowing attracted Mr Foster's attention. Informed that he had been detected Gronstein abandoned his attempts to follow Mr Foster. At this juncture his former suspicions of Xi's good faith must have returned with doubled intensity. Unfortunately for himself, Gronstein could not refrain from the pastime known in popular parlance as playing both ends against the middle. After he had telephoned Mr Foster, offering to reveal for a consideration the name of Hezekiah Morse's murderer, he notified Xi that he had one chance and only one to produce the rubies. Xi, a remarkably shrewd individual indeed, pretended to agree to Gronstein's proposal, and a meeting was set at a deserted spot in Lincoln Park. Whether the site was picked by Xi or by Gronstein I do not know."

"It was probably Gronstein's idea," I interrupted. "He seemed to have a weakness for that sort of rendezvous. His original suggestion to me was that we should meet at the Buckingham fountain."

"At all events it was a singularly imprudent move," Westborough resumed. "What transpired at their meeting is obvious. Xi, of course, had already stolen Mr Morse's revolver."

"Did he leave any fingerprints on it?" I questioned eagerly. Mack glowered at me in annoyance.

"He did *not!* There weren't any prints on the candlestick or on the back-door knob either. Go on with your yarn, Westborough. It's beginning to get interesting."

"But I have finished," Westborough asserted.

Mack's voice held a note of sarcasm. "Considering you've found out so much about your friend Zy, I thought you might know his name, too."

Westborough casually tossed a bombshell.

"I do know his name. I have known it since last evening."

"But—but—but—" Mack gulped.

"For God's sake, who?" I demanded.

Westborough spread his hands in a gesture of resignation. "I am sorry that I cannot tell you. I have no corroboratory evidence."

"No evidence at all?" I asked stupidly.

"None that would not have been considered too fantastic even by the witch burners of old Salem."

xxvi

Baines bowed as respectfully as usual upon opening the front door. "Hello, how's the head tonight?" I inquired.

"Much better, sir." He rubbed it a trifle ruefully. "You received my message?"

"Not until late this afternoon. I've been away from the office most of the day." I pitched my hat at the hall table. "Your message sounded rather mysterious, Baines. As though something strange has been going on here."

He helped me to remove my overcoat. "There has been, Mr Foster. I decided not to notify the police until I had talked to you first."

"Notify the police?" I repeated. "Was it that serious?"

Baines bowed apologetically. "Another burglary, sir."

"What?"

"I am sorry, sir."

"Last night?"

"Between two and three, sir."

So, while I waited at the Sherman for a Gronstein already lying stark and cold on a Lincoln Park bridle path, Morse's killer—the "Xi" of Westborough's fancy—had prowled again. Was he still looking for the purple parrot? I wondered. True, it had then been down at the police station, but Xi could scarcely know that. Not a word had been allowed to leak into the newspapers concerning the part played by the statuette in this baffling enigma. And the same object could readily explain his Friday night visit; his hurried search of Morse's desk, the volumes frenziedly yanked from the bookshelves. But, I told myself, it might be just as well to hear Baines before I embarked upon such a speculative sea.

Baines used no more words than were actually necessary, but for all that, and despite the interpolation of frequent "sir's," he told his story in a vivid, convincing manner. He had been awakened at about half-past two by a noise from the floor below. "Like someone walking around, sir." Putting on dressing gown and slippers he had descended the dark back steps to investigate.

"Nothing yellow about you, Baines," I observed. The butler smiled in a pleased manner.

"To tell the truth, sir, I often hear odd noises in this house. Boards rattling and so on, sir. I believe that most old houses are like that." He paused briefly. "I did not wish to summon assistance unless it was imperative, sir."

"Did you see the burglar?"

"I regret that I did not," Baines answered. "By the time I reached the second floor he was already going—I distinctly heard the front door close behind him, sir."

He added that he had gone downstairs and peered out into the street, but had seen no one. "Garbed as I was, I could scarcely investigate further, sir."

"Hardly," I concurred. I looked over Baines's spare frame, his head with its prominent bald spot, and shuddered. It was a minor miracle that the consequences had not been tragic. A man who could wipe out a tough character like Gronstein . . .

"You're lucky you didn't stop a bullet," I told him sternly. "Don't try a stunt like that again, Baines. This fellow—Westborough calls him 'Xi'—is desperate. He didn't hesitate two seconds to slug you with the iron candlestick, and the next time there may be some shooting."

Baines paled noticeably. "He was armed, Mr Foster. He had taken Mr Morse's revolver from the upper drawer of the desk."

"That was done earlier than last night," I told him. "As a matter of fact he took Morse's gun the night he knocked you cold."

"I did not notice that it was missing until this morning, sir," Baines informed regretfully.

"No reason why you should. Was anything else taken?"

"Not that I am aware of, sir."

"Are you really sure there was a burglar last night?" He drew himself up stiffly. "I don't mean that I'm doubting your word for one minute," I hastily interposed. "The only thing I question is what Westborough would probably term your 'paucity of data.' You didn't see the fellow; there's nothing missing except the gun, and we know it was taken before. The only thing you can be sure of is a few noises, and, as you said yourself a little while back, most old houses can produce odd night noises."

"There is something else, sir." Baines pulled open the drawer of the small hall table, and handed me a handkerchief. "I found this upon the study floor, sir."

It was a good quality linen handkerchief with a hand-rolled hem. A man's handkerchief with a small blue initial worked unobtrusively into one corner. The initial was the letter "T."

"T?" I knit my forehead. The only person whose name began with that letter that could be at all connected with Hezekiah Morse was Dr Trowbridge, and that was patently absurd. But of course the initial might not be a surname. If it referred to a Christian—

One name flared vividly across my brain. Thomas! Thomas Ray . . .!

"I'll have a look upstairs," I said to Baines, who bowed his acquiescence.

The study, however, was the same as it had always been. It was impossible to check all the books, of course, but the most valuable ones, including the three which had been removed the other night, were in their customary places. And nothing else appeared to be missing. Nothing, that is, but one of the iron candlesticks, and that was down at the police station.

Seating myself in the chair facing the desk I tried to think the thing out. But I could not rid myself of the obsession that the key to the mystery was in this very room, waiting for someone who possessed the acuity to discern it.

Westborough claimed to have discovered that secret, but there was nothing more to be made of Westborough. Speaking plainly he was a horse who wouldn't run. Mack and I had tried in turn threats and entreaties; we had stormed, pleaded, bullied and begged, but Westborough had been equally unresponsive to intimidation or cajolery. Fulmination and coaxing alike brought no more from him than an apologetically murmured, "Dear me, I am very sorry indeed, but I cannot tell you yet."

I asked him when he would tell us, and he replied, smiling, "I hope before the Greek calends." The joke passed over our heads, until Westborough explained that the Greeks had had no calends. Mack didn't think that was so funny, and for once I sided wholly with the detective.

But, with an obstinacy utterly at variance with his habitual mildness, the little man steadfastly maintained that he would divulge the identity of his "Xi" only when the proof was actually in his hands. And with that, perforce, we had to be content.

No, there was nothing more to be made of Westborough, I mused regretfully. His conclusions with regard to the purple parrot had been a brilliant burst of pyrotechnics, but—the burst which marks the end of the rocket's flight. Westborough had failed; it was solely up to me to save Sylvia from being indicted by the Grand Jury, before which she was to appear on Wednesday.

I considered my chances; they were probably about as good as of reaching the moon. Nevertheless, there was nothing to stop me from trying. And, since I had to begin somewhere, I began with the man whose name was at the moment uppermost in my thoughts. The man with the biggest motive of all for killing Hezekiah Morse.

That he had talked to me with a specious frankness I was by now entirely convinced. He had concealed an important piece of relevant information, for surely he must have known of Mrs Spendall's return to Chicago. And there had been two serious discrepancies in his story.

Westborough, with his uncanny predilection for the niceties of logic, had spotted one of them immediately. Vail had not given me a sufficient reason for his quarrel with Morse, a quarrel which he had admittedly provoked. True, Vail's temperament was perverse enough—both Mack and O'Ryan could testify to it—but it was scarcely that much at variance with his self-interest."

The other discrepancy was a trifle—but of the trifles which sometimes hang men. We had aroused Vail from a drunken stupor, and Hudson had declared that he had arrived home in a condition of uproarious inebriation. Yet Brenda Carstairs had told O'Ryan in the Water Tower Station that Vail had been sober when he left her—or, at the very most, not noticeably squiffy.

I was trying to decide just where that led to when my pipe went out and with it my entire train of thought. I reached for an ash tray, but there wasn't one in the room, so I went to the window to knock out the cold ashes against the window sill.

I stood there for a few minutes looking out into the street. No, Mack had been right. There couldn't have been a ladder from the sidewalk. Besides, a dozen people would have seen it if there had been. I filled my pipe reflectively and scratched a match outside the window to light it.

The flame provided sufficient illumination for me to notice the holes in the stonework—holes left when the former balcony had been demolished. The nearest one was a foot below the window sill and perhaps a foot and a half toward my left. I stretched out my arm and probed experimentally with a lead pencil. The hole was about half an inch in diameter and went into the stone a considerable distance—at least six inches, I judged.

I jerked suddenly away from the window. An idea had occurred to me. An idea "too fantastic even for the witch burners of old Salem," as Westborough had put it, but which, nevertheless, might well be the solution to the murder of Hezekiah Morse.

Doubtless, Westborough had traveled the same road. But Westborough had been blocked, and I meant to prove my case. Picking up the telephone book, I ran grimly through the "C's." The name was there, and I jotted down the address and number on a scratch pad handy to the telephone. Then I dialed; there sounded the irritating buzz which proclaims a busy line. I replaced the receiver and deliberated for a few seconds. I was almost sure I was on the right track, but it was well to "make haste slowly" as the proverb puts it. Much as I had resented Westborough's caution in this respect, I was forced to admit that it had been fully justified.

I lifted the receiver and dialed again. This time a husky contralto answered.

"Yes, this is Miss Carstairs."

"I'm Barry Foster. Captain O'Ryan introduced us at the station."

"Yes, I remember. You're Sylvia Morse's lawyer?"

"That's right. May I come over right away?"

She laughed banteringly. "Fast worker! Sorry, but I'm busy tonight. Any other time do?"

"You don't understand. All I want is to ask you a few questions." I added, earnestly, if melodramatically, "A woman's life may be at stake."

"Sylvia Morse's?"

"Yes. I won't take up more than half an hour of your time, Miss Carstairs, I promise."

"Well, there's a party on here, but we can talk in the kitchen if you have to make it tonight."

"I'll be over in fifteen minutes," I told her. "Thanks a lot."

Replacing the receiver I tore the address from the scratch pad and started toward the door. Then I remembered something that I had overlooked and rushed back into Sylvia's room. I took a photograph from its silver frame on her writing desk.

Baines appeared as I reached the bottom of the stairs.

"Are you leaving so soon, Mr Foster?"

"I'm coming back tomorrow—" I paused with my hand on the doorknob. "By the way, is tomorrow night Matilda's night out?"

"No sir."

"Then tell her to take it. I've a special reason for wanting her out of the house."

Baines bowed imperturbably. "I shall so inform her, sir."

I looked at my watch upon leaving the house and consulted it again when I reached the address on Delaware Place. Walking at a brisk pace it had taken me just eight minutes.

The building was a former stone mansion which, without quite obliterating its pristine grandeur, had been made over into an apartment house. I looked at the mailboxes in the vestibule and found a card reading "Brenda Carstairs—Jane Skipworth" and pressed the button. A buzzer sounded, I ran upstairs and met Brenda Carstairs, resplendent in black-and-gold hostess pajamas, in the hall.

"Mr Foster," she greeted me laughingly. "The man who simply can't wait a minute."

I grinned. "It was good of you—"

"Come on inside," she invited.

The high-ceilinged room boasted of a studio couch, covered with a black-and-white zigzag spread, several lamps with homemade shades, hand-painted "moderne" end tables and a number of scatter rugs to relieve the bareness of the really fine, old oak flooring. It also boasted an indefinite number of people (all talking at once while a radio blared full blast), and an atmosphere blue and foggy with smoke.

Brenda Carstairs mumbled introductions, someone thrust a glass into my hand, someone else offered a cigarette. It was a hospitable enough crowd, but I hadn't come for these diversions. Trying not to be too obviously rude about it, I explained that fact to my hostess, who at once led me into the comparative privacy of her kitchenette. There was just room for the two of us to crowd between the refrigerator and the gas range.

"Miss Carstairs—"

"Brenda, to my friends," she interrupted.

"Well, Brenda then. Are you and Tom Vail good friends?"

She shook her head. "Tom's a decent sort, but I don't know him particularly well. As a matter of fact, I—"

She paused abruptly. "As a matter of fact what?" I asked.

"Nothing."

"Miss Skipworth shares the apartment with you, doesn't she?"

"The rent is too much for either of us to swing alone."

"Was Miss Skipworth here the night Vail called?"

"Not that night. Jane was out on the South Side calling on Aunt Martha, who's as mean as they come but who may leave her a million bucks some day—if she doesn't up and marry a gigolo first."

"She was gone all night, then?"

"That's what I was trying to tell you."

"Pardon. You and Vail did a good bit of drinking, didn't you? I hope you don't mind my getting personal."

"Call that getting personal?" she gibed. "Yes, we were lapping them up pretty fast, I guess."

"How did the drinks affect you?" I asked hopefully. "Did you—"

She shook her head vigorously. "I see what you're driving at, Mr Lawyer-Detective, but it won't work. Things were pretty blurry, I admit, but I knew what was going on every minute of the time. Tom wrapped a wet towel around my head, and I laid down on the couch while he made coffee—pretty good coffee too. He made me drink two cups of it. Speaking of drinking I must be getting back to that bunch of bums now."

I caught her arm in time to stop her from opening the door. "Please, Brenda. Just a minute or two. You were lying on the couch and things were 'pretty blurry.' Why didn't Vail open the windows and let the room air out?"

"He did—while I was drinking the coffee."

"Not before?"

"No, I guess he didn't think of it before."

"How long did your period of partial stupor last?" The question, I noticed, had slipped out phrased in Westborough's best manner.

"You mean how long was I orry-eyed?" Brenda laughed. "Fifteen or twenty minutes, I suppose."

"And you could see or hear Vail during all that time?"

"Right! I told you your bright idea wasn't going to work. I know Tom didn't leave the apartment at all."

"But he did move around the different rooms, didn't he?"

"He was in here making coffee. And, come to think of it, he brought me a pillow from the bedroom."

"How does Vail carry his liquor?" I asked.

"Better than anyone I know," she replied admiringly.

"He was cold sober?"

"It didn't seem to have done anything to him at all."

"How did you know it was twelve-thirty when he left?"

"He said so, and then I looked at the clock. I didn't think it could be that late."

"Did you go to bed as soon as he had gone?"

"Don't be a goof," she jeered. "Wouldn't you? Not only that, but I dropped off to sleep the minute my head hit the pillow. If I hadn't thought to turn on the alarm I'd probably be sleeping yet."

"Do you have a watch?" I inquired.

"Yes and no. I have one, but it won't run. I've been putting off having the thing fixed until the state of the exchequer isn't quite so precarious. Say, I thought I had your scheme doped out swell, but now you go shooting down a new track. Where do these questions lead to?"

"I'm not sure they lead anywhere," I answered. "I understand that you and Vail were out for dinner?"

She nodded. " ''s God's truth,' the maiden said."

"And then you came here?"

"No, didn't I tell you? We flew to China."

I skipped the sarcasm. "Who opened the door downstairs?"

"Tom. I gave him my key, and he opened it like a perfect little gentleman."

"The same key unlocks the door upstairs?"

"That's usually true in an apartment, isn't it?"

"Therefore, Vail would naturally keep your key to open that door?"

"Of course," she nodded.

I inquired impressively, "Brenda, are you sure that Vail ever did return your key?"

"Gosh!" she exclaimed. "You've got hold of a honey of an idea! Come to think of it, I don't remember him doing it."

"But you found it in your purse the next morning as usual?"

"Yes," she corroborated, "it *was* in my purse the next day."

PART SIX

Tuesday, November 24

XXVII

I kept my promise to return to the Morse house the following evening. When Baines admitted me I was carrying under my arm a thin parcel wrapped in brown paper.

"Is there a board handy, six feet long, six inches wide and half to an inch thick?" I inquired.

"There is a pile of old lumber in the basement, sir. May I ask — "

"If you find a board like that, bring it up to the study," I directed.

Baines stood agape. "Very good, sir. But why — "

"I'm going to solve the mystery of who killed Hezekiah Morse," I proclaimed, and his mouth opened wider than ever.

"You are, sir?"

"Yes, old fellow," I laughed. "And you're going to help me do it. Are you on?"

"What shall I do first?" was Baines's answer.

"The board."

"I shall search for it at once, sir."

While he hunted for it I sat down at the downstairs telephone and tried to get Westborough. It was only fair to give him the chance to be in at the death. However, the little man was out, and the night clerk (probably the blond Swede I had noticed there before) didn't know when he would get back. The best I could do was to leave word for him to call me at the Morse residence and add that it was important. Larson (I remembered that was the night clerk's name) promised the message would be delivered, and I had to be content with that.

Baines came up from the basement, shouldering a plank of the size specified, and I helped to carry it up to the study. "That's just the medicine the doctor ordered!" I exclaimed.

He shook his head doubtfully. "I am still mystified, Mr Foster."

"Baines, did you ever puzzle over how Morse's murderer left the study?"

"It is very perplexing, sir."

"Perplexing is no name for it. Our killer—by the way, Westborough actually knows his name!"

"Not really, sir?"

"He does, but he won't call him anything but Mr Xi. Well, let's follow his example. Xi could make his exit from the study only through the window or by the door to Miss Morse's room! Take the door first: even if he went out before Miss Morse arrived, he'd have to go down either by the front or by the back stairs; there isn't any way he could leave the house without being seen. Therefore, the door's impossible; it's got to be the window—the window that was left unlocked."

"But that's equally impossible, sir."

"Is it? Come over here and I'll show you something." I led the butler to the window and triumphantly indicated the holes in the masonry. "See those, Baines? For some reason or another, they weren't filled up after the balcony was torn down. They're in a straight line, a foot below the window sill. One is eighteen inches to the left of this window and the other is an equal distance to the right of Vail's window. Now I'll show you what I bought this afternoon."

I unwrapped my parcel to reveal two oval-headed spikes. Each was a foot long and about half an inch in diameter.

"What large nails, sir!" Baines exclaimed.

I smiled. "Those, Baines, are spikes, and a devil of a time I had getting them. I went to three hardware stores before I hit on the idea of hunting up one that specialized in builders' hardware."

Baines shook his head in bewilderment. "I don't see what you are planning to do with those, Mr Foster."

"Just this," I said. Leaning out the window I inserted a spike into the nearest hole; it fitted snugly and penetrated to a depth of about six inches allowing half of its length to protrude from the wall. I had to lean far out of the window and stretch my arm a considerable distance in order to infix the second spike.

"Be careful, sir," Baines called in alarm.

"It's all over now," I reassured him. I stepped back to survey my handiwork. "There! Now we lay the plank across those two spikes, and we have a peach of a bridge between the two houses. Get the idea, Baines?"

He got it, all right, as I could tell by the sudden look of horror on his face. "Then the murderer, sir, is—is Mr Vail?"

"He is," I said grimly.

"I can't believe it, sir," Baines expostulated. "Is that also what Mr Westborough thinks?"

"As I told you he's never said what he thinks. But, unless he's a million miles off, I don't see how he could have any other idea."

"But Mr Vail was with a young lady until twelve-thirty," Baines objected.

"Wait till I get through tearing that alibi to pieces," I prophesied sternly.

"I can't believe it of Mr Vail," Baines mumbled, but he sounded as if he wasn't sure he could convince himself.

"If Vail is guilty you'll help me to bring him to justice, won't you?" I asked.

"Yes sir. It was a brutal, inexcusable murder, sir. And a very cowardly act to allow Miss Morse to be blamed unjustly, if I may say so, sir."

"First, is Vail's servant, Hudson, a particular pal of yours?"

"We often exchange pleasantries across the back wall, sir."

"That ought to make it easier. Call Hudson on the telephone and find out from him if Vail is going to be home this evening. If he is there's nothing we can do. But if he's going out, invite Hudson over to share a bottle of beer with you. I suppose there's some in the refrigerator?"

"At present there is not, but I can easily procure some. You're not actually going to enter Mr Vail's house, sir?"

I nodded determinedly. "If I find some spikes like these hidden there they'll make a mighty sweet exhibit for a jury."

"But if the window is locked, sir?"

I reached in my pocket for a small instrument, which was red-handled and which terminated in a small, sharp-edged wheel.

"This, Baines, is a glass cutter. It should be a simple trick to cut a hole around the catch, reach in and unfasten it."

Baines was profoundly shocked. "But that's housebreaking, sir!"

I admitted it and confessed I'd probably get several years in Joliet if Vail caught me and cared to prosecute. However, I had thought the thing out and had to take the chance. "And, besides, the risk will be negligible if the house is empty," I concluded. "Pick up the telephone and find out now from Hudson how the land lies tonight."

But Baines insisted on doing his telephoning downstairs. Never during his employer's lifetime, he explained, had he dared to use the study telephone, nor would he presume to do so now. A queer duck and no mistake! However, the makings of a good egg seemed to lurk under his starched exterior. He was burbling with excitement when he returned to the study a few minutes later.

"Mr Vail has left the house, sir."

"Good!" I ejaculated, stooping to pick up the plank.

"Unfortunately, Hudson cannot be here for another hour, sir."

"Another hour!" I echoed in dismay. I couldn't wait that long. So much depended on this venture! Sylvia's release—all our happiness together. I carried the plank to the window.

"Is Hudson likely to be upstairs?"

"Oh no, sir. He would be certain to be in the kitchen at this hour."

"Well, that ought to be safe enough—if I'm good and quiet."

I began to shove the plank out the window. It was heavy and awkward to balance. Baines, aghast at my temerity, rushed to lend a steadying hand.

"You won't go there with Hudson yet in the house, Mr Foster?"

"Baines, I've got to!"

I put on a pair of gloves—in case my plan miscarried, I had no wish to leave fingerprints all over Vail's rooms. Then I climbed out of the window and stood upright on the sill, supporting myself by reaching inside to hold the sash.

"Do be careful, sir," Baines pleaded.

Turning my head I glanced downward at the dark, empty street. There didn't seem to be much chance of being seen. I clung to the window embrasure and felt for the plank with my left foot. I am one of those who marvel at the feats of steeple jacks and window washers, and that six-inch plank looked appallingly narrow.

If I slipped—but I decided not to dwell on that. My feet rested upon the plank at last—right in the center of it between the two spikes. For one awful moment I swung there like Mohammed's coffin, and then my hand clutched the embrasure of Vail's window, and I stepped up easily onto the sill. Now that it was actually accomplished, I felt it had been easy.

I found the window unlocked so that my glass cutter turned out to be just excess baggage—not that I regretted it. I jumped inside and pulled down the shade. Then I stood there a few minutes in the dark and listened. But the noise of my own breathing was the only sound I could hear. It certainly did seem safe enough to go on with this venture. I had brought a small flashlight with me, and I pushed its sliding button. A beam of white light fell upon the blues and yellows of the huge bed. Should I begin my search in this room? It scarcely seemed logical that Vail would keep his spikes in the capacious drawers of that mammoth carved bureau. But the only sure way of finding out was to look.

A board creaked under foot; boards were always creaking in these old houses. And, thanks to my own impatience, Hudson was still downstairs. At such moments one's mind plays queer tricks. Once I swear that I actually heard his footsteps ascending the stairs. But, though I listened intently, the sound was not repeated, and I told myself that I had heard nothing but my own protesting conscience.

The bureau drawers, as far as I was concerned, were empty. I peered fruitlessly under the bed and then rummaged in a capacious closet, which had been built in the days when a closet was a giant cavern. Here were innumerable suits and a million or so shoes—but still no spikes.

Neither were they in the bathroom, but that wasn't a likely cache. I found a second bedroom; Hudson evidently hadn't visited it for some time because there was dust over everything. I ransacked a chest of drawers, then another bureau. I had so far found exactly nothing, and all the while time was slipping, slipping away from me.

"Where does he hide the damned things?" I asked myself.

Flashlight in hand—like any sneak thief—I stole across the hall. Another board groaned underfoot, and I stood stock-still. Presently, venturing to go on, I entered the nearest room. It was a small den, utterly at variance with the Spanish character of the rest of the house, but Vail had made it very inviting with a bearskin rug before the open fireplace and a number of large lounge chairs. It wasn't the sort of place where I could expect to find anything. However, I would have a look around. . . . I stiffened suddenly into immobility.

Downstairs men were talking. Two of them; I could even recognize the voices. And, though I wasn't mentioned by name, they were talking *about me*. For Hudson was saying in a voice frightened and alarmed:

"There's someone upstairs, Mr Vail!"

Vail! He was back in the house! Had it been a mistake about his date or what that had led him to return so unexpectedly? However, that question was of minor importance. Vail was here, and Vail was dangerous! I must admit that I threw all heroism to the winds and thought only of getting out as quickly as possible.

Tiptoeing cautiously to the door I saw, to my complete and utter demoralization, that Vail and Hudson were coming up the stairs together. There wasn't any way to get across the hall without being seen. I was cut off from my plank, and I couldn't leave the house. All I could do was to grope my way back again into the den in the dark, hoping they would go downstairs without finding me. But luck, like a capricious woman, threw me down at the moment I needed her most. I happened to brush against a book lying at the edge of the table, and it fell to the floor with a loud crash.

"Hudson, you're right!" Vail's exclamation came from just outside in the hall. "Someone *is* here!"

Their footsteps drew closer and closer to me. There wasn't another way out of this confounded den. I was trapped, and trapped neatly. There wasn't even a place to hide, except an obvious closet. However, poor concealment though it offered, it was decidedly better than nothing. I hurried inside and pulled the door shut behind me.

"The noise came from the den," I could hear Hudson conjecturing, and I thought angrily:

"The fat slob! Why couldn't he have been wrong for once?"

Then I noticed a glimmer of light under the closet door. "The noise was that book, Hudson," Vail declared with calm assurance. "It's been knocked on the floor."

Mentally, I kicked myself to Jericho and back. It would 've been so easy to have picked the thing up, but I hadn't even thought of it.

"He must be hiding in this room," Hudson whispered loudly. He sounded frightened, and I wondered if his heart was beating anywhere near as hard as mine was.

"Right," Vail agreed coolly. "And there's only one place he could hide."

As my heart continued its pile-driver blows against my chest I knew, only too well, how the hunted fox feels when the hounds ruthlessly unearth his last desperate hiding hole.

Vail shouted to the closet door: "I'll give you until I count three to come out of there. If you're not out by that time I'll start shooting." Calmly, deliberately, he began his count: "One! Two!"

There was no alternative. I opened the closet door and stepped into the den.

XXVIII

My eyes blinked as they met the light. The first thing I noticed clearly was that Vail's right hand was gripped about a serviceable blue-black automatic.

"Foster!" Vail cried. He added sternly, "What's the meaning of this?"

I remembered the maxim that a good offense is the best defense. It might work. Anyway, I had no other defense.

"It means, Vail, that I've uncovered evidence pointing to you as the murderer of Hezekiah Morse."

Vail motioned to Hudson to leave and slipped the automatic into his pocket. I watched the portly Hudson depart regretfully. I wouldn't have been sorry to have had him a witness.

"You have made a serious accusation," Vail declared icily. His eyes glinted narrowly, and his lips were set in an uncompromising straight line. "Well, Foster, I'm waiting for you to explain."

"You told me an interesting story the other afternoon," I began, "but even more interesting were the two facts which you left out."

Vail's steely blue eyes were fixed rigidly on my face.

"Well?"

"One of those facts," I went on, "is that Dorothy Spendall, your former mistress, has recently returned to Chicago."

Vail's tone would have chilled the interior of a refrigerator.

"And the other?"

"That Dorothy Spendall called on you Wednesday afternoon."

Vail started visibly. "You're bluffing. You can't possibly know that."

If the truth must be known I hadn't been able to prove it, but his reaction clinched the point.

"She called on you to demand some money," I continued. "I don't know how much, but more than you have in the bank—probably a good deal more. Your financial affairs are shaky; I've seen a Hill's report on them."

Vail moistened his lips. "That's rather a contemptible bit of spying, Foster. But go on."

"Mrs Spendall threatened to tell Morse all about your affair if you didn't pay her. Morse, descended from the Scotch Presbyterians of Dunedin, was a stern moralist. You've admitted that much to me. He wouldn't be apt to condone adultery. It looked very much as though your hope of marrying Sylvia was to be unfulfilled and, in addition, Morse would probably cut you out altogether from his will. You pleaded with Mrs Spendall for time, but she was obdurate."

Vail's face showed his perplexity. "I can't possibly see how you found this out, Foster."

"Then you remembered Morse's purple parrot," I pointed out.

"Purple parrot?" Vail repeated. "Are you crazy?"

"Don't try to pretend to me that you weren't acquainted with its secret," I admonished. "You knew—and you were probably the only person in the world besides Hezekiah Morse who did know—that its red eyes were rubies worth at least fifteen thousand dollars."

"My God!" said Vail. "Is that why—"

"Yes, that's why Morse was killed," I told him. "You could stall off the Spendall woman with the rubies, but you didn't dare to leave Morse alive if you took them—he would suspect you right away since you were the only other person who knew their value. And you'd be assured of at least a third share of the Morse estate if Hezekiah Morse died that night. Moreover, there was an excellent chance that Sylvia might feel herself obligated to carry out her grandfather's last wish. Cold-bloodedly, you determined to kill him!"

"*I* killed him?" Vail's lips compressed threateningly, but I hurried on.

"It's obvious to you by now, Vail, that I entered your house tonight by the very same method you used to get into his study."

"I haven't the slightest idea what you mean."

"Your portable bridge, however, clever as it was, might be deduced by the police, since you couldn't obliterate the holes in the wall. Hence, you arranged to have a witness who would swear that you were with her at the time of the murder, and to swear with the conviction that her words were perfectly true!"

"Are you demented?"

"You selected for this role a girl whose innate sense of fairness would lead her to the police station as soon as she heard you were accused. You knew it was safe to refuse, in pretended chivalry, to reveal her name; your alibi would be all the stronger because it appeared to be involuntary."

"Foster, I swear to you—"

"You can save your swearing for the witness stand, Vail. You'll be expected to tell the truth there. Do you want to know what you did on the night Morse was killed?"

"You're utterly wrong, but go on."

"I'm not wrong," I declared firmly. "When Brenda Carstairs handed you her key to open the door you slipped it into your own pocket, distracting her attention as you entered the apartment so that she wouldn't notice the key hadn't been returned.

"You encouraged her to drink until she had more than she could carry. You, however, remained comparatively sober; I have an idea that several of your highballs were poured down the sink when she was looking the other way. As soon as Brenda showed the obvious effects of alcohol, you suggested that she lie down on the studio couch in her living room."

"Well?"

"You didn't open the windows until *after* you'd given Brenda the coffee you made for her—that's another damning point against you, Vail. You were afraid the fresh air might revive her prematurely. It was essential for your plans that she should remain in a state of torpor verging on coma."

Seemingly absorbed in thought Vail returned no answer. I resumed my narrative.

"You went into the bedroom, ostensibly to get Brenda a pillow. While you were in there you set her alarm clock ahead—not less than half an hour. Brenda was in the living room but in her befuddled condition it was easy matter to escape detection while you moved the hands of her electric clock ahead by the same amount you had altered the alarm clock. Her watch isn't in running order, and there are no other timepieces in the apartment.

"Your next action was, of course, to revive Brenda. Here, you were skating on dangerously thin ice. If she failed to respond to the stimulant and lapsed into an alcoholic coma she was no good to you as an alibi. It would take too long to resuscitate her, and time was precious to you then. But your worst hazard was that if she became conscious of a lapse in memory, she wouldn't be able to testify that you were with her all the time. I imagine, Vail, that you were inwardly on pins and needles, as you forced her to drink the coffee and waited to see its effects.

"Fortunately for you, she revived, and you told her it was twelve-thirty. You emphasized the time pointedly so that she would glance at her clock to make sure you were right—another natural action. You are as familiar as I with the narcotic effects of alcohol. Brenda, in her own words, dropped off the minute her head hit the pillow.

"It took you less than ten minutes to walk to your home, where you let yourself in and tiptoed to your bedroom to avoid rousing Hudson. You inserted the spikes into the wall, as I did this evening, and laid a plank over them on which you could cross to Morse's study. You found his window open or at least unlocked. The slight noise you made as you stepped from the window sill wasn't sufficient to attract Morse's attention. You knew his remarkable capacity for sustained concentration. Standing directly behind him you seized the knife and stabbed. After you had placed his fingers about the knife in an attempt to simulate the appearance of suicide, you locked the hall door and were about to lock the door to Sylvia's room when a new danger occurred to you. If the medical examiner should conclude from the depth or direction of the wound that Morse hadn't taken his own life, the two locked doors would point to the window as the only possible egress. To assure your own safety you were willing to sacrifice Sylvia."

Would nothing break down Vail's assured serenity? I continued my résumé in curt lines.

"Yes, you sacrificed Sylvia by leaving the door to her room unlocked. Henceforth, in the eyes of the police, she would be the only possible scapegoat for the crime. You left your house as quietly as you had entered it and walked to Brenda's apartment. Admitting yourself with her key, you set back the electric clock to the correct time and then stole into her bedroom. She was plunged in profound sleep; there was little danger of waking her. You set back the alarm clock and returned her key to her purse. Your alibi was now unimpeachable. Even though the police forced an admission from Brenda that she had been intoxicated that night, she could and would persist in swearing that she hadn't lost consciousness and that you hadn't left the apartment before twelve-thirty.

"One more item, the final artistic touch, remained on your program. You stopped at a nearby tavern and rapidly gulped three large whiskeys; the liquor took effect and you arrived home in such a state of intoxication that Hudson had to put you to bed. I discovered the tavern-keeper this afternoon, and he was able to identify you from a photograph.

"Thomas Vail," I concluded, as impressively as I could make it, "that's the case I can make against you, and now I'm going to call the police."

But Vail held the ace of trumps in the squat and efficient automatic he had in his coat pocket, and uneasily I began to wonder if I hadn't acted nine kinds of a fool in so fully revealing my hand. I had broken into Vail's house, a fact which would make a strong defense for him if he were to conclude that I should be permanently silenced.

I shivered inwardly as I apprehended my full predicament. Then, realizing that I had now gone too far to be able to back down, I started across the room toward the telephone. Vail's voice arrested me.

But Vail's tone, I heard with relief, was not that of a killer.

"There is one serious error in your chain of reasoning, Foster. You said that I found the window unlocked and so was able to enter the study. What would I have done, Foster, if the window had been locked?"

My hand was already on the telephone, but I withdrew it abruptly.

"According to your theory," Vail went on, "I plotted an elaborate and involved procedure to establish an alibi for a murder which I could only perpetrate if a certain window happened to be unfastened. No matter how great Morse's powers of concentration, even you'll have to admit that I certainly could not force the window with a jimmy or break the glass without attracting his attention. Therefore, the success or failure of my plot depends upon that window, and the chances are that it would not be unfastened. The windows to Morse's study were usually locked as I was aware from my association with him. Now, if I had sufficient foresight to arrange such an alibi as you suggest, don't you think that I would also have considered that contingency?"

His logic seemed irrefutable. Was this, I wondered, the obstacle that had stopped Westborough?

"Your preliminary conjectures are true," Vail coolly continued. "Dorothy Spendall did call on me, and she did demand ten thousand dollars under threat of informing Morse of our former relationship. I don't mind admitting that my finances are at low ebb. However, your assumption that I then determined on Morse's death is the false foundation on which you erect your entire scaffolding. Instead I did what any decent man would have done under the circumstances. I told Hezekiah Morse the whole story, and that's the real reason why we quarreled."

Was the man telling the truth? For the life of me I couldn't tell. His voice carried conviction, and I decided that if Vail were lying he was a peerless actor.

"You still doubt me, don't you, Foster? Very well, I'll have to tell you that Brenda and I weren't alone in her apartment that evening. Another person also saw me leave at twelve-thirty, and that person was Dot Spendall!"

"Dot Spendall!" I echoed in disbelief.

"Yes. After I had gone to Uncle Hezekiah with the results you already know I kept my appointment with her solely for the pleasure of letting her know her guns had been spiked. Dorothy only laughed and said that she had never had any serious intention of telling him anyhow. I didn't know whether or not she was speaking the truth, but I gave her the benefit of the doubt and elected to bury the hatchet by asking her to dinner. At the restaurant we met Brenda, an old friend of Dorothy's, who invited us to her apartment."

"Why didn't Brenda mention Mrs Spendall to the police or to me?" I demanded.

"Dorothy confessed to Brenda that her name and mine had once been linked by gossipmongers and added that it would be better if they weren't coupled in the press. Brenda promptly agreed to take the entire matter of clearing me on her own shoulders."

"But you did stop at the tavern on your way home," I insisted.

"Certainly," Vail acknowledged. "That day had been rather disastrous for me. I had quarreled irrevocably with Uncle Hezekiah; I had been forced to give up my last chance of Sylvia. Under the circumstances you may understand why I didn't choose to go to bed sober."

Could I believe his story? What was true, what was false, and how could the two be sifted? Vail seemed to read my hesitation.

"If you want confirmation why not call Mrs Spendall at the Jetrock Hotel?"

I did so — and conducted a lengthy conversation with a tinkling little voice at the other end of the wire. Finally I replaced the receiver and shamefacedly extended my hand.

"Vail, I want to beg your pardon. I'm convinced you're innocent."

XXIX

I showed Vail my improvised catwalk.

"Ingenious! But you're not going back that way, Foster?"

"Not as long as you're willing to let me out the front door. One such trip is enough for an evening, I don't mind telling you."

"I should think so." Vail smiled as we descended the stairs. The door closed behind me.

The windows of the Morse house were dark; even the light in the study had been turned off. I felt a faint tinge of apprehension as I rang the bell. Baines seemed to be a long time in making his appearance. It didn't usually take him more than a minute or so to answer the bell. I pressed my finger upon the button and kept it there. I could hear the clamor of the bell within, but no sound of answering footsteps.

"Baines!" I hammered anxiously against the door. "*Baines!*"

Only a stolid silence answered. My uneasiness increased. Twice, I remembered, Baines had been in close contact with Morse's assassin. At neither time had Baines seen the man, but Westborough's "Xi" might well fancy that he had been recognized.

Xi — his identity was more of an enigma than it had ever been — might have decided to complete his murderous work tonight. And Xi was possessed of an uncanny secret which apparently enabled him *to enter the house at any time.*

I rushed back to Vail's door; I think I was a little mad. I rang impatiently until Hudson, alarm written plainly upon his podgy countenance, came to admit me, and then I brushed hurriedly past him. I found Vail in the Spanish bedroom upstairs. He was just changing to a dressing gown, and the blue-black automatic was reposing carelessly upon the top of the carved dresser.

"Baines doesn't answer! Something's happened to him!"

Vail's first move was to replace his coat, and his second to slip the automatic in his pocket.

"That bridge of yours is going to be some use after all, Foster. If it hasn't been taken down from the other side!"

However, it was still there. We started out the window together; then, like Alphonse and Gaston in reverse, argued concerning who was to go first. Vail insisted upon taking the lead, and I finally had to yield or waste still more time when—grim thought—we might already be too late.

Vail crossed the plank to the other house, and I waited on the window sill until he disappeared inside. Then I swung over after him. He switched on the lamp—that tall study lamp with its inner globular reflector—just as I climbed into the room.

"Doesn't seem to be much wrong here," he observed.

"Baines!" I called sharply. "Baines."

To my surprise and relief the butler's voice answered from downstairs.

"Yes, Mr Foster?"

My voice trembled from the sheer reaction. "Come up here at once?"

Baines halted in the doorway.

"Why, Mr Vail is with you, sir!" Perplexity was written in large bold letters upon his countenance. "But Mr Vail—you said Mr Vail—"

"I never made a greater mistake in all my life," I owned. Baines indulged in the luxury of one of his rare smiles.

"I am very glad, indeed, to hear it, sir. Mr Vail has been a friend of long standing."

Vail grinned acknowledgment as he restored the automatic to his coat pocket.

"Why didn't you answer the front bell?" I demanded.

"You rang, sir?"

"I nearly rang the bell off! Where were you?"

"I did leave the house for a few minutes, sir. To procure the beer with which to entertain Hudson."

Vail, I could see, was puzzled by this explanation, but I didn't enlighten him. I was beginning to feel foolish for having stirred up such a mare's nest. To cover my chagrin I asked exasperatedly:

"Didn't anything at all happen while I was away?"

"Mr. Westborough telephoned, sir."

"Did he leave a message?"

"He said that he would be here shortly, sir."

"How long ago was that?"

"Shortly after you left. At least an hour ago, sir."

I turned to Vail and admitted that I seemed to have brought him over on false pretenses. "However," I added, "now that you're here, why not wait for Westborough's slant? I promise you you won't be bored by him."

"Westborough? Oh yes, the little historian! All right, I'll wait for him, Foster."

"Is there anything else, sir?" Baines wanted to know. I pointed to the window.

"If you really want to be useful you can dismantle the Bridge of False Hopes and carry its components back to the basement."

His face remained immobile. "Very good, sir."

Vail had seated himself at the desk. "It's a theory of mine that one can get a clue to a person's thoughts from the scribblings he makes while he's telephoning. Suppose that Uncle Hezekiah had jotted down a few stars or triangles on this scratch pad—"

"I tore the top sheet off yesterday," I interrupted. "Anyway, there wasn't any scribbling on it."

"But there's a word written here now," Vail said.

"There can't be!" I objected. "The pad was blank yesterday, and nobody's been here since. Baines always uses the telephone downstairs."

"Your logic," said Vail, "may be correct, but it does not alter facts. There is a word here. Or—more exactly—there are five letters."

I crossed the room to see for myself. Vail was right—but how the devil did the writing get there? It was a small, cramped handwriting. One by one I puzzled out the letters: "P-O-S-T-E."

"That's not a word," I maintained.

"The only thing I can think of," said Vail, "is *poste restante*—the French equivalent of our general delivery."

"But that wouldn't make any sense!"

"Neither would anything else. Poster? Posterior? What else is there?"

"Try a dictionary," I advised.

"Didn't know Uncle Hezekiah allowed anything so modern in this library."

"Oh yes. You can consult the original authority. The work of the great John—"

I broke off abruptly. Words were rushing through my mind—words that I had heard before in this room. So startlingly vivid were they in memory, that I seemed to hear the very same voice repeating them.

"My favorite bit of Johnsoniana . . . when asked why he defined 'postern' as he—"

"Postern!" I shouted. "The word is postern. And that means that Westborough's been here!"

"How do you make Westborough out of postern?" Vail inquired. Even after I had explained he shook his head doubtfully.

"How could he get in if Baines didn't admit him?"

"He had a key; I gave it to him Saturday. Vail, he *was* here. No one else would write that particular word upon the scratch pad."

"Odd he didn't finish it," Vail remarked.

"He couldn't finish it!" I cried. "See the jerky trail on the last 'e'? He was interrupted!"

For a moment we stared at each other in silence, and then I picked up the telephone.

"It's time we called Mack in."

My mind had already visualized what must have occurred. Westborough had undoubtedly made a discovery of importance; perhaps even the very proofs he needed to divulge the identity of his "Xi." He had sat down at the telephone, his fingers toying with a pencil, his mind unconsciously dictating to them the letters. And then? A vicious blow from behind while he talked over the wire—or had that call been permitted to go through? A limp figure carried to a waiting car . . .

Mack was out, but expected in a little while. I left word for him to come at once and proposed to Vail that we search the house while we waited. However, I didn't really think that course would do any good. Like Gronstein, Westborough had known too much. Dangerous knowledge! This criminal had proved over and over again that he would stop at nothing.

I thought of Westborough's cheerfulness, of his unfailing kindliness, of the thousand and one likable traits of the little man. A cold fury shook me from head to foot. It was a blind anger, all the worse because there was no outlet upon which I could vent it.

"Damn them! If they've been able to—"

Vail rested his hand consolingly upon my shoulder. "Buck up, Foster. It may not be as bad as you think. Let's try to reconstruct his reason for telephoning. Undoubtedly, something must have just attracted his attention to Dr Johnson's dictionary, or he wouldn't have written those letters. Any ideas?"

But at that moment my mind was a complete and deadly blank.

"Could there be anything like a cryptogram connected with it?" Vail persisted. "Something on the order of a book code, perhaps?"

I said dubiously that the theory appeared to be pretty farfetched.

"Oh entirely," Vail agreed. "But why were the two volumes of that work taken from the shelf the other night? There must be some sort of connection. If—"

The doorbell sounded with loud, insistent clamor. Hoping that the appearance of Westborough would refute our conclusions, I rushed downstairs. However, even as I hoped, I realized that the little man would never venture to ring a doorbell so noisily.

It was Mack. Baines let him in as I came to the landing, and he brushed past the butler impatiently.

"Where's Westborough?"

"He has not arrived yet, sir. We expect him at any—"

"He was here!" I shouted. "He came while Baines was out. Come upstairs, and I'll show you."

When we were all in the study I pointed to the letters on the scratch pad—Westborough's pathetic beginning of a word. "This wasn't here before tonight. And you didn't write it, did you, Baines?"

"No indeed, sir. As you know, I never use this telephone."

"P-O-S-T-E," Mack spelled aloud. "What's the meaning of it?"

I explained our theory. Mack, somewhat to my surprise, recalled perfectly the Doctor Johnson incident. My impression had been that he hadn't paid it much attention at the time, but I was completely wrong.

"That's Westborough for you! Queer little codger! Full of stories like that—about people no one ever heard of who've been dead a hundred years or so." His frown deepened into a ferocious scowl. "If anything's happened to that little fellow I'll—"

"But Mr Westborough could not possibly have been here," Baines averred.

"Why not?" Mack demanded truculently. His nerves—like my own—were worn to razor thinness. "Foster said you were out. How long were you gone?"

"Scarcely more than fifteen minutes, sir."

"That's time for—hell, it's time for anything!"

Baines was quietly patient, as one explaining an obvious fact to a three-year-old. "But Mr Westborough could not enter the house in my absence, sir."

"Hell, that's right!" Mack exclaimed. "Foster, if you've been trying to kid me—"

"Westborough had a key," I said shortly.

"He had a key?"

"Baines knows I had one made."

"I did not know that it was intended for Mr Westborough, sir."

"Well, it was. I gave it to him on Sat—"

"That clinches it!" Mack proclaimed. He tore off the top sheet from the scratch pad. "This thing is evidence enough—even if there hadn't been something screwy about his phone call."

"Westborough called you?" Vail and I asked together.

"Yeh, it was him," said Mack. "I recognized the voice, but he didn't get a chance to say more than two words before the line went dead. I thought we'd been cut off, and I waited about five minutes for him to call back. Then I got a little worried and phoned his hotel. Night clerk—fellow by the name of Larson—told me that you'd called him from here, Foster. Said that Westborough had tried to get you just before he left the hotel and that he had talked to somebody at the number."

"He talked to me, sir," Baines informed. "At the time I received the message Mr Foster was away from the house."

Mack's stare was undisguisedly suspicious.

"Every one of you seems to have been out. Convenient for some of you, maybe."

Vail corroborated my account, but Mack would not listen to an explanation.

"We've wasted way too much time now. Baines, you and I'll take the top floor. Foster and Vail, you take this one. Sing out if you find anything."

Vail and I poked feverishly in closets, peered anxiously into dark corners, but could find no further traces of Westborough's presence. Equally unsuccessful, Mack and Baines rejoined us in a few minutes.

"The basement," Vail suggested. "It's the most likely place if he's—"

I don't believe he could have finished that sentence. I know that I couldn't have done it—even had Mack allowed it.

"Where's the basement, Baines?"

Descending the back stairs to the kitchen I was reminded of Westborough. He and I had come the same way when we were in quest of the canceled check from George Smith. Baines opened the door to the basement stairs, revealing a yawning dark cavern. "Turn on the lights," Mack growled.

Baines pressed the switch, and the cavern was converted into an ordinary, harmless basement. The butler reached behind the door for the ring of keys on the nail.

"Well?" Mack grumbled. "What 're you waiting for?"

"My keys, sir. They're gone!"

"Keys to what?"

"To the wine cellar and to several storerooms, sir."

"Now we *are* on the trail!" Mack shouted jubilantly. "I'll find that little guy if I have to kick down every door in the place."

But the kicking wasn't necessary. We found Baines's keys protruding from the lock of the first door we tried—the door to the same storeroom Westborough and I had visited the other evening.

Mack flung the door open unceremoniously, and we rushed inside. Someone had shoved an enormous wardrobe trunk a foot or so away from the wall; that was the first thing I noticed.

I hurried over there at once, and, in the space behind the trunk, lying ominously quiet, I saw Westborough. His hands and feet were bound with a length of clothesline; his mouth had been taped shut with adhesive tape.

As I shouted to the others my heart sank clear down to my shoes and stayed there. The little man's hair, sparse and silvery, was discolored by an ugly-looking clot of blood.

XXX

Mack's head shook gravely. "He's still breathing, but it looks like it had been a close call for the little fellow."

We carried Westborough, trussed as he was, to a sofa in the living room. While Mack cut loose the ropes and ripped off the adhesive tape, I went with Baines to procure hot water. Vail, almost as well acquainted with the intimacies of the house as the butler, dashed upstairs in search of bandages and an antiseptic.

If I had ever wanted evidence of the detective lieutenant's regard for Westborough it was furnished in plenty by the events of that night. Mack, who was as solicitous as a woman in his care, would allow no one but himself to sponge the little man's head. "Nasty bruise!" he exclaimed, holding a dab of cotton across the mouth of the peroxide bottle. "Could be a whole lot worse, though. I don't think it's going to need any stitches."

Westborough regained consciousness as the peroxide began to froth. A faint "Dear me!" was hailed by Mack with a shout of hearty relief; then the detective reverted to his normal gruffness.

"Hold still till I get this thing tied around your head." He wrapped the bandage with a skill which bespoke extensive first-aid training. "Well, who was it did the slugging?"

"I did not see my assailant," Westborough replied weakly, and Mack's face fell. "Dear me, I wonder just what implement was employed."

"The other candlestick?" I suggested.

"I do not see how that could have been feasible." His eyes, glancing about the room, came to rest upon a bronze statue of Minerva in full wartime panoply. "Perhaps that object—"

"Hold still," Mack commanded brusquely. He stopped his bandaging to survey the statue, which was about eighteen inches high and would have made a murderous club.

"Yeh, that baby might 've done it," Mack agreed. "We'll check it for prints."

"I fear that none will be forthcoming," Westborough declared. He sat upon the sofa as Mack tied the last knot in the bandage. "Fortunately, their evidence will not be needed."

"You mean you've got the goods at last!" Mack cried delightedly.

"Yes," Westborough confirmed. "All the necessary proofs are in my hands." He fumbled anxiously through his pockets, and I waited expectantly. "Dear me, I do not seem to have my spectacles," the little man sighed. "Strange, is it not, that one's eyesight should be so utterly dependent upon two curved pieces of glass?"

"What did become of 'em?" Mack growled. "Come to think of it, I—"

Baines produced the gold-rimmed bifocals from his own pocket. "They were lying upon the floor beside you, Mr Westborough. I took the liberty of cleaning them, sir."

"Thank you," the little man murmured, adjusting the bows over his ears. "Once more the world is revealed in its true perspec—"

"Who was the guy who hit you?" Mack asked bluntly.

Westborough asserted with conviction, "The same person who struck down Baines last Friday. The murderer of Carl Gronstein. The assassin of Hezekiah Morse."

"What's his name?" Mack demanded peremptorily.

Westborough smiled. "The chain of logical inference is the meal, the conclusion merely the dessert. Surely, you do not wish your dessert to take precedence over even the preliminary cocktail?"

Mack grinned. "Give me enough cocktails, and you can keep the whole dinner. But tell your yarn in your own way. I guess you've earned that."

"Shall we begin by adjourning to the study? There is a certain experiment which may only be demonstrated in that room."

"Okay if you're up to walking," Mack agreed.

"Indeed yes. With the exception of a slight headache, I feel very well." Rising to his feet he swayed dizzily. "Dear me, I fear that my tongue has played the braggart. Baines, will you be good enough to lend me your arm?"

Upstairs, Westborough seated himself in Morse's own desk chair. "You will be kind enough to close the door, Baines? I feel a noticeable draft. Thank you very much. And now, since Lieutenant Mack has kindly given me carte blanche, I shall begin by summarizing the peculiar difficulties we encountered in the solution of this problem. Obviously, the murderer had been able to make his escape only through Miss Morse's room or by the window. The total absence of footprints below, coupled with the lack of projections to which a climber could cling, determined me at a rather early stage to eliminate the window as a means of egress."

Vail chuckled. "Foster's one up on you there! He figured out how it could be done and nearly landed me in the hoosegow."

"Indeed?" Westborough murmured. "I should like to hear the details."

While my face burned a furious crimson Vail carefully outlined my mistaken conjectures. Westborough, however, did not greet the theory with the derision I had expected.

"A very ingenious hypothesis, Mr Foster."

"But way off the track, eh?" Mack guffawed.

"And yet each step is deduced logically from the primary assumption. It is remarkable how two such conflicting solutions can be presented for the same problem. I am reminded of the work of Lobachevski and Riemann in building their contradictory systems of geometry through the rejection of Euclid's unproved postulate to the effect that through a given point there can be one and only one line parallel to a given line. Lobachevski maintains that there can be either two or an infinite number (depending upon how the word 'parallel' is defined), and Riemann holds that there can be no parallels at all since every two straight lines intersect at a finite distance."

"What's that stuff got to do with the Morse case?"

"Very little," Westborough cheerfully admitted. "And yet the analogy is an interesting one. Riemann replaces the Euclidean two-dimensional plane with the sphere, and the Lobachevskian equivalent is the curious pseudosphere—a surface of uniform negative curvature. In three-dimensional space the differences are even more startling; however, I believe that I have cited enough to illustrate my point. Each of these three contradictory geometries is logically consistent throughout—just as are Mr Foster's solution and my own. But truth, to continue with the analogy, is in this instance non-Euclidean, and Mr Foster's Euclidean solution will not fit without a noticeable buckling and distortion—just as you cannot press down a flat sheet of paper uniformly upon the surface of a globe."

"You've been up in the stratosphere for about five minutes now," Mack grumbled. "Come down to earth and let me know who—"

"It may be logically inferred from the facts known to us," Westborough informed.

"Not merely once but several different times. To mention only one such analysis: the purple parrot tells very plainly the name of the person concerned."

"How do you figure that out?"

"Through Mr Morse's unsigned will. This document provides that Miss Morse, in the event she defied her grandfather's matrimonial wish, was to receive from him only this statuette. Why was the 'purple parrot' thus specified? For two reasons: it was valuable—the rubies, as we now know, are worth at the very least fifteen thousand dollars—and its value was unrecognized. Both of these qualities were necessary for the success of Morse's plan."

"What plan?"

"While Morse lived he did not wish to exhibit any signs of yielding. Neither, however, did he desire to leave his granddaughter entirely destitute. That conclusion is, I believe, fully justified; otherwise, Morse might easily have substituted any worthless object or the conventional one dollar for the parrot in his will. Miss Morse, however, was ignorant of the parrot's secret. Unless Morse planned to play a grisly postmortem joke upon his sole descendant, a hypothesis scarcely consistent with his character, some provision must have been made for apprising Miss Morse of the parrot's true worth. Shall we suppose that, at the same time he drew up the rough draft for the will, Morse also wrote a letter? A letter which he left with some trusted person to be delivered to Miss Morse only after her grandfather's death and, perhaps, only upon the event of her marriage to another person than Mr Vail?"

I couldn't see it. "Anything as important as that would have turned up before. Under the circumstances no one would keep such a secret."

"Unless motivated by his own self-interest," Westborough demurred. "Gentlemen, I think that Morse did leave such a letter. I think that it was opened and read by the supposedly trusted recipient, who thus became the only other person besides Hezekiah Morse to learn of the purple parrot's secret. And the name of that trusted recipient— Morse's murderer—is written plainly in Morse's unsigned will."

"I couldn't read it there," Mack sighed.

Nor could I.

"Then consider the bloodstained glove," Westborough suggested.

"There wasn't any such glove," Mack objected.

"But the glove, or its equivalent, had indubitably a real existence. Your men conducted a very thorough, painstaking search. Why was the glove not found?"

"Because it was carried out of the house," Mack snapped.

"Dear me, no. Let us try another line of thought. It is odd," he continued reflectively, "that among all of the possible suspects only one appears to have had traffic with underworld characters. Evidently the bootlegger, Giovanni Canzonetta, was among the least harmless—"

I shrieked a warning—too late! When or in what manner Baines had possessed himself of Vail's automatic I never knew. At that moment, however, it was enough that he had it and was holding it inflexibly.

"Stand together in that corner!" he barked. "All of you! And keep your hands up!"

XXXI

There were no heroics. Mack carried an automatic in a shoulder holster, but it might as well have been down at headquarters for all the use it was now. The detective made no attempt to reach it—a wise decision because a bullet can travel a good bit faster than the human arm.

"I have lamentably blundered," sighed Westborough. "I must admit that I had hoped for some overt act which might be construed as a confession. But I had not dreamed that—"

Nor had I! What a stupid, blundering amateur of a detective I had been! Bent upon a wild-goose chase next door when all the time the quarry was under my very nose! I had even asked that quarry to help in my misguided attempt—a joke for the high gods. Why hadn't I perceived the truth? Westborough had declared that the name of Morse's murderer was plainly written in the unsigned will, and now, perversely enough, I was able to read the riddle plainly. The five-thousand dollar bequest to Baines had not been granted because of the stirrings of Hezekiah Morse's conscience. Not in the least. Morse had demanded value received from the butler. Baines was the one who had been selected to impart to Sylvia the truth concerning the purple parrot.

Yes, Baines had learned the secret of the statuette and had killed Morse to secure it. That much was plain, but a myriad questions remained to be answered. The attack on Baines. Sunday night's burglary. The butler's undoubted alibi at the time of Morse's death. These were puzzling problems and clamored for a solution. I could answer some of them, perhaps. Obviously, it had been Gronstein who—

Baines's curt command broke into my thoughts. The butler had dropped his mask as completely as Uriah Heep had shed his supposed "humility" under similar circumstances.

"Hand over that gun, Mack!"

"It won't be healthy for you if I do," the detective warned. His tone was quiet, matter of fact. "The minute my fingers close around that baby, I just naturally itch to start shooting." He added with significant emphasis. "I can shoot about as well with one hand as the other."

"Take it from him, Vail," Baines ordered.

Vail shrugged his shoulders with assumed indifference. "All right with me if you want to take the chance. But I can shoot pretty fast myself, and I usually hit the mark."

"It would be safer if none of us were asked to remove Lieutenant Mack's weapon," Westborough said decisively.

"Then I'll have to get it myself," Baines said, taking a step forward.

"Try it," Mack coolly challenged. "Just try coming within two feet of me."

"Damn all of you!" Baines snarled. There was an ugly leer on his face. "Keep your hands in the air, then. You won't have to hold them there long. I'm leaving in just five minutes for the airport, and when I go I don't leave anyone behind to talk. Is that plain?"

"Entirely clear, I am sure," murmured Westborough.

"Think you'll get away with this?" Mack growled. "Baines, the force 'll nail you if you hide in Timbuktu."

Baines laughed loudly, unpleasantly.

"Don't try to reason with the murderous swine," Vail snapped.

"If it's the last thing I ever do I'm going to get the record clear," Mack proclaimed. "Baines, you killed Gronstein."

"The louse had it coming," Baines snarled.

"And you stabbed Morse."

"Fooled you, didn't I?" Pride surged strongly in the butler's voice. "You didn't dream how it was done. I was too clever for you—all of you."

"That statement is not quite correct," I objected. It was odd that I had any control over my voice. "You failed to fool Mr Westborough."

Baines's eyes were glaring furiously. They were no longer the eyes of a human being—they were those of a wild beast, a primitive jungle thing! "You were the one to tip me off he knew, Foster. Don't forget that."

I was not likely to forget. How could I have been such a colossal fool as to reveal that Westborough knew the name of Morse's assassin? But, as if that alone were not sufficiently stupid, I had brought Westborough to the house with my telephone call. I had let him walk squarely into the trap while I was away chasing wild geese next door. Dunce! Idiot!

Westborough might have been reading my thoughts. "Dear me, Mr Foster, you had no way of knowing!" His eyes—even at such a time—were twinkling. Then he continued: "Baines, I must confess to a reluctance to quit this life without the satisfaction of knitting together the few remaining loose ends. I trust that you will allow me the privilege of explaining your accomplishments in the manner in which they so fully deserve to be related."

Baines, to my surprise, had no objection to this extraordinary proposition. Indeed, he seemed rather pleased by it, if anything. Westborough's object was clear enough to me—I believe it was to all of us. He was merely playing for time, waiting for the unexpected incident which might upset the delicate balance of the situation, hoping that in some manner Mack would be enabled to reach his automatic.

I wondered why Baines had not seen through the scheme at once. However, Westborough had not underestimated by one iota the butler's colossal vanity.

"Let us commence with the supposed attack on Baines last Friday night," Westborough began. "Superficially, it might appear that Baines induced Gronstein to strike him in order to muddy the already murky waters. But Baines's object in staging the supposed attack was to divert suspicion away from himself while he appropriated Mr

Morse's revolver. Since he wanted the revolver only for one purpose—the removal of Gronstein—it would be hardly feasible to ask for Mr Gronstein's assistance. And, it is scarcely necessary to tell you, he had no other accomplice."

"Then Baines knocked himself cold?" Mack put in. He was playing up to Westborough's lead for all it was worth. "That's an impossibility!"

"In what manner?" Westborough queried.

"Why—why, it's obvious! Baines was hit on the back of his head. He couldn't do that to himself."

"The explanation is in the three books removed from the bookcases," Westborough informed.

"You tried to tell us that on the scratch pad," I exclaimed. "You started to write 'postern,' knowing we would think of Dr Johnson's dictionary?"

"I had wished to leave such a message, yes," Westborough confirmed. "I sensed a possible danger, and I felt it might be wise to scribble a few words which would be unintelligible to my assailant, but would be readily interpretable by anyone who had heard me relate the Johnson anecdote. I had not intended, however, to be quite so cryptic. Dear me, I fear that you were put to a deal of extraordinary trouble."

"We solved it," Mack grunted. "At any rate Foster did. But what do you mean about those three books? That doesn't make sense."

"Consider their position in the bookcase. They belong on an upper shelf—and we found the receding glass door open."

"I still don't get it."

"I see that I must be more explicit. You will remember that we found a rubber band on the floor—a *broken* rubber band."

"Now I see it," Mack shouted. "When you push back those receding doors, there's a knob sticking out—two knobs for each door. Baines simply hung the rubber band on one of 'em and balanced the candlestick on it. That your idea?"

"It is exactly my idea," Westborough corroborated. "Indeed, I made the same experiment myself prior to telephoning you this evening. I used one of the rubbers from Mr Morse's desk. The rubber was old and broke under the weight of the heavy candlestick, but it did not break immediately. No, there was an interval of a few seconds before the candlestick fell. That period provided Baines with ample time to stand below the suspended iron weight, bow his head and receive the full force of the blow. When the candlestick fell the rubber snapped away from the knob, and there remained nothing to tell the story but the open bookcase door, which we interpreted as the hurried work of a thieving prowler."

"Neat!" Mack exclaimed, his voice reverent. "Damned neat, I'd say! But when was Morse killed?"

For the moment, so absorbed were we in the unraveling of the puzzle, we forget that we were entirely at the mercy of a cold-blooded killer.

"Very close to midnight," Westborough returned. "Baines had at least a minute from the time he heard the voices of Mr Foster and Miss Morse in the hall below until

Miss Morse arrived upstairs. That minute was ample for him to affix the dead man's fingers about the knife handle, and make his escape."

"But she didn't hear him," I objected. "And all the floor boards creak."

"With the single exception of those on the back stairs," Westborough asserted. "You will recall how startled Baines was the other night at our unexpected appearance in the kitchen. Obviously, he had not been able to hear our approach. Nor could Miss Morse hear Baines tiptoeing quietly downstairs."

"You locked the study door to incriminate Sylvia!" I exclaimed hotly to the butler. "Baines, you murderous, lowdown scum! You—"

"Stand back, Foster, and keep those hands up!"

Vail's automatic didn't waver in Baines's hand. He wasn't five feet away, but it might as well have been five hundred. Baines could shoot as fast as he could pull the trigger; he could wipe out all four of us before one of us could get to him. And don't think for a minute that he didn't know it!

I obeyed instructions, my hands raising even higher in the air. I was beginning to be conscious of the muscular strain from keeping them uplifted so long.

"Consider another point," Westborough calmly invited us. "There was no outcry from the study; therefore, Morse had been given no opportunity to suspect Baines's intention. In some manner Baines had managed to enter the study, circle the desk, and stand behind Mr Morse without attracting his attention."

Now that it was too late my own mind was working at top speed. "The window! That's why it was unlocked! Baines didn't have time!"

"Time for what?" Mack grunted.

"Time to lock it. It was open when Baines came into the study. He offered to close it, and that gave him the chance to get behind Morse. He pulled down the window. Morse hadn't looked up from his desk—why should he? Then Baines snatched the knife?"

"Excellently reasoned," Westborough commended.

"It's the truth, all right," Baines owned. He was smiling—the nastiest smile I have ever seen. "It was a simple matter to reach his heart. I am quite familiar with anatomy— as you will soon have occasion to learn, gentlemen!"

"Dear, dear!" Westborough shuddered.

Mack shouted exasperatedly, "Think how we were taken in by the Sampson woman! We thought she was giving us the straight dope, and here she was in cahoots with Baines all the time."

"Dear me, no," Westborough replied unexpectedly.

"Are you crazy? She said he wasn't out of the room at twelve—that he'd been with her at least an hour before."

"Nevertheless," Westborough maintained, "Matilda is completely and utterly innocent of any complicity."

It was too much for Mack—and for me. It didn't make sense. It just wasn't possible.

"Yes," Westborough agreed, "it is rather reminiscent of Black Magic. I do not believe that I would ever have been able to puzzle out the secret if Baines, fearing a possible search of his belongings, had not concealed a certain book in the safest possible place of all—among the two thousand others in Morse's library. Since the opportunity to do such a thing occurred only while Morse was taking his walk at four o'clock in the afternoon, the crime had evidently been premeditated at least that long."

"What book?" Mack asked. "And why didn't we get on to it when we checked them with the index cards?"

"The necessary index cards had been provided—a very passable forgery, by the way. It deluded me completely when I made my first and only examination."

"How did you find out they were forged?" Mack wanted to know.

"It has never been proved," Westborough admitted. "As a matter of fact, both book and index cards had been removed when I came clandestinely to the study upon Sunday night to secure them."

"So that's why you asked for the key!" I exclaimed. "You were the burglar?"

"Yes, I was the burglar," Westborough confessed. "Dear me, I regret that such a drastic step was necessary, but I had no other alternative. Baines did not allow me to be alone in the study, and I did not wish to take the slightest chance of arousing his suspicions."

"What book was it?" Mack asked again.

"The author," Westborough returned, "is J. Milne Bramwell. But for the circumstance that the last name begins with the letters 'Br', the enigma might still be unsolved."

"What's his name got to do with it?"

"You will recall that Miss Morse mentioned verifying a certain quotation from one of Robert Browning's poems? Curious to see a first edition of *Men and Women*, I took the book from the shelf. When I returned it, my eye was caught by the title of an adjacent volume. It was a curious subject to be included in a library of this nature, and this volume, a third edition published in 1921, was scarcely old enough to appeal to Hezekiah Morse as a collector's rarity. I examined the index cards, found them in apparently perfect order, and foolishly allowed the matter to pass from my mind. When, several days later, it occurred to me to submit the cards to a handwriting expert, it was then too late. Although Baines's action in removing the book convinced me beyond all doubt that he was the guilty party, the same action, paradoxically enough, destroyed my hopes of proving it. There was only my word that the book had ever been in the library since I had said nothing about it upon that night. Unfortunately, I was so ill acquainted with the subject that I didn't realize until—"

"Shut up," Baines barked. "I'm through listening to you."

"You are not going to allow me to explain the nature of—"

"No, I'm sick of your yapping."

"You are not even interested in learning that your unwitting accomplice is now in the hands of a competent psychiatrist?"

"Damn you!" Baines shouted. "You've done it!"

"I fear so," the little man admitted gravely. "No matter what you do to us, you are unable to prevent your secret from being made public. And the arm of the law is extremely long, if I may remind you of that truism."

"Damn you!" the butler sobbed. "At least I'll pay off my score with all of you before they get me. Who wants to be the first? I'll let you make your own selection — if you don't take too long about it."

"Shoot and be damned to you," Vail said wearily.

"No," I objected, "let me —"

Westborough interrupted. "Dear me, there is really no need for these heroics. We are all quite safe because Baines is an extremely poor shot."

"I'm a good shot!" Baines exclaimed indignantly. "I did for Gronstein, didn't I?"

"Yeah, you can shoot," Mack laughed contemptuously. "In a pig's eye!"

"I am not as a rule a betting man," Westborough observed. "But I should like to make one wager, although it may be the last I shall ever make. Standing where you are it is utterly impossible for you to hit Mr Morse's surviving candlestick."

"I'd be likely to try it, wouldn't I?" Baines sneered.

"Of course," Westborough continued gently, "if you are afraid to make the trial, there is no more —"

"Afraid!" Baines snorted. His revolver barked, and the candlestick toppled from its shelf. "You lose that bet, Westborough, and you're going to —"

Never in all my life have I seen anything like the speed with which Mack's hand whipped his gun from the holster. Wheeling, Baines fired again; his second shot and Mack's first sounded at almost the identical instant. But Baines's bullet shattered harmlessly into the bookcase on the north wall, and Baines's automatic clattered to the floor while he clasped his bleeding hand in sudden and ludicrous surprise.

Stooping, Vail recovered the gun.

"My property, I believe."

PART SEVEN

Wednesday, November 25

XXXII

The state's attorney's office had nolle prossed the case, and Sylvia, liberated a scant two hours before, was now reveling in the luxury of a cigarette in her own living room. Westborough and I had been invited to lunch, and the clatter of dishes could be heard from the kitchen, where Matilda was bustling about to prepare the meal.

"There was so little evidence to establish our case," Westborough sighed. He was reviewing his entire solution for Sylvia's benefit. "On the other hand there were a number of significant signposts which pointed directly to Baines's guilt. Mr Morse's unsigned will clearly indicated the motive. There was also the problem of the glove."

"You never did explain that," I reminded.

"It is not difficult. In the event the glove had not been carried from the house, it would have had to have been destroyed within. There are not many methods by which this can be accomplished. Indeed, since no open fires had been lit that evening, the furnace was the only possible agency, and to this no one but Baines and Matilda had access. When I saw the cotton gloves employed by Baines for his basement chores, I realized that my embryonic hypothesis was in accord with the actual facts."

"Why so?" I inquired. "Those gloves weren't bloodstained, and there was a pair of them—just as there should be."

"White gloves soil quickly at work of this nature. These were suspiciously clean."

I hadn't noticed that! Shamefacedly, I recalled Sherlock's oft-repeated advice to Watson to cultivate the faculties of observation.

"Another important signpost was, of course, Dr Bramwell's book," Westborough continued. "Unfortunately, I did not realize that it was not a bona fide member of the Morse collection until some time later, when I endeavored without success to procure it through my felonious entry."

"Which reminds me that you left your handkerchief behind," I said. "It was yours, wasn't it? With a letter T on it?"

"It stands for Theocritus," the little man smilingly confessed. "A present from my sister-in-law. Dear me, how could I have been so stupid! I sadly fear that I am not at all qualified for a career of crime."

We all three laughed. Under the warmth of a cheerful blaze from the fireplace, Sylvia, I noticed gratefully, was fast relaxing into her former gaiety. The last few days had been a ghastly nightmare for her, but—like all nightmares—they had at last ended.

"However, Miss Sampson's headaches were the most important clue of all," Westborough asseverated.

"Matilda's headaches!" Sylvia exclaimed.

"She suffered from migraine, an affliction which may be treated with excellent success by Dr Bramwell's methods. Indeed, Miss Sampson actually did inform us that Baines had been so treating her."

"However, she called it Christian Science healing," I recalled.

"A misnomer—but doubtless employed by Baines to avoid alarming his patient," Westborough conjectured. "So many people have a profound distrust of this rather esoteric subject! Miss Sampson's pains were alleviated and effectively so, but, as we all know, through hypnotic suggestion."

"Hypnotism sounded like an incredible solution when you first told me about it," Sylvia declared.

"I had one of the wildest flashes of all," I confessed. "Regular horror-thriller stuff! I thought that Baines had sent Matilda upstairs to do the stabbing while he remained safely in the kitchen."

"Scarcely possible," Westborough objected gently. "If there is one doctrine with which practically all authorities are in accord, it is that a hypnotized subject invariably resists suggestions contrary to his moral sense. Had Baines ventured such commands, Matilda's violent rejection of them would have immediately terminated the hypnosis. However, Baines's actual procedure was much simpler."

"He just put Matilda to sleep and walked out of the room," I declared.

"Sleep is a somewhat inaccurate term, Mr Foster. Generally speaking, the hypnotic condition, whether slight or deep, is a conscious one."

"But," I objected, "you said last night that subjects upon awakening don't recall what happened while they were under."

"Yes, deeper hypnotic stages are nearly always characterized by amnesia with regard to the events of the hypnosis."

"It isn't clear to me at all," Sylvia averred. "I can see how Matilda couldn't know that Baines had been out of the room. But wouldn't she remember going to sleep? Surely she would have been able to remember that she had been hypnotized—and you said she didn't know it."

"That is the crux of the whole problem, Miss Morse, and I shall explain from the very beginning. Are you at all familiar with the phenomena of posthypnotic suggestions?"

"Posthypnotic suggestions?" Sylvia repeated. "Yes, I have seen them demonstrated. The hypnotist was only an amateur, but he did succeed in putting one of our group under. He told Billy when he woke up, he'd be thirsty and ask for a drink five minutes later, and that's just what happened. Right in the middle of his conversation, Billy blurted out that he wanted a glass of water. He said it so unconsciously that it made all of us laugh."

"That is a genuine example, but a simple one," Westborough told her. "Subjects can be made to perform all sorts of involved acts, some apparently grotesque, some extremely complicated and requiring a number of different operations to be undertaken in a prescribed sequence at a prearranged time. The only limitation is that they must not be acts which the subject would hesitate to perform normally. It is also possible to produce posthypnotic hallucinations, affecting any or all of the senses or even the unconscious processes of the body. Assuming that you reached the proper stage of somnambulism you might be caused, upon awakening, to see and hear an imaginary bird perched on one of these bookcases. The delusion might last for several hours, and during that time it would be extremely difficult to make you believe that your senses were playing you false.

"Posthypnotic negative hallucinations are as easily produced as are the positive," he went on. "In other words, the operator through suggestion can block out the normal perception of any designated object. Alfred Binet and Charles Féré cite the case of a young lady who was told that she would not see a certain gentleman in the room. When she awoke that gentleman was completely invisible to her. He put on his hat, and it appeared to her that the hat was suspended in empty space. He took off his hat, and she saw the hat, without apparent support, describing curves in the air. Binet and Féré, who term this condition systematic anaesthesia, claim to have proved by several experiments that the anaesthesia was real and not simulated."

"I still don't understand—" Sylvia started to say. Westborough, who was now warming to his subject, did not notice the interruption.

"Just as it is possible to block out the subject's normal perceptions, so it is possible to efface, either temporarily or permanently, any portion of his memory. Dr Bramwell, in his book *Hypnotism: Its History, Practice, and Theory* is very specific upon this point. You will understand why Baines took such trouble to conceal that volume in your grandfather's library when I read you a brief selection from it."

He paused to open the book which he had been holding on his lap.

"That isn't the actual copy Baines had?" I questioned.

"Dear me, no! That was irrevocably destroyed, but I was fortunate enough to secure another copy of this excellent and authentic work at the public library. Yes, here is the passage on page 110:*

" '*Owing to suggestion, the subject may have forgotten on awakening some or all the events of waking life.*

" 'This amnesia may occur in various ways:

" '(a) It may apparently be complete. The subject is then unable to recall anything connected with his waking life, and may even have lost the sense of his own identity. All memory of previous hypnoses is also forgotten.

" '(b) The amnesia may be limited by suggestion. Here the subject cannot remember selected events and ideas of his past life. For example, he may be unable to recall certain words or letters; or he may remember them, and yet be unable to utter them or write them down. This power of suggesting posthypnotic amnesia is sometimes of therapeutic as well as of experimental value. For instance, one of my patients, a nervous girl, was much frightened by seeing a friend in an epileptic fit and was unable to dismiss the scene from her mind. This was blotted out by suggestion and, although several years have passed since then, its memory has never risen either in the normal state or in hypnosis.' "

"Then, all that Baines had to do was to tell Matilda that when she recovered consciousness she wouldn't remember that he had hypnotized her that evening?" Sylvia pondered.

"Yes," Westborough confirmed. "Extremely simple, is it not? But, dear me, what an effective alibi it made! Miss Sampson, firmly believing that she was telling the exact truth, would have gone through even a lie detector test with flying colors."

"Did it take long to hypnotize her?" Sylvia inquired.

"Scarcely any time at all. She is a responsive subject, and we must keep in mind that on previous occasions Baines had induced several other hypnoses, each of which had facilitated his control."

"Was it also a posthypnotic suggestion that caused Matilda to look at her watch at such a convenient time for Baines?" I questioned.

He nodded. "Without doubt Baines suggested that she consult her watch at five minutes past twelve and suggested also that the act be remembered. Usually, post-hypnotic acts are forgotten immediately after their fulfillment."

"But how did Baines know she'd look at the right time?" I demanded.

"That is an excellent question, Mr Foster, and you may find my answer scarcely credible. Yet, I assure you, deep hypnosis is often associated with a phenomenal perception of time. Indeed, there is a voluminous and convincing testimony to the existence of these weird powers of posthypnotic time appreciation. Bramwell, Edmund Gurney, Delboeuf, and, more recently, Dr T. W. Mitchell, have conducted successful experiments along this line, of which Bramwell's experiments with the young lady he refers to as 'Miss D' may be taken as illustrative. Miss D was asked in hypnosis to mark a cross on a piece of paper at the expiration of a stated period—it might be as long as several days—and, without looking at watch or clock, to write down the time she then believed it to be. Sometimes the stated interval was expressed by such a phrase as '10,070 minutes' so that lengthy arithmetical calculations had to be carried out by her unconscious mind. In forty-five of the fifty-five experiments conducted, Miss D wrote down the correct terminal time at the exact minute the experiment fell due."

"Whew!" I exclaimed. "That doesn't seem pos—"

"I assure you that these are scientific facts, vouched for by recognized scientists."

"I won't argue with your authorities, but I want to ask you a few questions if you don't mind."

"As many as you like."

"On Monday you told us that you knew the name of Mr Morse's murderer but that you had no proof."

"The preceding evening I had discovered Dr Bramwell's book and the index cards missing from the library."

"But Tuesday night you declared to Mack that the necessary proofs were in your hands. Since Baines confessed you didn't have to produce your proofs, but, to satisfy my own curiosity, I'd like to know what they were."

"I had only one proof," Westborough smiled. "Miss Sampson's lost memory."

"What!" I ejaculated. "Matilda's memory came back?"

"It would be more accurate to say that it was restored."

"Restored? How?"

"Through the medium of another hypnosis. I persuaded Miss Sampson upon Tuesday afternoon to come with me to the office of a capable psychiatrist, who performed the simple experiment necessary. That had always been the one chink in Baines's armor, but, unfortunately, my knowledge of the subject was so limited that I did not fully realize his vulnerability until yesterday."

Westborough's reference to his "limited knowledge of the subject" was highly amusing after the exhibition he had just given, and Sylvia and I both exclaimed, "You seem to have learned a few things about it since."

He smiled, "I am blessed—or cursed, perhaps—with an inquiring mind. When my interest had been aroused I did take some steps to rectify my previous ignorance."

That was putting it mildly, but we allowed it to pass. We were both deeply grateful to this scholarly little gentleman.

"All right, just one more thing," I went on. "We were in something of a hole last night."

"Dear me, so we were," Westborough concurred, as though the recollection held slight interest for him.

"What made you think Baines would actually do anything so stupid as to turn away from us to shoot down that candlestick?"

"He is obviously obsessed by delusions of grandeur." Westborough returned. "A paranoiac! When his vanity with regard to his marksmanship was piqued he simply had no control over his actions. He had to achieve recognition from us at all hazards. But I take very little credit for seeing such a self-evident fact. Lieutenant Mack is the real hero of last night."

"He certainly did some straight shooting," I agreed.

"Don't!" Sylvia shivered. I rose to stir the fire; flickering yellow tongues darted up the chimney.

"Baines," Westborough continued, "confessed last night that he had once been expelled from medical school—the stigma must have resulted in what is often termed a psychic trauma. Working as a menial he was forced to bolster his ego by dwelling constantly upon his intellectual superiority; paranoia was a natural enough result. He played his butler's part well, but it was never more than a role, a species of psychological Iron Mask under which his injured soul festered."

"And to think," Sylvia said dreamily, "that it all started because of a miserable little bottle of wine."

"The wine," I said, "served as the spark to touch off the gas that was already in the cylinder."

She smiled at my cumbersome metaphor. "I was never very well acquainted with the contents of Grandfather's cellar. Is there really a wine called 'Est, Est, Est'?"

"Indeed, yes," Westborough confirmed. "I have enjoyed it upon rare occasions during my Italian sojourn. A clear topaz color, very similar to Orvieto." He paused. "I could cite a rather amusing story concerning it, one about a German Bishop, but here is Miss Sampson to tell us that luncheon is ready."

"First, your story," Sylvia insisted. "Please, Mr Westborough."

"Very well, then," he yielded. "The bishop, finding that it was necessary to make an Italian trip, sent his secretary ahead to make the arrangements. The secretary was specifically instructed to taste the wine of all the inns en route and to write the word 'Est' on the wall of the inn if the wine turned out to be satisfactory. At the town of Montefiascone, the secretary found a wine so superlatively good that, in order to do justice to it, he repeated his 'Est' three times upon the wall of the inn. Shall we finish this anecdote a trifle later?"

"No story, no lunch," Sylvia pronounced firmly.

"Hobson's choice!" he smiled. "The bishop, I must say, so thoroughly agreed with his secretary's verdict that he remained at the inn, drinking the wine, until his death. Hence upon his tomb the secretary had inscribed the epitaph: 'Est, Est, Est, et propter nimium est, Johannes De Fuger, dominus meus, mortuus est'."

Sylvia glanced toward me. "Translate it, Barry. You know Latin."

"Law Latin only," I qualified. "The first three words are as far as I can go."

"I know that much," she retorted, " 'It is, it is, it is' — you finish it, Mr Westborough."

" 'And through too much it is, my master, Johannes De Fuger, dead is.' "

"Only in this case it happened to be too little," I was thinking, as we went into the dining room.

THE END

* Acknowledgment is made to Rider & Company, London, and to J. B. Lippincott Company, Philadelphia, for their kind permission to quote the above paragraphs from Bramwell's *Hypnotism: Its History, Practice, and Theory*.

About the Rue Morgue Press

"Rue Morgue Press is the old-mystery lover's best friend,
reprinting high quality books from the 1930s and '40s."
—*Ellery Queen's Mystery Magazine*

Since 1997, the Rue Morgue Press has reprinted scores of traditional mysteries, the kind of books that were the hallmark of the Golden Age of detective fiction. Authors reprinted or to be reprinted by the Rue Morgue include Catherine Aird, Delano Ames, H. C. Bailey, Morris Bishop, Nicholas Blake, Dorothy Bowers, Pamela Branch, Joanna Cannan, John Dickson Carr, Glyn Carr, Torrey Chanslor, Clyde B. Clason, Joan Coggin, Manning Coles, Lucy Cores, Frances Crane, Norbert Davis, Elizabeth Dean, Carter Dickson, Eilis Dillon, Michael Gilbert, Constance & Gwenyth Little, Marlys Millhiser, Gladys Mitchell, Patricia Moyes, James Norman, Stuart Palmer, Craig Rice, Kelley Roos, Charlotte Murray Russell, Maureen Sarsfield, Margaret Scherf, Juanita Sheridan and Colin Watson..

To suggest titles or to receive a catalog of Rue Morgue Press books write 87 Lone Tree Lane, Lyons, CO 80540, telephone 800-699-6214, or check out our website, www.ruemorguepress.com, which lists complete descriptions of all of our titles, along with lengthy biographies of our writers.